THE ILLUSION QUEEN

THE ILLUSION QUEEN

T.E. DICKASON

Table of Contents

PROLOGUE

*O*n the island of Corazon, time was kept by the beating of a million hearts.

Few on the island were aware that long ago, in the lands now drowned under a raging sea, people once counted the passing of days, months, and years. Corazon's people had never seen the strange little machines their ancestors used to worship time. Ones with thin, metal knives slicing the day apart like a loaf of bread, cutting it into pieces so small few could take any nourishment or pleasure from them.

On Corazon little thought was given to what the next day held, for each new day was much like the last. The people took comfort in knowing barren fields would again fill with life, the redfish leaving frozen streams as fry would return full-grown in the bloom of spring, and they slept easy under a dark, starless sky that grew brighter by the light of a waxing moon.

This was the promise that kept peace in the land, and in every heart.

The promise that every person dies, but will be born again.

Except for one.

CHAPTER 1

Thick, black smoke rose from the pinnacle of the High Temple of Mir in a pillar so high it appeared to hold up the sky. The sight of it caused great unease in Corazon's people, for it was the only time they would know uncertainty in their lives. It signaled the body of their Queen was dying, and they would not know if her spirit would remain with them until the color changed from black to green.

Aleja would never shame herself to show any anxiety over the smoke, but she could understand and forgive the Queen's children, the simple people of Corazon, for such open displays of emotion. But what she heard from the wailing old woman prostrated before her was not something she could understand. And, it was her duty not to forgive it.

"Death..."

The old woman ground her forehead into the dusty floor of the amphitheater pit.

"...I beg of you, Daughter of the Queen of Corazon, Judge of Mir, and Instrument of Her Justice, give this man the death that took my son from me."

Muffled gasps from the crowd filled the amphitheater like a suffocating fog.

The old woman was a Caretaker, charged with the duty to raise the orphaned and abandoned children of Corazon. From her throne upon the stage above the amphitheater floor, Aleja saw a Caretaker's kindness in the old woman's tear-filled eyes, but also a face as hard and unyielding as the Guardians that flanked her.

The accused, an attractive youth with dark brown eyes and skin, stared at the Caretaker with a look of horror shared by many in the crowd. Seeing no compassion in the Caretaker's face, the youth pleaded with Aleja for mercy.

Disgusted with such a public display of fear, Aleja silenced the youth and called out to the Caretaker.

"To desire another to die is an evil of the Drowned World, the world our Queen saved us from." Aleja's voice, soft yet resonant, floated down from the stage and surrounded the Caretaker in echoes. "To utter such a request is as abominable as the act itself."

"You are wrong, Daughter." The Caretaker replied. "What does someone as young as you know about death?"

Aleja's face betrayed none of the insult she felt. It was true Aleja was young, but that was not unusual, for some Judges in the distant reaches of Corazon were even younger than she. Privately, for it would be abhorrent for a Daughter to admit it, Aleja prided herself over her self-control. Still, she could not allow the Caretaker to suffer no rebuke for her disrespect.

"In your grief you may have forgotten this Daughter serves you as the Judgment of the Queen. This Daughter will overlook your slight, but do not do so again."

Daughters never referred to themselves as "I" in public. Although Aleja was not one of them, she knew of Daughters who even refused to do so in private. Since the day the first wisp of smoke appeared from the High Temple, Aleja was certain one of they would be chosen to give her life to the Queen, for they were certainly more worthy of the honor. In the quiet moments of the day Aleja would tell herself this. But late at night, alone in her bed, she could not escape the shameful truth.

I don't want to be chosen.

"In the mind of every Judge of Corazon stands a Memory Palace." Aleja continued. "A grand structure filled with objects your eyes have never seen. Each one is a lesson from our Queen. And once this Daughter takes hold of one, she remembers every word the Queen once spoke with her own lips. All this Daughter is, all of her purpose, is to be the instrument of our Queen. The Queen who sacrificed her physical form long ago to give life to this island."

Aleja pointed in the direction of the smoke visible over the horizon of the amphitheater.

"You see the smoke, and must know what it means to a Daughter. Our Queen must live on to guide us, so every Daughter lives with the knowledge she may be chosen to be the Queen's Vessel. To have her life stripped from her body so the Queen's spirit may reside within."

"And you say a Daughter knows nothing of death." Aleja's fingernails scratched against the stone armrests as she leaned forward in her chair. "Yet this Daughter may know it before you."

Aleja paused. Feeling she had sufficiently chipped away at the Caretaker's confidence, she reclined in her chair and smiled. Her smile waned as the wind turned and the smoke from the High Temple billowed out towards the amphitheater like a storm cloud.

Aleja moved slightly, but awkwardly, as she searched for a more comfortable position in her chair. Even with the comforts of goose-feather cushions to soften the seat, sometimes Aleja went home with bruises in places that made her too embarrassed to share in the luxuries of Mir's bathhouses.

"How many days the sun has warmed this face is of no consequence to a Judgment." Aleja said after she adjusted herself. "But if you doubt the wisdom of ancients spoken through the voice of a young girl, then look to the wisdom carved in the stone around you."

Aleja gestured with open arms towards the reliefs carved into the walls of the pit. The reliefs, much like others gracing all the sacred pillars and temples in Mir, illustrated the story of the salvation and redemption of Corazon's people.

The amphitheater filled with screams as the Caretaker grabbed handfuls of stones and flung them at the carvings.

"Stories," she wailed, "they are just stories. Why should I care about lives carved in dead rock? I carried a life in my body, and had to hold it in my arms as it faded away."

The Caretaker pointed at the youth.

"All because of this man. What he took from me, the life of my only son, must be taken from him. It's the only justice that matters to me now."

Shouts and screams from the crowd rained down on the Caretaker.

"Heresy!" the crowd cried. "Banish her to the Wastes!"

This time, Aleja could not hide the shock on her face.

Aleja's Guardians cracked their staffs on the stone floor to quiet the crowd.

"Surely you do not mean to say your son, and yourself, will not one day be reborn on Corazon?" Aleja said.

"I am a Caretaker. I have fed and clothed many in my lifetime, but I have never seen a face I lost to death. Whatever life was in my son is gone. Forever."

Aleja shook her head.

"You are wrong. Our Queen will bring her people back to Corazon, again and again, in an eternal cycle of death and rebirth. This is her promise. This is truth."

There was a slight tremble in Aleja's voice, as if her own tongue doubted the words she knew to be true.

Aleja held out an open hand in the young man's direction.

"This was an accident, with no malice intended. The guilty man fell on your son from the top of a broken ladder. The Queen's judgment is fair and just. If a life is lost due to the accident of another, the living should take on the role of the dead."

"He was careless! Thoughtless and careless!" the Caretaker yelled.

"And he must die for this?" Aleja replied as calmly as she could.

"He must die for me! Those that love him must know the pain I feel."

"This man's death will not bring back a life." Aleja raised her hands to calm the crowd. "Vengeance offers no solace to grief."

The Caretaker laughed bitterly.

"You foolish young girl, what makes you believe I expect any solace? My grief will die with me."

Aleja's duty was clear. The old woman must be banished to the Wastes for her heresy. But what wasn't clear to Aleja was why she didn't do it the moment the woman uttered the hateful words. Perhaps the uncertainty about the Queen muddled her thoughts more than she realized. But even though Aleja herself could be punished if she did not apply the Queen's laws, she found she could not condemn someone who was in such pain.

The amphitheater hissed with whispered words. Aleja never felt so acutely aware of how many eyes were watching her. She took a deep breath to calm herself, closed her eyes, and receded into the depths of her Memory Palace to find an answer.

She found nothing. The uncomfortable thought crossed her mind she must have failed at some point in her training.

Or perhaps my training has failed me.

Aleja cursed herself for such a reprehensible thought. She opened her eyes, saw the doubt clouding the faces in the crowd, and wondered if their faces were a mirror of her own.

In a life where everything was assured and predictable, where even a mind could be forced into obeying order, Aleja felt lost. The countless judgments Aleja memorized since she was a child were of no use. As far as Aleja knew no one seeking justice had ever rebuked the Queen's judgment.

Aleja had to make a decision. For the first time in her life as a Judge, Aleja realized it must be her own.

"Give him the death that took my son from me."

The Caretaker's spiteful words rang in Aleja's head like the clanging of iron bells. Aleja felt she must say something, anything, if only to quiet the sound and give herself a chance to think.

Aleja looked into the Queen's blank, unfeeling eyes carved into the wall across from her.

If you will not give me the answer, must I find my own?

Aleja prayed the stone face would answer her, if only to break the silence of the amphitheater. But the cold visage gave her no comfort, and no response.

"Very well," Aleja swallowed hard, then stood up, "If this man is of no use to you, he cannot fulfill his duty to the Queen, therefore…this Daughter condemns him to die."

The young man fell to his knees and held his hands out to Aleja.

"How can this be?" He cried. "You cannot do this."

The crowd echoed the man's words, only more loudly, and with palpable anger. This time the crack of the Guardians' staves had no effect in quieting them.

Aleja looked at her guards. They were young and strong, with the swirling tattoos of the kraken's tentacles running down their arms, but did not carry the daggers of those tested by the hardships of the Wastes.

Would they have the strength to subdue this crowd?

Aleja moved between her guards, and filled her lungs with air.

"SILENCE!"

Aleja's voice tore through the amphitheater like a herd of charging horses. The crowd, now silent, stared at Aleja as if they couldn't fathom how this girl, who looked little older than a child sitting in the great stone chair, could have a voice of such power and authority.

Aleja waited before she spoke again. Only small birds, fluttering through the ivy covered columns behind her, dared utter any sound in the face of Aleja's withering stare.

"If you will not take this man as your son, then you will be free to live with vengeance in your heart and silence in your home."

Aleja walked down from the stage as she spoke. Once on the floor Aleja placed her hands on the Caretaker's shoulders.

"As you have said, this man must be given the death that took your son from you. So this Daughter decrees that when the sun rises, you must go to the place where your son died, climb a ladder, stand above this man, and fall on him."

A look of confusion came over the Caretaker's face.

"And if he does not die, "Aleja continued, "then you must climb the ladder and try again. You must do this, again and again, until your justice has been done."

The look on the Caretaker's face changed from confusion to disbelief.

"Or," Aleja's voice filled with a compassion that was both practiced and sincere, "you may accept the Queen's judgment, take this man as your son, and let him warm your heart and home."

When the Caretaker said nothing, Aleja feared what the crowd would do if she failed. But after a long and painful silence, and with head cast down, the Caretaker spoke.

"I accept the judgment of our Queen. I will take this man as my son."

Cheers erupted throughout the crowd. For a moment, amidst the shouts of praise to the Queen's mercy and wisdom, she thought she heard the crowd calling out her name.

I am just a Daughter. They should give no praise to me.

Aleja's heart raced. But whether it was from the fear of hearing her name or the exhilaration of it, Aleja could not tell.

Aleja looked at the Caretaker's face, and expected to see an expression of gratitude for sparing her from the Wastes. What she saw instead was a look of defeat. It was as if the Caretaker wanted to be banished all along.

Aleja pondered her decision after the Caretaker and youth were taken away. In not doing her duty as instructed, Aleja defied the Queen's law, and there would be consequences.

Aleja's head swelled under her headdress, a thin silver band split into two interweaving circles on her forehead. The circles were called the lemniscate, and were the Queen's symbol of eternal rebirth. She tried to ease her mind with thoughts of home, the warmth of her fire, the comfort of her bed, and the hearty taste of the pickled vegetables and steaming bowl of onion and seaweed soup that waited for her.

Once evening came, Aleja made her way towards the crowded street outside the amphitheater, and discovered she would not be going home. As usual, a palanquin waited for her under the grand archway of the amphitheater. But instead of the usual red curtained variety that would take her to the Temple of the Queen's Memory, where she would share with the Priestesses all she did and thought that day, this palanquin was covered in green.

The Queen's color.

Aleja walked towards the palanquin with legs as weak as willow reeds. A guardian drew the curtains and bid her to sit inside.

They're taking me to the High Temple.

Aleja looked up at the pillar of smoke just before entering the palanquin. In the deep blackness of the churning cloud she saw the first shades of a beautiful, forest green.

CHAPTER 2

It was obvious the Daughter waiting for Aleja in the palanquin was one of great importance, for the purpose of every Daughter was emblazoned upon the skin. The long tattoos of green and gold speckled feathers that ran down the woman's arm marked her as an Emissary.

Emissaries, messengers of the Queen, spent their lives travelling around the island overseeing the work done in the Queen's name. From the length and size of the feathers on the woman's arm and from wrinkles barely concealed by thick, black eyeliner, it was obvious she was a High Emissary.

Aleja's own right shoulder had the head of a snake, the symbol of Judges. Over time, if Aleja's work found merit in the eyes of her peers, the snake would sprout many different colored heads and coil around her arm and back.

Aleja bowed and then sat upright in a rigid, respectful posture. The woman reclined lazily in her chair. She returned Aleja's bow with a nod given more by her sleepy, almond shaped eyes than with her head.

The woman held a handful of seeds out for the waiting beak of a white cockatoo perched beside her.

Aleja was taken aback by the sight of the bird. It was unusual for people on Corazon to keep birds, for they were so common on the island that flocks of them darkened the skies even on a cloudless day. Most people, Aleja included, thought of them as pests.

The bird greedily devoured the seeds. Once finished, it stretched out its wings and crest to reveal beautiful feathers of light pink and yellow.

Aleja winced as the bird let out a satisfied squawk after its meal. The woman, seemingly unaffected by the ear-piercing sound, casually wiped the scattered remains of the meal out of the billowing pleats of her garment, an almost translucent blue peplos that glittered like the sky just before sunrise.

"Hermes wants another." The bird accompanied its demand with a nibble to the woman's ear. The woman laughed, gave the bird a playful rap on its head, and stretched her legs out from the slit in the side of her peplos. The golden anklets on her legs let out a ringing chime.

Even as old as the woman seemed, her legs kept the shape of one who spent her life trying to retain the beauty of youth.

"Please call this Daughter Aleja."

"Greetings Aleja. This Daughter may be called Kalim."

Aleja swallowed hard before she raised her head. She knew the name.

Kalim was High Emissary of Mir, who not only represented the entire city when travelling through Corazon, but also was one of the few who ever came into contact with the Queen herself.

Kalim plucked a grape from a wooden bowl by her side, placed it in her mouth, and chewed slowly.

"And as this beautiful creature has already told you," Kalim ran her fingers through the bird's plumes, "this is my friend, companion, and lifelong confidant, Hermes."

Aleja awkwardly nodded to Hermes, who bowed in response.

Aleja couldn't tell which of the two made her feel more uncomfortable; the annoying bird or its playfully doting, yet powerful, master.

"Hermes," Kalim said while holding a seed from its waiting beak, "I believe we should be going."

Hermes let out another ear-piercing shriek. The bearers lifted the palanquin and glided it forward as smoothly as if it were a ship setting out to sail.

Hermes squawked with delight at the sight of the seeds Kalim placed in a small wooden bowl attached to his perch.

Aleja smiled faintly at Kalim. Aleja's arms were still folded at her waist, and she fought the urge to rub her hands along her skin.

"What may this Daughter do for Kalim?"

"You may dispense with such formal talk." Kalim responded almost before Aleja finished speaking. "You are sitting in my palanquin, not on the judge's chair."

Kalim's smile did nothing to soften the bluntness of her speech.

"Although you appear to be a nice enough girl, I regret to tell you my visit is not for us to get acquainted. I am here to take you to the High Temple. Were you aware of that?"

"Yes."

"Do you have any idea why?"

"It is not my place to suspect."

Kalim smiled.

"It's not your place, yes, but you do suspect something. Or, at least, I would hope so. You're not like one of those empty-headed dolts who can't even say their own name, are you?"

Aleja shook her head. Kalim smiled, then plopped a grape into her mouth and rolled it along her tongue.

"So, go on." Kalim chewed as she spoke. "What do you suspect about the nature of this trip?"

"From the Palanquin's color and the sight of your distinction, this trip must be of some importance." Aleja said with a nod to Kalim's arm.

Tattooing was a common practice throughout Corazon, for it marked everyone's place in society. Aleja used the more formal word *distinction* for Kalim. Only simple people who worked with their hands referred to the marks on their faces, arms and shoulders as tattoos. "I must have been summoned to be informed about the Queen's health."

"It's interesting you think you are important enough to be told anything about that." Kalim's lips curled as if one of the grapes in her mouth had suddenly soured. "So, you did not suspect you would be summoned because of your own actions?"

"I considered the possibility."

Kalim raised one eyebrow. In the silence that followed Aleja felt compelled to elaborate.

"What I meant to say is, it is common practice for a Judge to be called to a temple for thought and reflection. So, I knew I would be called to reflect on my judgments today, but only when I saw the palanquin did I suspect–" Aleja stopped herself short, "–I mean, thought, I could be taken to the High Temple for something else."

"So, if you only suspected because of the palanquin, and not because of the seriousness of your actions today or from the sight of the smoke, then why are you so afraid now?"

"I apologize to disagree with you High Emissary, but I am not afraid."

Kalim laughed.

"Please spare me such nonsense. I admire bold people, not bold lies."

Aleja bristled at the accusation. A Judge's honor was based on her adherence to the truth. To be called a liar was the greatest insult anyone could give to a Judge.

"I'm not a liar."

"Is that so? Well, perhaps you're not lying to me, but you are certainly lying to yourself. You may be trained in memory and regurgitating the wisdom of our Queen, but as I'm sure you well know, Emissaries have developed different capabilities to serve the Queen's people. Namely, the ability to read someone. To know all you need to know the moment you see them."

"I know the duties and skills of all the Daughters of Corazon, High Emissary, for I left my life as a novice many seasons ago. More seasons than I can remember."

"Really? You must be a poor Judge then, for someone who looks so young not to recall the number of seasons since you first took your seat as Judge."

"I only meant–"

"I know what you meant girl." Kalim said with a dismissive wave. "You're baited far too easily."

Kalim leaned in towards Aleja and stared directly into her eyes. The smell of rose scented oils filled Aleja's nose.

"Tell me. Are you indeed Aleja? A Judge of Mir? A Daughter of our mother and savior, the Queen? Or did we pick up her sniveling servant on accident?"

No one had ever spoken to Aleja in such a fashion since she had become a Judge. Only a novice was supposed to endure such insults, and then only from a teacher, whose cutting sharpness of her tongue was only matched by the sting of her slap.

"How dare you!" Aleja shouted. "I am the Judgment of the Queen! You have no right to speak to me that way."

Kalim took a long look at Aleja and then broke into a laugh.

"What is it?" Aleja shouted. "What amuses you so?"

"You're quite passionate for a Judge aren't you? And so easily offended. I thought Judges were supposed to have a thick skin."

"Well," Aleja tried to control the tone of her voice to show she had regained her composure, but her words came with a slight tremble off her tongue, "I thought Emissaries were taught to be more charming."

Kalim laughed again.

"Yes, well, life teaches you its own lessons we all must take heed of. Like how to ease the fear in a young woman you're escorting to judgment."

"I'm not scared." Aleja replied sharply. "I'm not a child."

Even though I sound like one right now. I should be better than that.

"Well then, my little dew petal, perhaps you don't understand the stakes."

Aleja cringed upon hearing Kalim call her a "dew petal." It was an affectionate name when cooing over babies but to use it with young women was a most condescending insult, for it insinuated there was nothing more to her than a transitory beauty and once the day grew long there was nothing left but a withered leaf.

"I'm sure you've heard of the solitude in the Room of Reflection?" Kalim continued. "Most certainly you know of the poisonous vastness of the Wastes."

"Of course I know about such things." Aleja slumped back into her seat.

Kalim nodded.

"I would hope so. You hid your fear of them well. But one thing I'm trained to do, and have done for many years, is to see through the masks we wear every day. And all masks, no matter how much they conceal, cannot hide the eyes. Even now, as you tell me you're not scared, I see your fear in them."

"Perhaps that is true," Aleja's hands, rested on her thighs, involuntarily clenched into fists, "but why play games with me? You are my sister, why not reassure me?"

"I can reassure you of nothing."

"Then why are we even speaking?"

"What would you have me do instead? Stare at you in silence as you sweat through my seat cushions?"

"Yes, that would be preferable." Aleja replied curtly.

Kalim laughed out loud and clapped her hands. Hermes joined in with a laugh exactly the same as Kalim's, as if it were an echo.

"When my messenger told me a Judge from the dusty backstreets of Mir dared to condemn a man to die, I expected to meet someone with some fire. And yet this meek little creature crawled into my palanquin like a mouse hiding from a cat. It would do you no good to stand before High Chamberlain Taka like that, and I will not see a Daughter shame her sisters. So, 'Fill a belly with anger, and there is no appetite for fear' as the saying goes."

"That is not how the saying goes." Aleja interrupted Kalim, and uncharacteristically felt no discomfort at her own rudeness. "The expression is 'Fill a heart with love and it will not beat in fear' as one who has gained many seasons in wisdom should know full well." Aleja took a grape from Kalim's plate and plopped it into her own mouth with a smile.

Aleja expected to see the same mocking smile in reply, but rather, a shadow passed over Kalim's face.

"It has changed over time." Kalim said with what Aleja thought was a hint of sadness. Kalim took a handful of seeds and spoke brightly to Hermes. "Has it not, my pet?"

Aleja watched bewildered as Kalim lovingly stroked the bird. Kalim broke into laughter at the sight of Aleja's discomfort. Hermes, his bowl of seeds refilled, laughed even louder.

CHAPTER 3

Aleja's mouth watered at the smoky smell of roasting squid and fish drifting into the palanquin as it passed through Mir. Aleja envied the people drinking milky rice wine around the small grills lining the streets, sharing warm meals and conversation while she sat in stony silence with Kalim.

It was the eve of a Day of Rest, a day when only Caretakers needed wake before the first light of dawn. On this night the people of Mir stayed out late to drink and eat, with little concern to how they may curse their pounding heads the next morning.

Brightly burning torches lined the streets. Shadows danced across the palanquin's curtains in step with the joyous music that filled the air. It reminded Aleja of the shadow plays she enjoyed watching as a child. She would clap and scream in delight at the large, wooden puppets dancing in the light, completely unaware of the puppeteers controlling them in the dark. Aleja felt the puppets were so much nobler than the flesh and blood audience that watched them. Even when the puppets strayed from the Queen's path, they always found their way back to her. No one was ever banished in the plays.

Not like the real world.

The common perception of Corazon's people were of a plain and kind sort, but with manners as coarse and dusty as the ground they walked on. But they were grateful for the pleasures their Queen had bestowed upon them. They had food and wine to warm their bellies and companionship to warm their hearts. The dark pleasures of the Drowned World were long forgotten to them, and they desired for nothing more than what they had. But, as a Judge, Aleja knew it was not always true. Not all were satisfied. Some old, destructive habits still remained.

But it didn't matter what Aleja thought of the people personally. Even if Aleja were not in Kalim's palanquin, she would not have joined them. It would be unseemly for a Judge to spend time with the people she served. Aleja often watched them as she studied alone in her room, and would think about how little she knew about them. Sometimes Aleja was tempted to close the book and join them, but she never gave in to it. The words she memorized as a novice kept her will strong.

My life is not my own. I have no right to bond with the life of another, to offer what I cannot give.

Her only real contact with the Queen's people was with another girl who worked with horses at a small stable near Aleja's home. Although she was once terrified to even touch one, Aleja loved horses. They were almost mythical creatures to her, no different from the spiny, monstrous bears of the Yamanashi Mountains or the winged serpents of the Wastes Caretakers spoke of to scare unruly children. After seeing Aleja linger by the yards, the girl offered for her to take a closer look at the horses. At first Aleja demurred. Unaware that Aleja could not do any such thing without permission from a Chamberlain, the girl persisted and ultimately Aleja relented.

Afterwards, Aleja would furtively visit whenever she had the chance. She only helped with brushing the horses at first, but eventually Aleja learned to ride. She felt free when she rode. Not just from the domineering Chamberlains who would put a stop to it if they knew, but also from the constant press of her thoughts. When she was riding, the world outside the yard seemed to disappear entirely and the world inside her mind was quiet.

As the palanquin got closer to the center of the city the dusty, earthy smells of wood and grilled food were replaced by those of perfumes and spices. The sounds outside were lighter, softer, the conversations more refined. This was the part of the city where the high ranking Daughters, Consuls, and Chamberlains lived. Daughters of lower status, like Aleja, rarely ventured into such a place without invitation.

Aleja felt the palanquin rise up as they crossed one of the bridges that led to the High Temple gardens. Once inside the garden the lilting sounds of the inner city were replaced by the chirping of insects and birds.

"This is where I take leave of you, my dear." Kalim said as the palanquin stopped.

"You won't come with me into the High Temple?"

"No. As Emissary of Mir I am charged with attending to the grubby matters of this world. The Temple Maidens attend to the dream world."

"The dream world?"

Kalim smiled.

"Why, the world of the Queen of course." Kalim tittered. "And remember my little dew petal, whoever you stand before in Judgement, whether it is the High Judge, High Chamberlain or even the Queen herself, do so without fear."

"Why do you care?"

"Because you don't just represent yourself, but all Daughters. We are an example to all the people of Corazon."

"So it has nothing to do with me."

"Why should it? Such shameful ego you have, girl. You are one of many. Never forget that."

Despite the contempt in her voice Kalim smiled, and then held out her arms for the parting embrace all Daughters gave one another. Aleja hesitated, glared at Kalim warily, but then relented. After a stiff hug, Aleja took the hand of Kalim's guard and exited the palanquin.

Aleja stood before one of the four gates of the High Temple. The High Temple was in the center of the city, and was the central hub of a large circular road known as the Wheel. The Wheel cut through the city, forming a marker between the inner and the outer sections, an invisible wall between those who served the Queen with their heads, and those who served with their hands.

Towering aqueducts bringing water into the city ran along roads that formed the spokes of the Wheel. The aqueducts fed directly into the upper reaches of the High Temple. From high above, the immensity of the High Temple and the aqueducts looked like a giant red spider crawling through the city.

Aleja stared at the figure standing before the gate.

A statue of the Queen, more than twice Aleja's height, loomed over her. In the light of the torches the black statue seemed to glow with hints of gold.

The statue's eyes were fiery red rubies, the nostrils enlarged as if drawing in a deep breath, and lips curled in an animalistic snarl. The clothes and armor of the statue were tattered, as if torn in battle, and her chest was exposed through the shredded breastplate.

The left arm was raised high and held on to a blade consumed in fire. The heat from it warmed Aleja's face in the cool night air. The right arm reached out as if it meant to grab Aleja and drag her into the temple.

As a small child, Aleja screamed the first time she saw the statue. Until then she had only known the Queen as the mother to the people of

Corazon, who loved them with a depth of feeling none could ever comprehend. But at that moment the Queen was more a monster than a loving mother.

It was Aleja's first lesson of what it means to love and protect your children. In order to inspire devotion, you must invoke fear.

Beyond the gate was a humble stone walkway overgrown with soft moss and creeping vines. Five women, each holding torches in their hands, stood on the walkway. Aleja knew them to be Temple Maidens from their colorful tattoos of carp swimming up a roiling stream. The fish were a symbol of the gifts of food that supported the Queen and her people on the long sea journey from the Drowned Lands to Corazon.

The Temple Maidens kept their hair long, and wore elaborately threaded headdresses that wove into a lemniscate across their foreheads. The paint around their eyes, and the sheen of their diaphanous peploses, glittered in the torchlight. Each Maiden radiated an intimidating beauty.

Without a word, the Temple Maidens beckoned Aleja to follow them. Aleja couldn't help but imagine the statue's fiery eyes following her as she walked to the High Temple.

Admit it. You are afraid.

Aleja tried to calm herself.

Breathe, Aleja, breathe.

After a few breaths she felt her pulse slow. And yet, Aleja did not dare look back as she walked into the darkness of the High Temple halls, for fear she would see the statue following her. The Temple Maidens walked in a tight circle around Aleja as they led her to the center of the temple, a large room known as the Syncronia.

Aleja blinked as her eyes adjusted to the brightness of the Syncronia. Even though the maze of hallways seemed to get darker with every turn the Syncronia was well lit, not just by torches, but also by light reflected on the mirrors hung on its towering walls.

A glittering mosaic of colorful pieces of tile covered the wall across from Aleja. The Queen's face dominated the center of the mosaic, her black hair wove through images depicting Corazon's history like seawater through a rocky shore.

Aleja first saw the mosaic during her initiation as a novice. Then the room was full of children. All girls, full of energy and excitement, blissfully unaware of the challenges and discipline to come.

Aleja did not realize the toys she played with, the tops that spun in such vivid colors, the little metal figures that bent and danced near flames, would be the first objects she would place in her Memory Palace. They would replace, first in her hands and then in her memory, the toys she once played with in her village.

It was the first step in forgetting her previous life.

Like the Priestesses who served in the Temple of the Queen's Memory, who were the living records of all the Daughters' experiences, Aleja was gifted with the Painted Eye. She could recall sights so vividly it was as if she were actually seeing them in front of her. Yet, despite this gift, Aleja's memories of the time before she became a Daughter were fleeting and quickly forgotten. She remembered the feel of a loving touch, the smell of clay, the sound of an ocean. The memories were nothing she could see, so Aleja dismissed them as nothing more than a passing feeling. If they could not be seen, then they must not be real.

A smooth, glassy image of a ship leaving Corazon for the Stone Islands caught Aleja's eye as she approached the mosaic.

Aleja did not understand why people chose to leave the Queen's protection to live on the Stone Islands. On the mosaic large predatory birds, their talons opened wide and stained with blood, threatened to dig into the flesh of the people picking through the Stone Island's rocky shores for their meager sustenance.

The Yamanashi Mountains were also depicted on the mosaic, but without any representation of the wild and mysterious people who lived there. Aleja wondered why include the mountains if you would not also show the people? And if the mountains were unimportant, why would they be placed so close to the image of the Queen?

Aleja dismissed her questions upon approaching the solitary man who stood at the base of the Queen's neck.

He had a shaved head and was dressed in the tight, wrapped clothing of a Guardian, yet in a deep green color rather than a light brown. The man faced away from Aleja.

"High Chamberlin Taka," a Temple Maiden said with a bow, "the Daughter named Aleja is here for your guidance."

Taka nodded his head, but did not turn to face Aleja. Each of the Temple Maidens left her with a parting embrace.

Aleja knew Taka to be quite old, for he guided the city of Mir as High Chamberlain long before Aleja was born, but his posture was of a young, vigorous man. He stood legs apart, his hands behind his back. The tight wrappings of his clothes strained against the muscles of his arms and legs.

Taka's eyes were focused on the mosaic. The red eyes of the ram's skull tattooed on the back of Taka's head stared down at Aleja.

The mountain ram was the distinction of the Chamberlains, the ones who selected the young girls of Corazon to be Daughters, chose who would be Corazon's Guardians, and made sure they all served the Queen. The face of the ram skull covered most of the back of his head. The segmented horns curled around the sides of Taka's temple before ending in points at the base of his ears.

Aleja had never seen a ram skull where the horns extended so far.

Taka turned to face Aleja. He stared at her with eyes as blue and deep as the ocean surrounding Corazon. Most of Corazon's people had brown eyes with skin and hair to match. Blue or green eyes were so rare Aleja actually thought they were lost to her people.

"Did you know that long ago," Taka began, in a voice oddly high pitched for someone with such an intimidating presence, "when the stars were too numerous to be counted, when the living outnumbered the dead, that the people of the Drowned World greeted those they did not know by grasping hands?"

"No, High Chamberlain. This Daughter was not aware of such a custom."

"Of course. Do you wonder why we don't do so?"

"It would not be proper."

"And why is that?"

"A person does not want to dirty the hands of another, or does not want to presume they will become intimate companions. Only those who share a purpose may share an embrace."

Taka leaned in towards Aleja. There were signs of many seasons on his face, as there were on Kalim's, but his flesh had none of her softness. The muscles in his face were tight and gave him a slightly skeletal look.

"Would it shock you to learn our ancestors once kissed the lips of the dead? That they stayed with the empty body for days in a room with food left to decay like the body of their loved one? I must ask you, what do you think of such customs?"

Aleja's nose and mouth scrunched involuntarily as Taka spoke. The revulsion she felt at his words built in her throat, and she swallowed hard before she replied.

"Forgive my ignorance, High Chamberlain, but this Daughter does not understand the question."

"If you were to guide our people as our Queen has," Taka said, his face drawing ever closer to Aleja's, "would you permit such customs?"

"This Daughter would not. A body without life serves no purpose above ground, and until taken back to the ground it is a source of corruption. Its proper place is in the urns that let it liquefy and drain into the earth. It is then purified as it feeds the fruits and vegetables that sustain the living. Only when it has given back what it took will our Queen bring the life back into this world."

"That is correct. Yet, you speak of corruption. Have you ever seen the living being corrupted by the dead?"

"Thanks to the graces of our Queen, this Daughter has not, High Chamberlain."

"Then how do you know such things are true?"

Aleja struggled to keep a straight face at the question. It would be wholly inappropriate to laugh in the face of High Chamberlain Taka, but Aleja almost did so. Aleja's exhaustion and hunger had almost consumed her wits. The apprehension she once felt was now replaced with a weary annoyance.

"Because this Daughter is a living witness to the memories of the Queen and her people."

Aleja held out her hand, palm upward, in the direction of the mosaic. Taka looked with her at the images entangled in the Queen's hair. Men, women and children in piles, the flesh and blood of each melting into the others. The bodies' thick, poisoned veins bulged through the pallor of their skin. The mass of dead looked like they were entangled in a large, blood-stained spider web.

Horrible creatures with heads of animals and skin that shined like the metal mined from the Yamanashi Mountains rode horses over the dead, and strange ships floating in the sky rained fire down upon the living.

Taka looked upon the mosaic and nodded his head.

"It is time for your reflection." Taka said abruptly. "Go inward to your Memory Palace and recount the Parable of Thirst."

Aleja closed her eyes and took a long, drawn out breath. In her mind she was no longer in the Syncronia, but rather in a room where all the tables and shelves were covered with objects of every shape, size, and color. On a stand by the window there was a cup made from blue glass. Aleja admired how it sparkled in the orange glow of the setting sun.

Aleja picked up a small figurine of an earless man with a slash of red paint across his face. Upon picking up the figurine, the story became clear in her mind. Aleja opened her eyes, and began to tell the tale.

CHAPTER 4

*F*our men were lost in the Wastes. They had neither food nor water and were on the verge of death when they found an old man sitting on a large stone. The old man held a pitcher made of common clay. In front of him were four glasses, one red, one green, one black, and one blue.

"You are halfway to salvation my brothers," the old man told them, "but I cannot guarantee you will leave the Wastes alive. All I can offer you is a drink from this pitcher to take with you for the rest of your journey."

"In the red glass the pitcher will pour the most delicious wine, the green the juice of sweet fruits, the black the beautiful dreams of the liquid lotus, and in the blue, only plain and pure water. You may make any choice you like but you will choose for life. If you make it out of the Wastes alive, you will know no other taste on your lips for the rest of your days"

The first man, a wastrel, chose the liquid lotus. "What is life if one can't dream?" he said, deaf to his companions' pleas to change his choice. The second man, a drunkard, chose the wine. "What is life if one can't rejoice?" he said when the others protested. The third man, large in appetite and size, chose the juice. "What is life if one can't savor its sweetness?" he reasoned. The fourth, a simple and selfless man, chose the water.

"Water is life." He said in his defense as the others mocked him.

The old man filled their cups and sent them on their way. The wastrel danced and sang with imaginary women, and as the dream took hold of him, laid down in the poisonous, red sand and buried himself alive. The other three, unable to wake him from his dream, left him to his death.

The drunkard kept with his companions for a while but the wine began to swell in his head. The joy of his drunkenness turned to sorrow and his companions left him after he fell into a slumber from which he did not wake.

The juice nourished the portly man for a time, but its sweetness began to corrupt his body. A new and stronger thirst grew in him with every drink. Over time it created madness in him, and in desperation to weaken the sweetness of his drink he mixed it with the bitter, poisonous sand. He then drank it, and died.

The simple man wandered alone. Despite the fates of his companions, at times he envied them in their deaths. For the man knew that he too may not make it out of the Wastes, and he cursed the tastelessness of the water that cured him of his thirst but would bring him neither salvation nor joy.

But when he did make it out of the Wastes, he was welcomed home with a great celebration. A great feast was held in his honor, it was then he found the old man's words were true. For no matter what he placed in his mouth, whether it be a sweet wine or roasted fish, all he could taste was water.

Yet the man did not curse his fate. He rejoiced with his family and friends, savored the warmth of his home and bed, and was thankful for every breath he took for the rest of his life.

CHAPTER 5

Even with Taka staring coldly at her, Aleja told the tale flawlessly. Every voice, every motion, was performed exactly as Aleja learned it as a novice. Aleja opened up her hands to her side to show the tale was finished.

"Do you know why I asked you to tell me the parable?" Taka asked with a withering stare.

"This Daughter does not assume to know the mind of the High Chamberlain." Aleja said, choosing not to elaborate further. She thought other parables may have been more appropriate for this reflection, and wondered why she was even asked to do so at all.

Perhaps I'm not here to be Vessel, or to be punished for my judgment. Did I unknowingly commit some other offense?

"What is the lesson to be learned from it?" Taka asked.

Aleja felt annoyed at the question. The parable was one of the most basic lessons of the Queen, and somewhat beneath one who had accumulated as much of the Queen's wisdom as Aleja. The parable illustrated the reason the people of Corazon satisfied themselves with "simple pleasures" and cast aside the "poisoned pleasures" of the Drowned World.

"That joy must be sacrificed to achieve true happiness and contentment." Aleja answered quickly and confidently.

Taka scoffed.

"You disappoint me, Daughter," Taka stared at Aleja. "I would have suspected someone who used her own judgement rather than the Queen's would have a different interpretation of the story than the one she was forced to memorize as a novice. Have you given the parable no thought at all since you became a Judge?"

Aleja took a calming breath before her answer.

"I have, and have rendered Judgement using this parable before."

"Then what other wisdom have you gained from reciting it during the few seasons you have served our Queen as a Judge?"

Aleja realized with a growing anxiety she had never interpreted the passage in any other way than what she was told as a child. Still, she did not want to give Taka the satisfaction of stumping her.

"I find the wisdom of the parable taught to me so long ago has been sufficient for my judgements."

Taka smiled.

"Clever girl."

Aleja's heart froze at the sight of Taka's smile. She realized her answer inadvertently exposed the shallowness of her understanding more than confessing to it would have done. It was a prideful offense Daughters could be punished for. Aleja thought of the isolation she would have to face in the Room of Reflection, and struggled to keep the fear of it from showing in her face.

"Clever, but not wise." Taka said. "For wouldn't the truly wise admit to knowing nothing rather than foolishly attempt to deceive others? Would it help you to hear of my perspective on the parable?"

"Yes, High Chamberlain," Aleja nodded gratefully, hoping a reinterpretation of the parable was the extent of Taka's planned consequence. "It would honor this Daughter to receive the wisdom of one who has served our Queen and her children so well."

Taka smiled wanly, and then turned to face the image of the Queen. Again, the unforgiving red eyes of the ram stared down at Aleja.

"It is true people must deny joy to bring about true happiness and contentment. But, in order for people to survive, the poison of choice must be taken away."

"I don't understand High Chamberlain."

Taka looked back at Aleja, his face grim. He drew in close, and stood over Aleja as he spoke.

"Nor would I expect you to, for as a Judge, your duty is to recite the lessons and judgments of the Queen you have committed to memory. You are a cipher, nothing more."

"But weren't the men in the parable given a choice?"

"Only to teach us of its dangers."

"But wine, the dreams of the lotus. They are all still choices we have."

"They are representations of the choices of the past, for they are pleasures the people of Corazon know and understand. The people of Corazon have been spared knowledge of the poisoned pleasures, those that fed the ego of humanity and destroyed the bonds between the people and their world. The temptations that caused all the land to be swallowed by the sea, the air to be poisoned, and brought all life to the brink of death."

Taka held out his hands towards the images on the Mosaic.

"We are told by our Queen how to greet the living, and how to handle the bodies of the dead, so we may not be plagued by the disease that once ravaged our people. Whether or not to hold a stranger's hand may seem like a small thing, but our Queen's teaching was, and always will be, heeded nonetheless. So now, such habits, such...choices...are forgotten."

"You gave the old woman a choice. One you had no right to offer. This woman still held humanity's murderous habits in her heart. She was to be condemned, banished to the Wastes. It was good her son died before spreading his seed, for now his mother's poisonous hate will not live on beyond her. And yet, even after her blasphemy, you let her walk out of the Amphitheatre with the illusion she was the one who decided the fate of the young man." Taka looked back towards the mosaic, his eyes watering with tears. "She decided, and not, our Queen."

"So you see, Daughter. The dead do not corrupt the living, only the living can do that." Taka turned and looked into Aleja's eyes. "You did that."

Aleja, overcome by the force of Taka's emotions, knelt down before him and hung her head down.

"This Daughter sees the error of her ways, High Chamberlain." Aleja said through her tears. "How may she undo the damage she caused?"

"She cannot." Taka's voice was as cold as his eyes. "Should I fix my own error of appointing you as a Judge? Would it undo any of the evil of the Drowned World you tolerated today?"

Aleja furiously shook her head no. She wondered if Taka noticed her tears, and if he would be swayed by them.

"That is why you are not to judge in your own fashion. You are to only recite the judgements of the Queen. Your dereliction of duty has poisoned those who witnessed the woman's hateful nature. You are not to give the people a choice. You must know your place, now more than ever, for the Queen has decreed it."

Aleja saw Taka's feet turn away and heard his slight, muted steps as he walked towards the mosaic. His footsteps slowed the closer he came to the wall.

"Look up, Daughter. Know your place in the world. See if you have any choice in it."

Aleja hesitated. She could not bear to see the judgement in Taka's eyes or in the image of the Queen. Taka knelt down beside Aleja and helped her to her feet. He whispered into her ear.

"Do not weep, for this is a night of celebration. The Queen has chosen her Vessel."

Aleja heard rumbling as a large stone door opened somewhere behind her.

"She is waiting for you, Daughter. In the Room of Reflection."

Aleja trembled as she raised her head to look at the mosaic. She could not suppress the gasp that escaped her lips at the sight.

The face staring down from the mosaic was no longer the Queen's.

It was Aleja's.

CHAPTER 6

During the uncountable days Aleja spent in the Room of Reflection there was little light, little food and no comfort. Just a thin mattress lying on a stone floor and a single circular opening to let in a strange, shimmering light. For food, a clay plate sparsely appointed with rice, a sliver of fish, and pickled vegetables was left in the room while Aleja slept.

Aside from the trickle of water running down one of the walls there was only a pot of tea to wet her throat. The tea had a pungent, bitter taste which only her deep hunger helped her drink down.

Aleja thought she experienced isolation before in her home, but it was nothing like this. There was no Chamberlain to guide her reflections or even a servant to attend to her. There was only the lifeless eyes and silent lips of the people carved on the wall to keep her company. A monstrous relief of the Queen dominated one of the walls. The carving looked so real that as the day grew long it seemed to move in the shimmering light.

After meditation, and usually before finishing the last of the tea, Aleja would turn away from the Queen's judgmental gaze and fall into a deep sleep.

Even though Aleja was sent to the Room of Reflection to purge herself of her memories, to empty her mind so it may be open to the Queen, to her frustration every time she destroyed an object in her Memory Palace to erase its memory she would find it renewed when she awoke. Just like the pot of tea and clay plate set by her mattress.

And every night, in her dreams, she was haunted by the image of her own face on the Syncronia wall and what it meant for her life.

But it never really was my life was it? Aleja thought as she swished the bitter tea down her throat. *It's pointless to think about it. It doesn't matter why I was chosen. The Queen has her reasons, and only my sinful pride makes me question them.*

She dreamed of standing in the Syncronia before hundreds of people, all screaming for her death, and felt a cold steel blade brought to her throat. It was so vivid Aleja was surprised to see herself still in the room when she woke. Aleja did not get up from the mattress to eat. She leaned over, poured some tea, and brought it to her lips.

She thought about the judgement she made, and the reprimand she received from Taka for it. She knew Taka's lesson was true, but in her heart, she could not accept it.

I don't care what the Queen would have done. I did the right thing.

On a day when the tea's bitter taste was especially strong, Aleja threw her clay cup against the wall in disgust. It shattered on the relief of the Queen carved into the wall, covering her face in a waterfall of inky green. Aleja remembered how the old woman did the same with rocks, and how the crowd responded.

Heresy!

Undoubtedly, whoever came in at night to clear the tray would report this back to Taka. Just as likely, it would earn Aleja more days in the Room.

Aleja cleaned the Queen's face using the length of her peplos, and then set about cleaning up the bits of broken pottery. Aleja jerked back her hand at a stinging pain and saw a small shard sticking out of the tip of her forefinger. Blood welled up around it.

After pulling out the shard, Aleja sucked on her finger to stop the bleeding, but to no avail.

Aleja traced her bloodied fingers over an inscription carved into the bottom of the cup. Images of home flashed through her mind. But not of the small, white house she kept in Mir, or even the temple she lived in as a novice, but the land the Maidens of the High Temple made her forget.

The Clay lands. The land of her birth.

Aleja remembered the small stream that trickled down a rocky hill she played on. The rocks in the hill gave way to rows upon rows of grapevines hanging from ropes threaded through old, grey wooden stakes that stood rigid in the hard clay. As a small child, Aleja delighted in walking under the dangling vines to pick the few grapes her small hands could reach.

Aleja would give the grapes to her "Grape Mother", the woman who cared for her, who was as solid and sturdy as the rocks jutting out of the hillside. As Aleja stood proudly over her harvest, Grape Mother smiled, deepening the lines that cracked her aged face.

Grape Mother humored Aleja for a time, then resumed her duty to the village. It was the same duty her own parents had, and theirs before them, and on and on in a line that was longer than the rows of grapes threading the hillsides.

Grape Mother, who was the last in the village to say goodbye to Aleja when she was taken to Mir to become a Daughter, was not Aleja's birth mother. Aleja had no knowledge of her birth mother, nor did she recall ever seeing a face which resembled her own.

But it did not matter. The village raised children. It was not so important who birthed you. What mattered was you were cared for.

To the rest of the village the old woman was called "Cracked Clay", but to Aleja, she was "Grape Mother", and Aleja was her "Grape Child".

It was the name Aleja chose for herself, and the one she kept till her first day as a novice. The day the Temple Maidens stripped off her clothes, dusty from days of walking through the dry hills and valleys, and replaced them with a clean, white linen gown. Then the teachers shaved off all the hair from her head, even her eyebrows.

The Temple Maidens told Aleja to let her tears flow so she could forget her old life. They asked Aleja to draw pictures of all the things she missed about her home and then, once finished, burnt the drawings in front of her.

Her Grape Mother was the last memory the Temple Maiden's forced Aleja to forget. Aleja cried as they burned her drawing of Grape Mother sitting by a moonlit window, gazing at ships in a distant bay as she sang Aleja to sleep.

"When the ashes wash away, you will no longer be Grape Child." The maidens said in unison as they rubbed the ashes of Aleja's drawings onto her face. "You will be a novice. And when you learn how you will serve, the Queen will choose a name from the old world to begin your new life as her Daughter."

The maidens did not know Aleja had already chosen her name, and snuck it into the High Temple with all the skill of a thief hiding a precious stone. Rather than cut her off from her childhood home, the name bound her to it, and kept the memories of her childhood hidden in her heart.

The room grew dark, as if a giant shadow passed over the opening.

The smoke from the temple. It must be fully green by now.

Aleja imagined the joyous and relieved expressions on the people's faces, but did not need a mirror to see she did not share in their happiness.

Why am I to wait here? Are they torturing me? Breaking me down? Isn't the Vessel supposed to be celebrated before the day of her sacrifice?

Aleja thought back to her meeting with Taka, and to how his deep blue eyes, and the red eyes of the ram, stared at her.

Could he see my fear? My unwillingness to let go of my life? Is that why I'm here?

It dawned on Aleja as she picked up the last of the cup with her bloodied hands that maybe this was what Kalim was trying to protect her from. If she hadn't shown fear, they would not need to break her down like this.

Aleja traced the lines on the broken clay cup. A trickle of blood ran down the shattered edge and a single drop fell on the floor.

There was a thunderous roar from the walls the moment the drop hit the floor. Aleja looked up, then stared in horror at the walls. The eyes of the people and animals carved in the walls came alive, and their mouths were no longer silent. They stared at Aleja and filled the Room of Reflection with the sound of their screams.

CHAPTER 7

The screams sent Aleja scurrying to the corner of the room where her mattress lay. She put her hands up to her ears to block out the sound. The people and animals on the walls changed from stone into flesh, and then decayed as their screams quieted to a pitiful whimpering sound. The smell of rot filled the room, making the bitter smell of the tea sweet by comparison.

Aleja looked at the carving of the Queen. Beams of pale, grey light poured out of the Queen's eyes and mouth, and she let out a terrifying moan that silenced the others.

Aleja searched the walls for a door, but found none. Her hands franticly moved over the stone, hoping to chance upon a latch. The Queen's cry grew louder, and vibrated through the floor and the walls.

The Queen's gelatinous body stretched out of the stone like the tentacles of an octopus through a fisherman's net. The pale grey light of the Queen's eyes shone on Aleja's face.

Aleja crumpled into the corner as the Queen came closer. The Queen's mouth grew wider. Aleja screamed as the Queen grabbed hold of her, and began to swallow Aleja head first.

As the darkness consumed Aleja she heard only a voice, sweet and soothing, calling out to her again and again.

"Come to me, Daughter of Light."

Aleja's body went limp. She felt warm. It was like drowning, but without pain or fear.

"Come to me," the voice said repeatedly in a watery echo, "come to me."

Once her body was completely consumed Aleja suddenly felt the sensation of wet grass beneath her feet. Aleja was surprised to see she was standing on solid ground. It was night, and the dew on the grass was cold. Aleja looked in wonder at the garden around her, and then took a deep breath of the lavender scented air.

The Queen was gone. Aleja, as far as she could tell, was alone.

The muddy ground squeezed between Aleja's toes as she planted her foot firmly forward and walked into the night.

The night fog, tinted blue from the light of a luminous moon, gave the garden a ghostly appearance. The air was filled with an odd, chirping sound similar to the sounds of insects.

Through the fog Aleja saw a house on the top of a small hill. There was a candle lit in one of its windows, a pale yellow light muted in the haze.

Aleja followed a path of small stones that led to the house.

She heard a child cry from the window. It was a soft, pitiful sound. Aleja's heart broke at the sound of it.

"Don't cry," Aleja called out as she rushed toward the house, "I'm coming!"

A wind blew past Aleja and almost knocked her down. The wind brought goose-pimples to her skin, and not just because of the chill in it. A voice carried with the wind as it blew up toward the house.

"Hush, my child, do not fear."

The curtains billowed and the light from the candle went out.

Aleja stopped in her tracks.

"Is anyone there?" Aleja called out. There was no response, only a faint echo of Aleja's own voice. No longer hearing the child's cries, Aleja walked slowly forward.

The side of the house was white and weathered. Ivy vines crept into open windows and threaded a roof that was little more than a wooden frame.

Aleja entered the house through its only door. The walls were covered by ivy. There was a patch of small, blue flowers on one of the walls. Aleja pulled apart the vines to get a better look at them, and then fell backwards with a startled shout.

A pale face, its mouth disfigured into a leering grin, stared sightlessly at Aleja from behind the lush curtain of ivy. Aleja turned away and covered her mouth to halt her scream.

There were others staring at her from the walls. The whistling wind blowing through their open mouths sounded like a deathly sigh. Aleja swallowed her fear and looked closely at the faces.

Masks. They're just masks.

Aleja spun around at the sound of the door slamming shut behind her. Another mask hung above the door. The pupils of its eyes were pinpoints, and the blue irises clouded as the fog outside the house. The mask's white skin sagged, and the bloodless lips gaped at Aleja in expression of pure misery.

As Aleja drew closer to it something fell from the mask. Aleja picked it up and felt a familiar, nauseating texture on her fingertips.

Skin. Dried and leathery.

It was an ear.

It's made of skin, Aleja realized with horror, *human skin.*

Aleja threw the ear to the ground and frantically wiped her hands on her peplos. A fresh gust of wind blew into the house and the ear skittered across the floor back towards Aleja. The whistling sound from the masks grew into a wail.

The wailing was so loud it shook the rafters. Debris crashed to the floor. Aleja tore through the ivy covering a window as the house began to collapse.

The ivy over the window was thick, and had now turned brown and hardened. Aleja's hands bled as she tore at it.

Behind Aleja, where the human face was nailed above the door, she heard the child crying again. Aleja's heart raced. She grabbed the vines with both hands and tore them from the window.

There was a loud, cracking sound overhead. One of the rotted beams broke free and swung down. Aleja ducked as the beam slammed into the window and broke through the wall. Once the dust settled Aleja saw a hole just big enough for her to crawl through.

The child's pitiful cry grew louder as Aleja crawled on top of the fallen beam and squeezed her way through the opening. Just as her head broke through the hole she felt a dry, crackling caress on her leg. A withered hand slowly ran down the length of her thigh before grabbing hold.

Aleja looked back at her leg. Through the leaves Aleja saw the skin mask's glassy, clouded eyes, now wet with tears, staring at her. Its childlike cry changed to mocking laughter that sounded like a flock of screeching birds.

With her free leg, Aleja kicked at the creature's face until it blew apart like dried leaves in a windstorm. The skin mask's hand lost its grip on Aleja's leg, and she crawled out of the window and fell.

But instead of hitting the ground outside the house, Aleja fell into water. She struggled to swim up, but only sunk deeper with every stroke.

Aleja opened her mouth. She readied herself to free the last of her breath and let go of her life. In the darkness she did not see the bubbles escaping her lips, nor did she feel the tears that joined the water filling her lungs.

But she felt a hand. And with a force more powerful than all the waves crashing down on Aleja, the hand pulled her up, and dragged her coughing onto the muddy ground.

CHAPTER 8

Once Aleja coughed up the last of the water she looked up at the woman standing over her. The woman had long, unkempt hair that covered most of her face, and was dressed in a muddied, thin chemise like those worn by the young girls who dove for pearls off the coast of Mir.

The woman squatted besides Aleja and pulled her hair from her face. She regarded Aleja curiously, as if she were an exotic animal.

"You are fine." The woman said. Her voice had an odd, lilting quality. Aleja couldn't tell if what she said was a question or a statement.

"There are others here." Aleja's own voice was near panic. "They attacked me. Chased me."

The woman held her hand to Aleja's face. Her touch was calming. Aleja felt her mind and body ease almost into sleep.

"Don't worry." The woman said. "The lost children are far from here."

"The lost children?"

"Yes." The woman said simply, and then stared out into the fields that surrounded them.

It was still night, and from the looks of the willowy grass, Aleja believed she was in the middle of a large field of rice paddies. Aleja spotted a flock of white herons in the distance walking through the water that covered the ground, the birds' thin legs pierced the glassy surface with delicate precision.

Aleja looked back at her savior.

"How are you named?" Aleja asked.

The woman's laugh was childlike.

"Don't you know me, Aleja? I am your Queen."

Aleja stammered for a bit, and then quickly knelt on both knees before the Queen. Aleja placed her hands in front of her in the shape of a triangle, then lowered her forehead into the space. She felt the coolness of the muddy earth.

Aleja waited silently for the Queen to address her. She would not presume to begin a conversation with a Goddess.

But instead of addressing Aleja, the Queen gently helped her stand and then picked up something from the mud.

"Look, Aleja. Isn't she beautiful?"

The Queen held a small, ugly creature close to Aleja's face. The fat bodied creature, with dark, slimy skin and spindly legs, stared at Aleja with large, bulbous eyes. She saw its chest and cheeks expand as it made the peculiar chirping sound Aleja heard throughout the garden.

"Yes, she is, my Queen." Aleja said with a gulp. "Quite beautiful."

The Queen smiled and knelt down on both knees in front of Aleja.

The Queen caressed the creature tenderly.

"I wanted to bring them here, to the island. I loved to hear their song at night when I was a child. My first summer away from them I hardly slept at all. I wanted this for my children." The Queen said with a sweep of her hand towards the rice fields. "But your world is still too harsh, and they are too fragile for it. The poisons of this world seep into their skin. They would certainly perish out there. Here they are safe, except from the herons. This one has injured her leg, and now I must decide what is to be done about it."

Aleja could see one of the legs appeared swollen and limp. The creature drew the other neatly under its chest as the Queen ran her finger along its head.

"If I let her go she would be too slow to escape the herons, and certainly too slow to swim from the fish. She will die. I have the power to heal her Aleja, but, I ask you, should I?"

The Queen's gentle caress grew harder, and her hand slowly wrapped around the creature in a fist. The creature let out a croak, and its bulbous eyes stretched further out of its head.

"Or should I end its misery now?"

There was a sickening, squishing sound as the Queen squeezed the animal.

As ugly as the creature was, Aleja could not stand to see it in pain. Without thinking, she grabbed hold of the Queen's hand and pried her fingers loose.

"You have taught us life is sacred." Aleja said with her head bowed. "If one can help preserve it they should do everything in their power to do so."

"I would heal her," Aleja said, almost blushing as she did so, "if I had the power."

The Queen drew close to Aleja's face. The large, dilated pupils of the Queen's sensuous eyes stared directly into Aleja's.

"You believe so, and yet you judged one of my own children to die."

"Yes, I did. It was a mistake."

"A mistake?" The Queen replied playfully. "How does one know what is a mistake and what is not?"

Aleja was taken aback. She tried to think of an answer, but found she could not.

The Queen looked out towards the rice fields and placed the creature on the ground by the water. She drew her hair behind her ears and squatted on her bare feet. She looked like a simple village girl. Aleja saw nothing of the fiery, demonic Goddess that guarded the High Temple gates.

"Even if I heal her, I cannot protect her from every danger, even here." The Queen spoke as the creature sat limp in the mud. "More than any other I want her to live on, to continue singing her song. Do I destroy those who wish to harm her? Or do I let nature run its course? I ask you Aleja, which one would be a mistake?"

Aleja thought for a moment. She was sure there was a decision made in the past which could be applicable, even to a situation as bizarre as deciding the fate of such a small, ugly creature as this. But if there was, Aleja was ashamed to admit she did not know it.

"I don't know, my Queen. I'm sorry." Aleja said. "I don't have the answer you seek."

To Aleja's surprise the Queen seemed pleased with her response. The Queen released the wounded creature back into the water and smiled. She traced the creature's limping swim with her finger in a wide, zig zag pattern along the surface of the water.

"Nor do I." The Queen said.

The Queen pulled off a piece of the water's surface and held it out to Aleja. It was a mirror. Its smooth black surface rippled like the water it came from. The Queen placed the mirror in Aleja's hands.

"Take this back with you."

"What is it?" Aleja asked.

"The darkness that will guide you through the blinding light."

"I'm sorry my Queen. I don't understand. What is it for?" Aleja said as she took the mirror from the Queen's hands.

The Queen did not answer Aleja's question.

"Trust in the path you have chosen." She said with a loving caress to Aleja's face.

"I thought I was chosen to be your Vessel." Aleja stared at her reflection in the mirror. Even though Aleja felt confused and anxious, her image stared back at her with a resolve Aleja did not feel. "What path have I chosen?"

The Queen embraced Aleja. When the Queen drew back her face changed. It was black, and as smooth and reflective as the mirror. But the eyes were not a fiery red like those of the High Temple statue, but rather, dark and full of stars.

"If I told you," the Queen said, her voice a whispered echo, "it would not be your path."

Aleja looked deep into the eternity of the Queen's eyes, and felt no fear. There had never been so many stars in the night of Corazon's sky.

"A life of knowledge without experience is like a book that has never been read." A circle of stars and fire surrounded the Queen as she spoke. Cracks of light pierced her skin, and her body broke into pieces. The Queen's body was engulfed by the fire pouring from her wounds. The Queen's disembodied arms carried Aleja into the light. "Trust in yourself, and yours will be the book which will never burn."

The Queen, the field, the herons, all disappeared in the blinding light of the flame. Only the mirror remained.

CHAPTER 4

Aleja woke to the coolness of a wet cloth on her forehead. Her throat was parched and her voice croaked as she asked for water. Eyes closed, Aleja drank from a clay cup placed to her lips. Her thirst overtook her. Aleja grabbed the cup and swallowed the water in a gulp.

"Go slowly," said a voice by her bed, "you may not be able to keep it all down."

Aleja opened her eyes and saw a beautiful young woman standing by her bedside, her hands folded delicately at her waist. She seemed to glow in the soft, orange light pouring into the room from the window by Aleja's bed. Although the Daughter introduced herself in the manner all Daughters did, Aleja found it unnecessary, for the beauty of Sara, the Maiden of the High Temple, was famous throughout Mir. Seeing her now, Aleja thought the stories did her beauty no justice.

Sara was everything Aleja felt she herself was not. Slender and tall where Aleja was angular and short, with a delicate nose the shape of a dew drop before it fell from the petal of a rose. Aleja's own nose, a rounded stump that barely protruded from her circular face, was her least favorite feature. Sara looked as young as Aleja, but with her grace and talent she quickly achieved the rank of Maiden of the High Temple, and was responsible for overseeing the duties of all the Temple Maidens.

After a bow Sara turned to call back to a servant waiting in the shadows.

"Bao, fetch more water."

The servant, a short, stocky woman in the later seasons of her life, bowed and quickly filled the pitcher. She returned and stood by Sara's side. Aleja recognized the look on Bao's face that she saw in so many of Corazon's common people. A look of simple, sweet kindness. The look of a child that never grew up.

"This Daughter knows you are used to living alone." Sara's translucent, delicately tapered peplos, billowed in the breeze sweeping through the room as she spoke. It was as if the wind also adorned Sara to accentuate her ethereal beauty. "But so you may be more comfortable, the Temple Maidens have chosen Bao to be your house servant. She is simple and plain, but has served in the High Temple all her life, and will attend to your needs unquestioningly and without hesitation. Please tell this Daughter to send her away if this is not the truth, for one of the Temple Maidens could see to her duties. Do you wish her to remain in your service?"

Bao picked at her fingers as Sara spoke, and glanced up slightly from her lowered head as Sara waited for Aleja to respond.

"Yes, Sara. I wish her to be here." Aleja held out her cup towards Bao.

Bao, now smiling, walked briskly towards Aleja. Sara helped steady Aleja's hand as Bao filled the cup.

"Where am I?" Aleja asked.

"You're home." Sara held her arms out and smiled with pride at the resplendent furnishings of the room.

Aleja looked around. The room was wide and spacious, with red stone walls, and filled with ornately carved furniture. From what Aleja could see from her window it was obvious the room was far higher in the sky than her modest home beyond the Wheel. She looked out the window, and imagined she could see the roof of her old home.

"This is not my home." Aleja said.

"It is the High Temple, the home of our Queen, and her Vessel." Sara replied.

"Vessel?" Aleja shook her head, as if trying to rattle her senses to clarity. "What are you talking about? What happened? How did I get here?"

Sara sat beside Aleja and dabbed her forehead with the cloth.

"You were unconscious in the Room of Reflection. The Temple Maidens brought you here upon High Chamberlain Taka's command. The Queen has chosen you to be her Vessel, and now you must be treated as an honored guest. But for now, Vessel, please try to rest."

"Call me Aleja."

"My apologies Vessel, but there is no longer any Daughter named Aleja, for those chosen to house the spirit of our Queen are only to be named Vessel."

Aleja looked over at Bao, who was sitting by the large, wooden entrance door, dipping cloths into a bowl and then folding them into a large, neat pile on the table. Tears welled in Aleja's eyes as she watched Bao smile with every towel she prepared.

Sara turned back to Bao.

"Those will be sufficient, Bao." Sara pointed at the rapidly accumulating pile of towels. "Thank you."

Bao cast a nervous glance at Aleja, who gave Bao a nod to show she was to stop.

"May I ask you something, Sara?" Aleja said, while still looking at her servant sitting by the door.

"The Vessel may ask anything of me, for my duty as Maiden of the High Temple is to serve the Vessel."

"I understand that outside this room, and in the company of others, I must be known as the Vessel. But I ask you, as one concerned for the comfort of another under her care, that in private you refer to me as Aleja." Aleja fell back upon her pillow and looked up at Sara. "I am sorry to cause such conflict in you, sister."

Sara shook her head and smiled. She sat next to Aleja, and gently wiped away the tears pooling in Aleja's eyes.

"There is no conflict. You are under my care Aleja. This Daughter will do as you wish."

Aleja nodded her head in thanks. Sara took her by the hand.

"Tell me Aleja, what is troubling you? Unburden yourself."

"Memories."

Sara looked quizzically at Aleja.

"I mean, I remember some things but, I can't tell whether it was real or a dream."

"Is there a difference?"

Aleja scoffed.

"To Judges there is."

"What is the last thing you remember?" Sara asked, showing no offense to Aleja's sharp reply.

Aleja paused and bit her lip. Sara motioned for Bao to get another cup of water.

"My face. On the mural." Aleja said with a shudder.

Aleja hoped Sara would look confused. But there was no change in her expression.

"I was hoping you would tell me I must have dreamt it." Aleja said.

Sara took the empty cup from Aleja and placed it on a night stand by the bed with a motion so graceful the cup almost seemed to float away on its own.

"No." Sara drew a blanket up to Aleja's chest. "I can assure you it was not a dream."

"What does it mean?"

"The Queen has chosen you to be the Vessel of her spirit. She will take her place in your body, your memories will become hers and..."

Sara paused, as if unsure to continue.

"...your body will no longer be reborn into this world."

Sara, her eyes now glistening like Aleja's, tugged the blanket a little higher up to Aleja's neck.

"I know what it means to be the Vessel." Aleja said. "What will happen now?"

"You will be honored for your sacrifice to our people. Till the day of the ceremony you will live here in the High Temple under the care of the Temple Maidens and will follow the guidance of High Chamberlain Taka. High Emissary Kalim will escort you when you go outside the High Temple. The Guardians will strengthen your body to receive the Queen's spirit, and the Herdmasters will teach you to how ride a horse."

Aleja felt her spirits brighten. Even though it would be without the shameful thrill of riding horses without permission from the Chamberlains, the prospect of riding a horse from the Queen's stables more than fully compensated for it.

"I'm to ride a horse?" Aleja said breathlessly.

Sara nodded.

"Why?"

"For the procession around the Wheel. On the day of the ceremony."

"The ceremony?"

"When the life in your body is removed, and the Queen's spirit takes its place."

Aleja shuddered again, and silently cursed herself for it.

"Yes, of course." Aleja exhaled. "What are my duties before then?"

"You must greet those from all over Corazon who will come to Mir to provide tribute. Games and celebrations will be held in your honor. People from all over Corazon will come to see you lead the procession. After the ceremony the Temple Maidens will change the green smoke to red to signal all the temples in Corazon that the Queen's spirit has taken on new flesh."

Sara paused, took a cup from Bao, and held it to Aleja's lips.

Aleja's next question came out quickly and awkwardly.

"When will the Queen take hold of my body?"

Sara wrapped her arm around Aleja and held her close. Aleja was ashamed Sara could now feel her trembling.

"The ceremony will be on the night of the next full moon, when light and dark take equal hold of the sky. You will know the day approaches when the rains come to Mir, and the color of the Yamanashi Mountains change from green to gold and red."

"I see." Aleja's smile was brief and sad.

Sara drew Aleja in close.

"It is a great honor, Aleja." Sara said softly, "The greatest the Queen can bestow upon a Daughter. When people think of the Queen they will see your face, and your memory will live forever in her."

"But why was I chosen, Sara?"

"I don't know. Only the Queen does, and if she did not tell you then it is not for me, or any other, to say."

Aleja shook her head and cursed the tears stinging her eyes. To feel any sense of sadness over this was only because she could not abandon her sense of self, and was unworthy of the honor. It dawned on Aleja that until now she never felt any real hope or fear she would ever be chosen, for there were thousands more suited than she. She felt safe in her mediocrity, of going about each day no different than the next, of never believing she would be something more. Her talent in memory, her ability to act as Judge, was all she felt she needed in life. And now that was gone.

Sara took a comb from the nightstand and ran it gently through Aleja's hair. Aleja relaxed, and eased her head into Sara's lap.

"Have faith the memories will return, Aleja." Sara said, as if she had read Aleja's thoughts. "You have made a memory palace of facts and judgments in your mind and each will hold firm. But you have seen the Queen, who is not just our mind, but also our heart. It is natural to be overwhelmed by feelings in her presence. Details are the stone that shaped your mind, but emotions are the vine that grows steadily over the rock, and over time, can crack through the wall and reshape it, hold it together, or tear it apart. As a Temple Maiden I accept this as truth. A Judge may cut at the vines, but I believe the roots are still in the ground, waiting to grow."

"Which is exactly why I made no such attachments to people or places." Aleja interrupted. "Even after my days as a novice were done."

"In your memory palace, is there anything personal to you?" Sara paused and placed the comb on the nightstand. "Anything you have ever held dear?"

"No, we are trained not to include such things. Personal items have memories associated with them that cloud judgment. There is nothing about my childhood I remember. Only that I am from the Clay lands and that there was a–" Aleja stopped short. A glint of light from across the room caught her eye. A mirror, which looked exactly like the one the Queen gave her, dark and with sharp, angular edges, sat on a dresser on the far wall. The light from the window shimmered across its surface, and Aleja saw an old woman's face staring back at her in the glare.

My Grape Mother. Yes, I remember her.

"What is it?" Sara asked.

Aleja paused. She thought back to how the Temple Maidens took her childhood memories from her. She wanted to trust Sara, wanted to confide everything, but held back just the same. She didn't want any risk to the memory, even if it was soon to be taken by the Queen.

"Nothing." Aleja smiled at Sara, who gave one in return, and then asked to take her leave.

After Aleja granted permission Sara got up, and then bowed deeply. Aleja gave an awkward nod in response.

"I will tell High Chamberlain Taka you are well." Sara said. "Would you like me to show you around the High Temple after the sun rises?"

"Yes, I would. Thank you, Sara." Aleja said.

Sara went to the door after their parting embrace, and closed it with a bow in Aleja's direction. Once Sara left the room, Aleja walked around her new quarters. Bao got up from her chair by the door and followed her only a few paces behind.

The room was open and spacious, with latticed walls to separate the dining area from the other parts of the room. Two doors framed by large, open windows led to the balcony outside. There was a large stone bath, even bigger than those in the public baths near her old home.

Beyond the bath Aleja noticed a small room off to the side, almost hidden from view by two pillars positioned by the entrance like stone sentries. The room was dark, windowless, with only a small, simple cot for a bed and a small wooden table no bigger than a chair.

Nightmarish scenes of the misery the people of Corazon left behind in the Drowned World covered the walls. At the far end of the room, across from the entrance, was a relief of the Queen. This vision of the Queen was like the one that greeted Aleja at the entrance of the High Temple. Her many arms ended in claws gripping bloodied weapons, a hideous, fanged scowl was on her face, and her eyes gleamed red from the gemstones placed under her heavy brow. Aleja thought back to the Caretaker's heresy in the amphitheater.

They are all just stories. Carved in dead stone.

Memories of meeting the Queen in the rice patties came in waves. Although the details were frustratingly hazy, Aleja felt the warmth of the Queen's kindness, the comfort of her presence. And then, as she stared at the terrifying carving on the walls, a voice inside Aleja said words she would never dare to speak aloud.

That is not the Queen.

"Meal ready Daughter." Bao said awkwardly from behind Aleja.

"These are your quarters?" Aleja asked, "You are to eat here?"

Bao nodded.

Aleja looked over the meal on her table. Light from the fiery sunset poured in from the latticed windows onto the table. The water in her cup glittered.

The sight of it brought back memories of sitting alone in her room, eating silent meals and shutting out the world.

Aleja shook her head emphatically.

"No. You will not eat there. Not tonight Bao. Not ever."

Aleja pulled another chair up to the table for Bao, and bid her to sit down. Bao did so reluctantly, and looked distinctly uncomfortable as Aleja took her place at the table. Before Bao could even think to serve her master Aleja placed a slice of warm, fatty red fish on her plate. Bao broke out into a smile at the sight of it. They bowed at their food, and said the customary prayer over it together.

"Thank you for giving me your life."

CHAPTER 10

The next morning Sara led Aleja through a labyrinth of hallways that were almost a mirror of the streets of Corazon. The High Temple was massive. A city within a city. At the center was the Syncronia which, like the High Temple itself, was the hub of a large hallway that circled around it.

Sara's novice Ulaa followed in silence a few footsteps behind them. She stood just out of view, watching her teacher, as Sara walked Aleja through each room and explained its importance.

The activity in the honeycomb of narrow, inner-hallways was far more bustling than the wide circular hall. Attendants rushed through the halls, carrying freshly washed sheets and clothes, trays of food, oils and perfumes. So intent on their purpose, to Aleja's amazement, the attendants gave only cursory nods to Sara as they passed by.

Sara not only didn't seem to mind, but made sure to give way to them.

Aleja did not believe such wonders existed in the world. The city outside the High Temple was a sea of plain, white clay houses with red tiled roofs. There was the occasional flourish, mostly in the markets, where food vendors, jewelers, hairdressers, and taverns all tried to attract interest with colorful drapes over their doors and colored glass in their windows.

But it was nothing like what Aleja saw inside the High Temple.

Sara led Aleja through rooms lit by towering light wells, steep holes in the ceilings that filled rooms with pillars of light. The light was reflected throughout by the numerous mirrors hung on the walls and by the smooth marble floors. The frescos here were not faded, but filled with glorious color, and the reliefs carved into the walls showed no sign of wear. The interior rooms, not lit by the light wells, were illuminated by large crystal lamps that lit each room in pale blues, forest greens and deep maroon colors.

Although much of the High Temple was reserved for the Chamberlains to oversee the work of the Daughters and Guardians, there were diversions. There were menageries of exotic and colorful animals, misty garden courtyards, cavernous halls filled with music sung all day by choirs of Temple Maidens, and, most spectacularly to Aleja's eyes, a room with a domed roof that looked as large and far away as the sky.

The roof was decorated, like much of the mosaics and reliefs in the High Temple, with scenes of the Queen's history. In the domed room the mosaic on the ceiling showed the Queen leading her people hand in hand towards a hole in its center that let in the blinding light of the Sun.

All doors in the High Temple were open to Sara save two. The location of one, the Queen's chambers on the uppermost levels of the High Temple, was unknown even to Sara. The other, Sara told Aleja in whispered tones, led to a library filled with maps, ancient texts, and other things forbidden to the people's eyes.

The door to the library was guarded by a silent pair of Guardians. Both large and formidable looking, with the daggers of the Queen dangling from their belts.

"I always wondered why those who survived the Wastes would be able to keep the daggers they were given." Aleja said to Sara. "How could someone once banished be trusted?"

"Because they returned to the Queen's embrace." Sara explained.

"But why let them keep the daggers? There are no dangers here."

"Because it is the ultimate symbol of our trust in them. What more could you do to show someone you trust them with your life than give them the power to take it? Those who survived the Wastes are the strongest and most faithful of all Guardians, for the trials of the Wastes taught them how much they need the Queen and each other. To ensure their own protection, they must protect us all."

"But do all those who survive return to the Queen's embrace?"

"The few who do survive. Yes."

"How do we know?" Aleja persisted.

"I have seen them return." Sara replied.

"What if some refuse to return? Maybe they stay with the Yamanashi people once they reach the mountains?"

Sara slowed her steps.

"You are quite clever, Aleja. I have never considered the possibility."

Aleja blushed, and said no more.

Sara placed both hands on a pair of large doors and gave them a push. The heavy-looking doors opened with little effort, and the hinges holding it to the walls made no sound.

Once opened, the sound of rushing water poured out of the room. Aleja entered the wide expanse of the room with eyes and mouth wide open. Waterfalls poured from the massive reliefs of the Queen's face on each wall and emptied into channels that created a circular island in the middle of the floor.

Aside from a large, stone pyramid in the center of the island, only the walls had any sort of decoration. The floors were smooth, black marble. The bridges over the water channels were nothing more than a marble slate.

Water came from the Queen's mouth and from holes hidden in the waves of her hair. The holes were large enough for a person to crawl through. Sara explained attendants climbed into the holes to scrape off the sediment that built up in them.

"Actually, all of the water channels need such cleaning." Sara explained as she pointed to a small panel in the wall. "This whole temple is filled with narrow crawlspaces to access them. So many I don't think anyone knows all of them."

"Where is the water coming from?" Aleja asked. It seemed a shame to her that water taken from the lakes of Corazon would be used only for a decorative effect.

"It is not the water from the lakes." Sara said. "Rainwater is collected along the Aqueducts stretching all over Corazon and is brought here."

Sara led Aleja over one of the marble bridges. It seemed impossibly thin, and Aleja walked with delicate steps over it, as if afraid it would break underneath her.

"There is a deep channel in one level of the aqueducts where the water runs uncovered. It is a beautiful section of the aqueduct, the sound of the rushing water is quite soothing. Temple Maidens sometimes walk it while resting from their duties."

"I would like to see it."

Sara's face went flush. Aleja forgot the walkway was one of the sections Sara was not to show her. Anything outside of the High Temple was forbidden to Aleja now.

"Forgive me, Sara, I forgot…"

Aleja trailed off, knowing further apologies would only shame Sara more. To her relief Sara smiled and waved off Aleja's apologies.

"There is no need, Aleja. I only hope you like what I am able to show you."

"Oh yes, this room is impressive." Aleja replied quickly. "I'm sure it is a good place for reflection."

"I'm sure it would be. But that is not its purpose."

"What is its purpose?"

Sara smiled.

"What do you divine its purpose to be?"

The two women stopped short of the small pyramid in the center of the room. Aleja turned in circles to look for some clue that would give away the room's purpose.

The room was the size of the Syncronia, though much less ornate. Although a healthy stream of water poured from the Queen's mouth little else poured from the holes hidden in her hair. As she looked at the Queen's face Aleja noticed there were also holes where the Queen's eyes should be.

Not a drop poured from them.

Aleja looked down at the channel. It was filled less than halfway.

"The Syncronia is the visualization of the Queen's mind and memory," Aleja said as Sara smiled and nodded, "this must be the heart, for the blood of Corazon flows here."

Sara clapped her hands in delight.

"I couldn't have explained it better. It is not only the representation of how the Queen gave her physical life force to reseed and replenish Corazon, but it's also how we divine the health of Corazon now. The Chamberlains come here to determine if the yields will be good. When not a drop falls from the Queen's lips, or a heavy stream pours from her eyes, then we know things in our land are out of balance."

Aleja looked up at the Queen's sightless eyes.

"Have you ever seen such a thing?"

Sara shook her head no.

"Never. Since I have been here the water has been steady, more or less."

"Where does the rainwater go? Once it's passed through here?"

"Most of it is used to clean out the floors below. It then empties into channels bargemen use to take waste from the city."

"What of the baths?"

"They are filled from water from the Yamanashi Mountains. The water is so pure, so clean, Aleja. It is one of the few pipes that does not divert anywhere else in the city."

"Sara, I know I am to take my baths in my room, but, I don't suppose just this once I may see the large bathhouse and take mine there?"

Sara's novice Ulaa looked nervously at her mentor as Aleja spoke. Sara's smile was confident and assured.

"I don't remember the High Chamberlain forbidding it, do you Ulaa?"

Ulaa, trying hard to look unconcerned, shook her head quickly.

"Well then, permit us to take you there." Sara said and then outstretched her hand towards Aleja.

Sara guided Aleja to the pyramid, and then appeared to disappear into its walls. Aleja then noticed the opening was cleverly and carefully constructed to give the illusion the wall was unbroken.

I wonder if the entrance to the Queen's chambers is hidden in such a way. Perhaps we passed by it without even knowing. What other hidden passageways could I find here?

Aleja took one last look at one of the reliefs of the Queen. Just before she went through the door and descended the stairs, she saw a single tear drip from one of the Queen's eyes.

CHAPTER 11

It took the length of the day for Sara to show Aleja the expanse of the High Temple. It felt like more walking than Aleja had done in a lifetime. By the time Aleja took her meal in her room, she was almost too tired to lift a bowl of soup to her lips. After the meal, Bao almost had to carry her to bed. Bao held Aleja at her waist, and she could feel the strength in the woman's arms.

The bed was large and comfortable. Aleja's body, warmed and relaxed from the bathhouse, rested easily into it.

The High Temple bathhouse was the largest Aleja had ever seen. There were many rooms, some so hot bathers wore wooden sandals to walk on its floors and others with water so cold Aleja feared her heart was about to stop when Ulaa poured it over her head to cool her. The bathhouse rooms were filled with laughter and relaxed conversation as warm and hazy as the humid air. Some of the bathers swam in the larger pools or rested on bridges crossing over them. After finishing their baths Aleja, Sara, and Ulaa sat with feet dangling in pools filled with little fish that nibbled on their toes as they ate sweetcakes and talked.

It was a dark, moonless night. The dark filled Aleja's room save for the light from a small, blue crystal lamp casting a faint glow by the mirror. Aleja's eyes grew heavy as she stared at its water-like surface. The mirror seemed to sing to her as she drifted into unconsciousness. Just as sleep was about to overtake her, Aleja was startled by the sound of shattering glass.

Aleja threw off her blanket and got out of bed. The dust stirred up by her blanket swirled and glittered in the mirror's strange blue light.

The mirror grew with every step Aleja took toward it until it was as large as the entrance to the Syncronia.

Aleja walked into the mirror and was consumed by its darkness. All around her was nothingness. She felt no floor under her feet as she walked onward into the abyss.

Aleja heard a man's voice calling out to her in the dark. Somehow, she knew it was the voice of her father. She even knew his name.

Amedeo.

Aleja looked at herself. She was a young child again, back in the Clay Lands, seated at his simple wooden table.

Aleja's father was a solitary man, a stranger to most in the village, including Aleja herself. No one had ever told Aleja the man was her birth father, but Aleja suspected it was so. Something in the eyes, she thought. The way he looked at her. Different from the others.

It was the night before Aleja was taken to Mir to become a Daughter. Her father had dinner with her alone. After a silent meal he showed Aleja a book. Aleja had to be told what it was, for she had never seen or heard of one before.

"This is how people remembered once." Aleja's father said as he let her gently turn the fragile pages. "It was how we shared our thoughts with others."

Aleja remembered the crinkling sound of the stiff pages as she carefully turned each one. Her father pointed to something written on the page. The lines and dots went in all directions. To Aleja it looked like a black raindrop splashed upon a pale stone.

"This is my name, Amedeo." Her father said with his finger on the page.

"Where is Grape Child?" Aleja responded excitedly.

"It is not here. There is no such name among the ancients. You must know you will no longer be Grape Child. You will forget that was once your name."

Aleja began to cry. Amedeo held her. Aleja felt comforted by his embrace, but not by his words. Her father told her all names, all people, all things must one day pass into nothingness. It was how things in this world were supposed to be. He said the people of the village loved her, but she was too special of a child to stay with them. She would be going to a place where there were other children like her, a place where she would start a new life.

"To become a Daughter, your old life must be cast off like a snakeskin." Amedeo told her. "The Daughters will make you forget everything. This village, your Grape Mother, and your name. You will not even remember me speaking to you now."

"Why?"

"So you can serve the Queen, and our people. You must receive a name from the ancient world. You cannot have a name of the Clay People."

"I won't forget my name." Aleja yelled through her sobs. "If they try to make me, I will scream it in their face."

Amedeo laughed and hugged Aleja. His laughter was warm, and it made Aleja smile.

"I know you won't forget, Grape Child. That is why I want to show you this."

Amedeo pointed to another one of the strange markings in the book.

"This is the ancient language of the Queen."

Amedeo drew his finger along one of the words.

"And this is the name you will have when you become a Daughter."

He took Aleja's hand and traced over the name with her finger. She continued to trace until the ink seeped into her skin.

"There is magic in this name. It is your past, it is your future, and it is who you are now. You must trace it so your body will remember the shape of this name. After your training the Temple Maidens will place your hand on a mirror as black as night. The mirror is how they talk to the Queen, and once your hand is placed on it they will hear your name." Amedeo pushed her finger harder onto the page as she traced. "Know this name. Inscribe it into your bones. Burn it into your mind's eye, and we will always be with you. Grape Child, and the land she loved, will survive."

"What is the name?" Aleja asked as she traced it repeatedly.

"Aleja." Amedeo responded with a bittersweet smile.

"It's strange. I don't like it." Aleja protested. "It has no meaning."

"Not to you, not now." Amedeo said as he closed the book. "But when the time is right, it will."

Amedeo took out a paper. He placed a piece of coal chalk in Aleja's hands.

"Now, Aleja, write your name."

As Aleja traced her name on the paper she heard a strange music. It was as if her new name was being sung to her, in a voice more beautiful than any she had ever heard.

Amedeo smiled. He handed her a clay cup, the water inside red from its color. Aleja reached for it, but it slipped from her hand and crashed onto the floor.

Amedeo looked at Aleja with tired eyes, as if all the life in his body had been poured into the cup that now lay broken on the floor.

"Pick it up, Aleja." Amedeo said, his voice weary.

Aleja looked down at the shattered cup. The water quickly absorbed into the red earth floor. Amedeo took a piece of the cup in his trembling hand and held it before Aleja.

The piece had changed. It was no longer clay, but now gleamed like black glass.

"You must make it whole." Amedeo said as he placed it in Aleja's hand. She felt a slight pinch in her palm, and looked down. Aleja screamed at the sight of her hand bloodied from a deep cut.

Aleja awoke with a gasp. Bao stood by her bed.

"You have good sleep, Daughter?" Bao said with a bow.

Aleja nodded, her eyes fixed on the mirror. It was back to its normal size, and still propped on the dresser across from her bed.

Bao looked over at the mirror, and then back at Aleja. She whispered quietly to Aleja, looking slightly over her shoulder at the attendants waiting behind her.

"It sing to you, too?"

Aleja stared at Bao in disbelief. Bao smiled back at her.

Aleja was about to ask what Bao meant when the door to her chambers was thrust open. A familiar, and unwelcome, voice echoed through the room.

CHAPTER 12

"Is that girl out of bed yet?"

Kalim cut through the line of Maidens by Aleja's bed. She stood over Aleja with hands on her hips.

"Slept well enough, did we?" Kalim smirked.

Aleja looked up at Kalim and blinked.

"I thought we would meet you outside?"

"I hate waiting." Kalim snapped back.

She turned back towards the Maidens.

"What are you? A bunch of pretty statues? Prepare the Vessel for riding."

The Maidens scurried towards Aleja and almost climbed over each other to be the one to help her out of bed.

Sara entered the room just as the Maidens removed Aleja's tunic.

"High Emissary Kalim," Sara said sweetly, "thank you for gracing us with your presence. May this Daughter be of some help to you?"

"I am just fine, thank you." Kalim said with a dismissive wave. "It's the Vessel you need to concern yourself with."

"Yes, thank you High Emissary," Sara replied with a slight bow, "but it was this Daughter's understanding that you would wait for the Vessel outside the High Temple."

"The High Emissary hates waiting." Aleja said before Kalim had a chance to respond. "More than she hates rudeness, apparently."

Aleja smiled sweetly at Kalim, who gave Aleja a bitter one in return. Sara stepped through the group of Maidens and stood next to Kalim. Aleja noticed the slight movements Kalim made to stay clear of coming in contact with Sara. No one else took any notice.

"Apologies, High Emissary," Sara whispered. "But we are acting in accordance with High Chamberlain Taka's wishes, and would not have kept you waiting if you did not arrive before sunrise."

"The High Chamberlain has his schedule, and I have mine." Kalim pointed to a Maiden holding breeches in her quivering hands. "Make quick with dressing the Vessel, and don't worry yourself about her morning meal. We have food in my palanquin. From this day on I want the Vessel at my palanquin before dawn breaks."

Aleja noticed Kalim never looked at Sara, even when addressing her directly. It was rude, but felt odd even for one as brusque as Kalim. It was almost as if Kalim couldn't bear the sight of her.

"Am I to feast on seeds with your bird this morning?" Aleja said as Maidens hurriedly tied the breeches tight to her waist.

"Hermes has already eaten, but if you would like his scraps you may have them."

"Your bird eats better than many in Mir." Aleja said as a chemise was pulled over her head.

"Certainly." Kalim tittered. "He has more refined tastes than most."

Aleja and Kalim shared cold stares. The air was heavy with an uneasy silence.

"The Vessel will be prepared the next morning as you have instructed, High Emissary." Sara said suddenly. "This Daughter will make sure the attendants have the Vessel ready for the morning ride and will be waiting for you outside the Temple gates."

"See to it. Don't make me call on her again like I am some simple house servant."

Kalim responded with her back to Sara. It infuriated Aleja to see Sara being treated with such disrespect.

Did Sara offend her? Or is she just jealous of her beauty?

Although it was difficult for Aleja to imagine, especially when Kalim was scowling, she heard Kalim was once as revered for her beauty as Sara was now.

The uneasy silence between Aleja and Kalim accompanied them as they left the High Temple and rode through the gardens to the Queen's stable.

Once there, Aleja and Kalim were greeted by a delegation of stable workers led by the Herdmaster of Mir, a cheerful old man named Turik. He was an unusual sight. Men in Mir preferred to be hairless, even to the point of shaving off all the hair on their head. Baths in Mir were filled with the sounds of yelping pain as attendants plucked each hair off men's bodies. Turik's squinting eyes peered out at Aleja through thick bushy eyebrows. He had a broad toothy smile framed by a beard braided like a horse's mane.

Turik approached and bowed.

"Greetings, Vessel. It honors us for you to enter this humble stable."

"Humble? You consider the Queen's stable to be humble, Herdmaster?" Kalim quickly replied.

"Although it bears her name, High Emissary, we deem it not worthy of her. We strive every day to make it so." Turik said after some hesitation.

"Well, perhaps you need to strive a little harder. I hope at least it is worthy enough for the Queen's Vessel." Kalim's smile dripped with condescension. "We wouldn't want to see the Vessel riding a mangy donkey for her procession."

One of Kalim's attendants held Hermes on a golden perch. Kalim casually fed the bird a handful of seeds as Turik fumbled out a response.

"A, uh, donkey?" Turik's ears turned red. "No, the Vessel will ride the finest breed. If you would permit me, High Emissary, let us show–"

"Show us in? Yes, please." Kalim interrupted. She motioned for Aleja to follow her, then walked past Turik towards the stable. Turik, the top of his bald head as red as his ears, scurried ahead of her to lead the way.

"Why must you be so disrespectful?" Aleja whispered sharply to Kalim as they approached the stable.

"Exactly whom have I disrespected?" Kalim replied loudly.

"This Herdmaster." Aleja's whisper was now more like a hiss. "The Maiden of the High Temple."

"Oh, have I? I wasn't aware. Exactly how did I disrespect them?"

Aleja stumbled out a response. She didn't think she would have to explain it.

"Well, from the way you speak to them. You wouldn't even look at Sara as you spoke to her."

"Sara, is it? Have you become friends in so short a time?" Kalim reached back to pet Hermes. The bird let out a screech into Aleja's ear.

Aleja wanted to say she considered Sara a friend, but felt embarrassed to admit it out loud, and knew Kalim would mock her for it.

"The Maiden of the High Temple has been most helpful." Aleja said after a time.

"As she should. It is her purpose to make us comfortable. We are not duty bound to do the same for her."

"Still," Aleja protested quietly, "basic respect for another Daughter–"

"What exactly is my purpose on this island?" Kalim interrupted. "What do I do to serve the Queen?"

Kalim's question was punctuated with the sound of a horse angrily snorting in one of the stables. There was the sharp sound of hooves against wood, and the muffled commands of the stable hands as they tried to subdue the animal.

Aleja, curious, looked towards the stable. Turik walked into her vision and hurriedly redirected her towards the yard.

"This way, this way. The horses are this way." Turik said with an anxious look towards the noise coming from the stable.

Aleja turned her attention back towards Kalim.

"To serve as representative of the Queen." Aleja replied to Kalim's question. "To see her will is carried out throughout Corazon and mediate between disputes of those who serve her."

"Yes. And how does a mother mediate between squabbling children? How does she get them to bow to her will?"

Aleja thought for a moment. Kalim did not wait for a response.

"Either through love or fear. It has not been in my nature to inspire love, so I chose fear. I'm sure your new friend has made great use of the love she has cultivated among the Temple Maidens, but love is as temporary and tenuous as a spider's web." Kalim nodded towards Turik readying the horses in a line for inspection. "Fear is the spider herself."

Aleja watched as Turik got both his attendants and the horses into their proper positions. It was clear they were not quite ready to receive the Vessel, and his embarrassment showed.

Aleja looked at Kalim, who smiled back at her. It was clear this was exactly the effect Kalim wanted to have on Turik.

Aleja was sure the next morning's ride would proceed much differently. More smoothly, although probably with little joy.

The horses, ten in all, stood steady before Aleja. She was surprised at how docile they were. Aleja thought stallions in service of the Queen would have more fire in them. These were all beautiful, but broken.

As Aleja's hand ran along their necks and haunches, she felt only pity for the animals. She felt nothing of the thrill she expected from being so close to them.

Aleja's hand delicately grazed their faces. Aleja searched for a spark in them, some hint of the wildness of the Horselands outside the walls of Mir, and was disappointed she found none.

"Do none of these old nags take your fancy?" Kalim hissed impatiently behind her.

Aleja ignored Kalim and went towards Turik.

"Are there others in the stables I might see?"

The bells in Turik's beard rang as he shook his head.

"My apologies Vessel, but you first need to learn to ride. These horses are the ones most suitable for you."

"So there are others?"

The Herdmaster opened his mouth in reply but was cut short by the sound of yelling from the stable behind him. The crowd, and even Kalim, cried in alarm as a muscular, black stallion leapt over the stable gate and then galloped into the yard.

Stable boys and girls, one with head bloodied, another holding his arm in obvious pain, chased after the horse with ropes and sticks. Some in Aleja's attendance tried to get in front of the horse, only to leap face down into the dirt to escape being trampled by the stallion.

The stallion was saddled, but clearly not tamed. It charged towards the open fence leading to the High Temple Gardens. A quick thinking Guardian bravely went to close it, and almost payed with his life as the stallion knocked him over with the force of its turn.

The stallion charged towards Aleja. Even from a distance the horse's eyes met hers.

Aleja froze at the sight. She knew she should jump out of the way but her legs felt stuck in the dirt.

A Guardian grabbed her arm, but as strong as he was he could not move her. It was as if she was a stone set deep into the ground. The Guardian's grip slipped and he fell as he tried to pull her out of the horse's path. The horse charged with incredible speed, but to Aleja everything seemed still. Dirt flying from the horse's hooves seemed to hover in the air like feathers floating in a breeze. The yelling and chaos of the yard seemed muted, as if it were coming from deep underwater, but the horse's breath and the rhythm of its heart pounded in her ears. Even from afar, she felt a connection with the animal she never did with any horses in the stable by her home outside the Wheel.

Aleja felt a flash of anger she wasn't sure was her own. The anger of a magnificent animal born free, yet kept in confinement until it was as broken as the others. She also felt the giddy pleasure of finally breaking free, and laughed as the stable hands fell face first into the mud while running from the horse's charge.

With the wall of horses behind her and the stallion charging ahead, the muddied Guardian finally pulled Aleja to the side while another readied a bow to shoot the animal down.

Aleja snapped out of her daydream.

"No!" Aleja yelled at the Guardian readying his bow.

She ripped her arm free from the Guardian and ran towards the stallion. Any arrow from the Guardian's bow would have to go through her first.

Aleja heard Kalim shout, and felt her hand as she too tried to stop Aleja from running to the stallion.

"Aleja stop!" Kalim screamed.

The Herdmaster, distracted by the horses now breaking rank and running through the field, could only manage to shout a futile command as the horse charged directly towards Aleja.

Aleja's heart pounded as hard as the stallion's hooves did against the earth. She held her arms outward as if to embrace the animal, who showed no signs of slowing down or of veering from Aleja's path.

"Kill the creature!" Kalim yelled. "Save the Vessel, you cowards!"

Aleja did not see the arrow release from the bow. She only heard the sound of trampling hooves and the angry bray of the horse. Nor did Aleja feel the arrow graze her head as she dodged the horse, grabbed the reins, and swung herself onto the horse's back.

The arrow would have found its mark right between the horse's eyes had it not been for Aleja pulling the animal to the side. A warm trickle of blood ran down the back of her head, mixing with the sweat quickly building on the nape of her neck.

It took a moment for Aleja to realize she was now riding a horse charging at full speed. In her sudden terror she wrapped her arms around the horse's neck.

The horse bucked, and almost sent Aleja flying off the saddle. Aleja managed to grab the reins before she toppled off the animal. She tried to get control not so much of the animal, but of her own body on the saddle.

Aleja's fear turned to exhilaration as she barreled past the crowd of people staring at her with eyes and mouths open wide. She laughed out loud at the sight of Kalim trying to get her to stop, only to trip and fall backwards into the mud. Her concentration broken, Aleja almost flung herself off the other side of the horse. Aleja groaned as she pulled on the reins to straighten herself. This time the horse did not buck or try to fling her from its back.

But the stallion did not follow her lead. Aleja held on tightly. She felt the burn of the leather straps in her hands, her thighs straining to hold herself tight to the horse's sides. Her feet struggled to find their way into the stirrups flailing wildly below.

There was nothing Aleja could do but hold on as the stallion stormed towards one of the lower fences as if to leap over it. Even if the horse was able to clear the fence Aleja knew she would be thrown by the force of the jump.

But rather than feel fear at the thought, Aleja felt strangely at peace. She relaxed her thighs, and rested her head near the horse's neck.

Jump then, one of us will be free.

Aleja felt a subtle shift in the horse's pace, and just before it reached the fence it turned and slowed to a trot. Aleja pulled on the reins to bring it back towards the stable. The horse fought only for a moment, but then responded to her. She pulled back to slow the stallion down, and found her footing in the stirrups.

The horse stopped. Kalim led the attendants rushing up to Aleja, yelling obscenely as she did so.

"What were you thinking? Who were you trying to kill? You or us?"

Aleja laughed at the sight of Kalim, who was distinctly less impressive when covered in more mud than jewelry.

"I was just eager for a ride." Aleja replied nonchalantly.

Kalim scoffed, but for once was speechless.

Turik rushed up to Aleja's side. She felt the horse twitch slightly, but calmed him with a gentle caress down his neck.

"Vessel," Turik exclaimed breathlessly as he took hold of the reins, "I was not aware you were able to ride so skillfully. Forgive me for insulting you with such a poor selection of horses. I should have given you a choice."

Aleja nuzzled the horse's mane. She smiled down at Turik.

"It's alright, Herdmaster. It doesn't matter, I think this horse chose me."

Kalim sauntered up besides Turik and glared up at Aleja.

"Honestly, such nonsense. You threatened the safety of the Vessel by letting that beast out." Kalim turned back towards the Guardian who fired the arrow at the horse. "And you could have done far worse with your misguided shot."

The Guardian, who stood slumped behind Kalim, fell to his knees and planted his face into the ground.

"Punish me for my stupidity, High Emissary. I would rather die with honor in the Wastes, than live without it in Mir."

Kalim let out a mocking laugh.

"As foolish as your shot was, I suppose it pales in comparison to standing before a charging horse. But as I am in no position to lay punishment on the Vessel, we shall have her punish another." Kalim turned back towards Aleja. "What would a Judge give this Guardian for that scratch on your head?"

Aleja placed two fingers on the back of her head and felt a hot sting at the touch.

Kalim looked up at Aleja expectantly.

"What should be his punishment?"

Aleja knew the punishment was painful and public. She was sure Kalim knew it as well.

Is this another one of your little games, you old spider?

"A Judge administering the Queen's justice the way she proscribed it would have part of the Guardian's distinction stripped off his skin, in full view of his sisters and brothers." Aleja said.

Aleja looked at the Guardian still kneeling with his face in the mud. His decision was foolish, she thought, but done only to save her. Aleja did not have the heart to punish him so.

Kalim nodded as if giving her approval.

I won't give you the satisfaction. Aleja thought with a smile on her face. *I won't aspire to be feared like you.*

"But since you are asking the Queen's Vessel, not one of her Judges, I believe this Guardian should simply be required to practice in front of them. He will suffer damage to his honor, but will also be able to regain it in their eyes as his skills improve."

The Guardian peered up from the dirt. Mud and tears framed his eyes.

Kalim's smile disappeared. She looked at the other Guardians, who stood ready to apprehend their comrade.

"So be it. Guardians, you heard the Vessel. This man must practice every evening until the master decides he is worthy to walk the streets again. Now take him away."

The Guardians pulled the man from the ground and did as Kalim bid. Before he was taken away, he looked Aleja in the eyes and mouthed the words, "thank you".

Aleja nodded, then turned away from him and looked towards Kalim. The look in her eyes was far less appreciative.

"Still willing to practice justice in your own way, I see. What exactly did you learn in the Room of Reflection?"

Aleja took Turik's hand and dismounted.

"Enough." Aleja said as she landed on the ground.

"I don't suppose you learned to ride a horse there?" Kalim said.

Aleja did not reply. She handed the reins over to Turik and thanked him.

"We shall be making inquiries to the stables in Mir." Kalim said, seemingly indifferent to Aleja ignoring her. "High Chamberlain Taka will be very disappointed to hear they are allowing Daughters outside the Wheel to ride the Queen's horses."

Aleja glared at Kalim.

"There's no need. I never rode a horse until today."

Kalim scoffed loudly.

"What have I told you about lying, Vessel?"

Aleja shrugged her shoulders and turned towards Turik.

"He's beautiful. What's his name?"

Turik stared at the fence where the horse jumped into the yard. An arrow was now embedded in its post.

Aleja was happy to see Turik's warm smile return to his face.

"You may not believe this, Vessel." Turik said with a chuckle. "His name is Arrowchaser."

CHAPTER 13

The rains came early to Mir.

It did not wait for the leaves of the tangled oak trees to brown and fall to the ground, or for the thick flocks of birds to fly over the city as they fled the northern skies to the sanctuary of the Marsh isles, lands sheltered by the Southern Cove and the Queen's decree no human shall set foot on them.

Aleja listened to the rain hitting the slate roof as attendants dressed her, applied glittering paints to her face, and perfumes to her body. The sound calmed her, even if it was a reminder the time for her ceremony was drawing near.

Every stroke of brush on her face, every bracelet or necklace, every shred of cloth she wore had to be approved by Taka. He would never speak to Aleja or the Maidens. Taka would only nod his head if he liked something, or if he did not, flick his hand as if he were swatting at a fly.

Kalim, when she was also present, was equally brusque with her appraisals, but more verbal.

Aleja couldn't decide which she liked least, Taka's silent stare or Kalim's sharp tongue.

Whichever I must endure at the moment, I suppose.

When she wasn't riding Arrowchaser, Aleja only looked forward to her evening meals with Bao. Although Bao was more of a listener than a talker, Aleja felt the weight of the day lighten when they ate together. The food was hearty and warm, and instead of the bitter tea Taka and Kalim's attendants constantly served her she was allowed one glass of wine to wash it down. Thanks to Sara, the tea usually ended up in the drain.

"I can't drink that." Aleja told Sara one day as she prepared it. "It reminds me of the Room of Reflection."

Sara deftly poured Aleja's tea into her own cup and drank. She did it so subtly the other Maidens didn't notice.

"Our little secret." Sara said with a wink.

Aleja was pleased Sara didn't even question her. Ever since, even though Aleja knew the tea was brought to her room, Sara made sure it was dumped or switched it out before the scent could reach Aleja's nose.

But that was as much freedom from Taka's control Sara was able to give Aleja. Since her first day's ride with Arrowchaser, Aleja found she was no longer free to walk around the High Temple, even with Sara. After the incident Taka decreed Aleja was to have someone by her side at all times.

When she was not riding, training, or being adorned with what seemed to be every scent and jewel in Corazon, Aleja was confined to her room. Of all the things Aleja endured as Vessel, she liked being adorned the least. On the first day Aleja felt the flicks of the Maidens brushes were pleasant, almost soothing. Now each one was like an itch Aleja could not raise a finger to scratch.

"That's it." Taka said once an oaken crown was placed on Aleja's head.

Taka turned to the Maidens and held out his hands.

"Thank you for the work you have done for our Queen. You have given her children a living vision of their Queen they will hold in their hearts till their last days." Taka turned to one of his junior chamberlains.

"The wait is over. We will allow the delegations to see the Vessel tomorrow."

Taka clapped his hands together and bowed to the attendants, sending shockwaves of amazement through the crowd at such a display of support from someone as critical as Taka.

The Maidens were reduced to tears and all decorum was lost as they hugged and shared in their joy, provoking the first relaxed smiles and laughter Aleja had seen in days.

Yet despite their happiness, Aleja stood unsmiling.

After Taka left, Aleja asked for a mirror.

The mirror she looked into was not as clear as the one given to her by the Queen. This one was polished metal, and her reflection stretched around the edges, distorting the contours of her face.

A stranger stared back at Aleja, her face patterned with bolts of glittering blue streaking from incredulous eyes.

Everything about Aleja's features was exaggerated by the paint. Her skin was darkened to remove all sight of her freckles and made a striking contrast to the golden, interlocking lines painted on her hands and arms. Aleja's lips were a luscious green, like the creamy jade earrings dangling from her ears. The thin, oaken crown was not as heavy as others Aleja had worn, the ones made from the metalworkers in Jin. This crown, made from the trees at the foothills of the Yamanashi Mountains, was carved into thin spirals. Gossamer threads of silver held the branches in place and gradually covered them as the crown rose up into several points above her forehead.

Aleja took off the crown and handed it to an attendant. The attendant took it and placed the lemniscate band on Aleja's head in its place.

"Prepare my bath." Aleja said as she stared at herself in the mirror. Her reflection stretched in the edges of the polished metal in a way that made the thick blue lines around her eyes appear to lift off her face.

"You have no time for a bath." Kalim called out from a dark corner of the room.

Kalim walked into a rectangular column of bluish light descending from one of the room's many light wells.

Kalim smiled in the way she always did when bearing news she knew Aleja didn't want to hear.

"Are you so ready to end the day?" Kalim said. "What a waste. You have so few left, and there is still so much to do."

"Oh, you mean I will get to stand in a different place today? Well then, what are we waiting for?"

Kalim sighed.

Aleja held up her hands, which, although softened by the lotions her attendants applied to them, still bore raw, red blisters from the horse's reins.

"My last ride with Arrowchaser was a little rough." Aleja said. "Herdmaster Turik suggested I rest for one day."

"He is in no position to decide that. Besides, if you hurt it is your fault." Kalim glared at the attendants, who were busy at work pretending not to notice the spat, and twirled her hand at them. Aleja noticed they picked up the pace immediately. "You're pushing too hard with that beast."

"We push each other."

Kalim let out another sigh.

"Yes, I forgot you made another friend. Anyway, you have balance training today, or have you forgotten?"

Aleja closed her eyes. The very mention of training created a sudden and acute ache in her arms and legs.

"I never forget, High Emissary. Anyway, I don't think it's necessary. You heard the High Chamberlain. I look like a Queen, I don't need to act like a monkey."

Kalim laughed.

"Certainly, although a monkey is not as likely to fall from a horse or a palanquin as you are. That would indeed be an inspiring sight for the people to remember. The Vessel flopping on the ground like a fish thrown onto a dock."

"There are several sunrises before my procession, Kalim. Surely one training could be missed? Besides, I think I stood perfectly well today."

Aleja turned to the Maidens removing her jewelry.

"Don't you think so?"

"Oh yes, Vessel, quite well." The Maidens replied eagerly until they caught sight of Kalim's stare.

The Maidens quickly quieted themselves and removed Aleja's gown with cowed heads. They then helped Aleja into her zona, the knit brassiere and briefs she wore for her training.

"Not as well as you may think." Kalim said, "You have far to go before you show the grace worthy of our Queen. Now let the Maidens clean the paint off you so we can finish this day before the next dawn breaks."

Kalim was silent on the way to the training grounds, but occasionally smiled at Aleja as if she was keeping a secret from her, although Aleja couldn't fathom what it may be and was almost too tired to care. But her curiosity was aroused the moment they arrived at the Guardian's training ground. Whatever it was, she could tell something was going to be different about this day.

Instead of going to the small, musty interior rooms as usual, Aleja was taken to the large, open atrium in the center of the building. Rather than painted murals of wrestling Guardians or acrobats jumping over charging bulls, Aleja would get to train surrounded by the golden light of the setting sun.

The facilities in the atrium were much the same as those in the interior rooms. Smooth balls of stone and leather, long balance beams, one about a full foot wide and the other not much wider than a rope, various weights to build strength, and mirrors to examine her form.

The young commander in charge of her training was tall and lean, with skin almost as dark as his black hair. Aleja's heart skipped at the sight of his face. It was beautiful enough to be chiseled into the walls of the High Temple.

Aleja turned to Kalim. Kalim took notice of Aleja's sudden apprehension, and smiled back at her.

"Should we tell them we're here?" Aleja said, her voice betraying the sudden nervousness she felt.

Kalim looked at the Guardians.

"Oh, I wouldn't want to interrupt them. Why don't we watch for a while? It's not every day a woman gets to see such displays of…strength."

Aleja and Kalim watched the men, dressed only in briefs, as they began impromptu wrestling matches. After she had her fill of watching the commander make short work of his comrades, Kalim stepped out of the shadows of the pillars that framed the atrium.

"We would like to begin." Kalim's voice echoed across the grounds.

The men stopped in their games and rushed up to Aleja. The commander bowed deeply and the others quickly followed suit. Aleja could hear them trying to catch their breath in short, muffled gasps.

"High Emissary Kalim, I apologize for not greeting you at the entrance." The commander said through quick breaths. "The ground is prepared for the Vessel's training."

The commander looked at Aleja with sharp, piercing eyes. Aleja suddenly became aware she had been staring at him for some time and awkwardly looked away.

Kalim gave Aleja a sly, sideways wink.

She changed my trainer. But why? Is this just another one of her games?

"So I take it you are to see to the Vessel's training?" Kalim said.

"Yes, that is my duty High Emissary. Please cast me aside if you believe me unworthy."

"What is your name, Commander?"

"Ivo."

"Well, Commander Ivo," Kalim said, "you certainly appear worthy. Just remember your duty and obligation is now to strengthen, and protect, the Vessel. The body our Queen will inhabit for her next lifetime with us."

Ivo nodded.

"I understand, High Emissary."

Ivo pointed to a stone bench at the edge of the atrium. Aleja caught her gaze following a bead of sweat slowly rolling off his shoulder and through the ridge by his bicep.

"You may take a seat there if it pleases you, High Emissary." He said.

"As it so happens, I have another engagement." Kalim turned to Aleja. "Vessel, I will leave you in Ivo's capable hands."

Aleja looked at Ivo. His eyes were not just green, but laced with thin strands of gold. A sudden and unexpected feeling of panic came over Aleja at the sight of them. It was as if her stomach was already beginning to do the somersaults Ivo was about to assist her with.

Aleja took a quick breath and bowed slightly to Kalim.

"That will be fine, High Emissary." Aleja said in the most dignified voice she could manage. "Thank you for your assistance."

"I will take my place then." Ivo said with a deep bow, then made his way to the training floor. Ivo's comrades followed in a line behind him.

Once they were out of ear-shot Kalim reached over and grabbed Aleja by the arm. Aleja followed Kalim's eyes as they gazed at Ivo.

"Just remember," Kalim said with a wink, "never wish to end a day before its time."

CHAPTER 14

"We will go easy today Vessel." Ivo said as he walked Aleja towards the training area. The ground in the courtyard was covered in lush green grass and was lit by a massive light well above.

"The ground is not so wet, but you may not be used to training on it." Ivo said.

"How could the ground be so solid?" Aleja said, her voice lilting slightly as the tips of the grass tickled the bottom of her feet. "It's been raining for days."

"The ground covers a field of stones that helps with drainage. We also had the opening of the light well covered. Some of the rainwater drains off the roof into a channel that feeds into the Water Hall in the High Temple. I imagine it must be flooded by now."

I wouldn't know. I haven't been able to walk about the High Temple since my first day there.

"The water is running quite heavily, yes." Aleja replied.

As much as she hated the lie Aleja felt desperate to keep the conversation going, and didn't feel like making Ivo uncomfortable with a complaint.

"Did the Vessel ever hear the Evening song here?" Ivo asked as he looked up at the light well.

"No, the Vessel is expected back at the High Temple when the first candle of night is lit."

"Well, if my lessons find the High Emissary's favor, perhaps the Vessel will be permitted to listen to the Evening Song with us." Ivo said. "The way the sound travels through the open windows of the well and echoes through the halls is quite beautiful. It would be a great honor to share with you our devotion to the Queen."

"Undoubtedly." Aleja said. "But the Vessel is expected to do so at the High Temple only."

It was only a moment, like the blink of an eye, but Aleja saw Ivo wince at her reprimand.

I must be tired. I'm starting to sound as nasty as Kalim.

"But the Vessel will see if she can listen here." Aleja said with a forced but pleasant smile. "Apologies Commander, it has been a long day. May the training begin?"

"Yes, of course, Vessel." Ivo said with a bow mirrored by the guardians standing in wait behind him.

To Aleja's surprise Ivo did not direct her to the balance beam, but rather to an open area encircled by a line of white sand. Ivo directed her to stand across from him as another guard took his place by Ivo's side.

"Have you much training in the Gentle Way?"

Aleja blanched. The Gentle Way was how Guardians referred to their methods to subdue and control people who are a threat to either themselves or others. No Daughter ever received training in physical arts that could cause harm to others.

"None, of course, this Vessel was a Daughter, not a Guardian."

"So you know none of the forms?"

"No, that's not what I meant." Aleja was so flustered by Ivo's apparent surprise she momentarily forgot how to refer to herself. "Why would any Daughter ever need it? A Vessel is to stand before her people, she is not even to speak to anyone. "Aleja paused, then laughed as the thought occurred to her. "Much less twist their arm backwards."

Aleja was relieved to see Ivo smile at her joke.

"That is an excellent point, Vessel. But after hearing about the difficulties you were having I thought, perhaps, it was because of a certain inflexibility in your training. Or, if you'll pardon any offense I may give, inflexibility in your body."

"Excuse me, Guardian. Daughters are taught stretches and poses, which keeps us quite flexible."

"Yes, you are correct Vessel, and forgive any offense I may have caused, for it was not my intention. But, if I may give my opinion."

Ivo waited for Aleja to nod her assent.

"Stretches do help the body maintain flexibility, especially for those who must do their work in sitting positions, but stretching eases a body out of rest. The Gentle Way shows you how to move not just in a fight, but also how to move when you walk, stand, or run. Dancing would also be a good way to teach movement, but it is not what I know. You are right, your duties will not require you to twist an arm, but you may enjoy learning how."

Aleja regarded Ivo skeptically, but was convinced by the sincerity in his voice. Most Guardians were very proud of their skills. But unlike Ivo, none desired to share them. Aleja couldn't tell if it were pride on his part or pure foolishness. Charmed by Ivo's lack of guile, Aleja decided to give it a chance.

"Fine." Aleja responded, then took a seat on one of the larger balancing balls, and pointed to another guardian. "But demonstrate it first."

Ivo smiled and then nodded. Without warning Ivo's comrade approached him from behind and attempted to get Ivo in a headlock.

If Aleja blinked she would have missed everything. Ivo grabbed the attacker's hands, and despite being a full head taller than him, slipped through the opening in his arms and moved behind him. The man yelped as Ivo pushed upwards on his arm, which was now bent awkwardly behind his back.

Ivo quickly released him. The two exchanged a quick embrace, the chamber echoed with sound of hands slapping bare backs. Ivo turned to face Aleja.

"It was so fast," Aleja said with admiration, "I almost didn't see it happen."

"It must be, Vessel, for no move is successful when the opponent can see or predict it."

"You are so much taller than he," Aleja pointed to the other man, "yet you seemed to shrink as he came at you. How was that possible?"

"That," Ivo said with a satisfied smile, "is what I want to show you. That is what the Gentle Way can teach you, how to find comfort in your body, to make it bend to your will, and make it do the most extraordinary things. Tell me Vessel, if someone was to grab you in anger, what would you do?"

Aleja had to think. She never considered the possibility. Violence was rare, even in a city as large as Mir, and violence against a Daughter unheard of.

"This Vessel does not know. Perhaps grab the attacker's hands and pry them off?"

"What about grabbing your own hands?"

"What?" Aleja shook her head.

Ivo smiled and held out his hands to Aleja.

"Let me show you."

Aleja nodded and let him grip her by the arm. He showed her the proper way to stand, legs apart so the space between them was a triangular shape.

"Good," Ivo loosened up his shoulders, "now grab your own hand, and pull it towards yourself as quick and hard as you can."

Aleja did so, and to her surprise not only pulled herself free, but also slammed her elbow into Ivo's jaw, sending him sprawling to the ground. The guardians watching let out a loud whooping sound.

"I'm sorry, I'm sorry, I'm sorry!" Aleja shouted out as she knelt by Ivo's side. "Are you hurt?"

Ivo rubbed his jaw and shook his head. His comrades laughed as they helped him to his feet.

"Not at all, Vessel." Ivo said after stretching out his jaw.

Another guardian, older than Ivo, thick and stocky, slapped him on the back.

"Now you know why I keep telling you to shut your mouth in a spar." The Guardian turned to Aleja. "Thank you, Vessel, we've wanted to teach him that lesson for a long time!"

Everyone laughed, including Ivo, as much as it appeared to ache his jaw.

"I'm sorry, Commander." Aleja said. "Perhaps I'm not meant to learn the Gentle Way."

"I disagree. But let's start with something less aggressive. After all, I promised the High Emissary I wouldn't endanger you." Ivo grinned. "Maybe I need to worry more about myself."

Aleja smiled. She no longer felt tired.

"Well then," Aleja said, "what are we waiting for?"

CHAPTER 15

leja stood on the balcony of her room at the High Temple and took a deep breath of the evening air. She asked Sara for a moment alone, and despite Taka's command she be escorted at all times, her friend granted it. Although many in Mir were already wearing thick tunics to keep out the chill, Aleja was dressed in a light, linen peplos. A constant breeze blew over the balcony, wrapping the fabric tightly to her and covering her skin with goosebumps.

Rather than return inside, or cover her arms with cloth, Aleja began to move.

There was a tiredness in her body, but Aleja did not desire sleep. As the moon waxed Aleja's dreams became more vivid. Sometimes she dreamed of her father, sitting at his table as she traced her name, or trying to fix the clay cup that always broke and bloodied her hands. In other dreams she was in the garden, on good nights sitting quietly with the Queen listening to the sounds of insects. On bad nights she was trapped in the house, fighting with the skin-masked creatures trying to pull her into the vines. It was as if the Queen and the creatures were battling for control of her thoughts. Every dream, bad or good, began with Aleja being absorbed by the mirror.

There was nothing she could do about the mirror. Taka ordered it placed there, and moving the Queen's mirror was one command Sara would not defy.

The wind rushed the smells of the sea over the balcony. Aleja took a deep breath, then wrapped her arms around an invisible opponent. She moved one leg gracefully in front of the other, and then simultaneously swept her other leg and turned as if leading her partner in a dance.

Aleja had only been with Ivo for a few sessions, but already learned much from his training. Every activity, even holding a cup, now felt different. Even Arrowchaser seemed to respond better to her after Ivo's lessons. Aleja no longer pulled too hard on the reins to guide him, but led with subtle pressure from her thighs or a slight touch on his neck.

Aleja positioned herself into the first form. It was simple, almost no different from the stretches she practiced most of her life. Her legs splayed in a triangle shape, knees bent slightly, and hands slowly rose up to the center of her chest.

The first form was the basis of all the techniques of the Gentle Way. It was a way of moving that kept one as solid and sturdy as a stone, yet lithe and smooth as running water.

Most of her time with Ivo was still spent on balance, but she did not find it as tedious as before. With Ivo's help she corrected the small but important details on the balance beam that once sent her crashing to the ground.

And, unlike times with other trainers, she did not flinch when Ivo needed to hold her body into position. She only hoped he could not detect the slight quiver she felt at his touch.

Aleja ran her hand along the balcony railing. It was thick, about the width of her hands set side by side. Aleja leaned over the railing to look at the ground far below her. Her room was little more than halfway up the High Temple, yet there were days when her balcony was covered by clouds.

Aleja lifted one foot onto the ledge, and then the other. She held on tight to the railing in a squat position.

Stand up, Aleja. You won't let yourself fall, trust yourself.

Aleja took her hands off the railing and slowly stood up, moving her legs apart to establish a firm base as she did so. She took one cautious step forward with arms held outward like the wings of a bird. When her balance held she took another forward step, followed by one back, and with each step picking up speed until she was moving across the ledge as if she was on the sturdy floor of the training ground.

Turn after turn her balance held, and Aleja couldn't contain her laughter. Aleja leapt into a spin and landed facing outwards towards the city.

Aleja looked down. High as she was above the ground, the conical shape of the High Temple ensured a fall would only take her three stories until she slammed into slate or stone.

It would be enough to destroy the Vessel. Poor Taka would be so sad.

Aleja laughed, and then took another spinning leap.

It's alright if I fall. The way I feel right now, I could probably fly.

Aleja took a few more prancing steps and then launched into another spin. She stopped mid-spin at the sound of the balcony door opening.

The Maidens stared at Aleja with mouths open wide. To make matters worse Sara was also there, and was creeping slowly towards Aleja as she danced her insane dance on the ledge.

Aleja lost her balance. Just as she was about to topple over Sara wrapped her arms around Aleja's waist and pulled her to the balcony. The Maidens rushed forward and helped pull Aleja up from the floor.

Aleja held on tightly to Sara's arms as they walked back into her room. Much to her own surprise, Aleja couldn't stop laughing.

"What were you thinking?" Sara scolded Aleja. It was the first hint of anger Aleja had ever heard in her friend's voice. "If anything happens to you what would happen to us? Do you think any of us are strong enough to survive the Wastes?"

Aleja stopped laughing. At the sight of Sara's anger she burst into tears.

Sara sat with Aleja and put her arm around her.

"I'm sorry to scold you so, Aleja. It's just that, I let you have some time alone because I trusted you. It hurts me that you broke that trust."

"Don't be sorry, Sara. You're right. I didn't want to hurt myself, I just…"

A Maiden handed Aleja a cloth to wipe her eyes.

"What, Aleja?"

"…wanted to feel free."

Sara pulled Aleja close as a Maiden handed her a cup of water.

Aleja thanked the Maiden, one of the many who were now staring at her with baited breath.

That was stupid. I put them all at risk.

Aleja didn't think any would tell Taka, for they would also be punished if he knew. None would have anything to gain from it. But just as Aleja came to that conclusion she noticed Sara's novice, the young girl named Ulaa. She was pouring the tea brought to Aleja's room, and staring at Sara with a strange smile on her face.

CHAPTER 16

Aleja sat before her own massive image in the Syncronia as the delegations of Corazon prostrated themselves before her. Aleja was seated in a massive chair that glittered like a star, with the Queen's mirror placed behind her head. She wore the oaken crown Taka chose, and her peplos and the paint on her face was a kaleidoscope of color.

As usual in public functions, Aleja was instructed only to give each person a gracious bow after they had shown her their offering. Then a Guardian would guide the delegation away and the Temple Maidens would take the gifts from Aleja's sight.

As splendid as some of the gifts were, Aleja could only think about how she would gladly trade them all to see Sara again.

Sara was not exiled, Aleja was thankful for that at least, but was sent to the Room of Reflection, and was no longer responsible for Aleja. Her novice Ulaa now had that duty.

Aleja made sure to give Ulaa a hard time on her first day. Once Taka heard he summoned Aleja to the Syncronia and berated her.

"You can go back to the Room of Reflection if you miss her so." Taka yelled at Aleja. "She was there only to serve, not to grow close to you, or you to her. What is the purpose of the Vessel making any attachment to her life anyway? It is the Queen's life now, not yours!"

Aleja spent the rest of the day confined to her room, wanting to throw the Queen's Mirror off the balcony if she could only walk a foot without her every step being watched. Except for the presence of Bao, who continued on with her meager duties oblivious to the tension around her, Aleja no longer looked forward to her time in the room as respite from Taka or Kalim. And on days like this, when there was no time with Arrowchaser or with Ivo, when she sat all day to listen to each Chamberlain prattle on about her sacrifice, Aleja had to bite her tongue to keep a scream from escaping her throat.

Whenever Aleja felt herself drifting, being too slow with her recognition of each delegation, Kalim gave a slight cough from behind her chair. Taka spoke for Aleja to each delegation, with a smile on his face for their benefit, but daggers in his eyes for Aleja.

Aleja's apparent lack of appreciation for the gifts from the small villages of Corazon filled her with some remorse, for these people were giving her the best of what they had. But the obvious, insufferable pride the city delegations had for their gifts annoyed Aleja beyond any such guilt she may have felt over her ingratitude.

The last delegation came from Jin, which some called the Golden City for the way the gilded pavilions and jewelry of its people glowed in the sun. The city was wedged between the Yamanashi Mountains and the sea, and prospered from the richness of both. Unlike the other coastal city Andrid, whose ships took the lost souls of Corazon to the Stone Islands and to the Wastes, Jin's ships circled Corazon bearing the metals of the Yamanashi, both the harvests of the sea and the fields, and never returned to Jin empty of riches.

Jin's delegation was large, consisting not just of Chamberlains and Emissaries, but their beautiful Temple Maidens and imposing Guardians bearing decorative chests of impossible size. The sound of the chests thudding to the floor was as much a physical presence in the Syncronia as the delegation.

The High Chamberlin of Jin, a withered old man named Maran, led the delegation. His physical presence gave little hint of the power he held in Jin, and of his influence over all of Corazon.

At first sight Aleja thought Maran harmless, even amusing, in the doddering, fidgety way he ambled towards the stage. Maran walked slowly, almost painfully so, and often stopped on his way to pat the heads of the children who lined the path with bronze plates of figs and grapes in their little hands.

Maran seemed to lose his sense of place at times. He would smile genially as one of his embarrassed attendants redirected him back towards Aleja.

But as Maran walked closer to present Jin's gifts, Aleja felt the little life that was left in the old man awaken, like dying coals stoked into a roaring fire.

Maran drew in close to Aleja, far closer than any other delegation dared. Aleja did her best not to show any reaction to the sourness of his smell.

"It is the great honor of Jin to express our gratitude to our Vessel." Maran said with a deep bow. "The Evening Song will celebrate your sacrifice, and your memory will live on in the beauty of the voices who sing it."

Maran's voice was thin but expressive. His hands moved constantly as he spoke.

The chests opened, and as all eyes looked to the contents of them, Maran walked closer to Aleja.

Aleja, startled by Maran's boldness, looked him in the eyes. There was an odious delight in them. His hands skimmed near her body like birds gliding over water to snatch a fish into their greedy beaks.

"Ohhhh," Maran exclaimed airily to Taka, who looked as uncomfortable as Aleja now felt, "our Queen could not ask for a more fitting Vessel for her spirit, could she High Chamberlain Taka?"

Maran's voice oozed like honey, yet its sweetness was sickly, like the smell of fruit rotting in the sun.

Taka nodded, but said nothing. Whether Taka did not wish to engage with Maran, or simply wanted to signal his praise was sufficient homage and the delegation could take their leave, Aleja could not tell. Either way, Aleja saw enough of Taka's silent hostility to recognize it in his reaction to Maran.

If Taka hoped Maran would take his leave, the old man did not oblige him.

As the Temple Maidens and Guardians pulled the gifts from the chests and displayed them to the crowd, Maran took his place in-between Taka and Aleja and whispered into her ear.

"The Vessel is fine. A worthy gift to our Queen. I'm sure the High Chamberlain takes much pleasure in the beauty it will bestow upon her. But what of the spirit that now clings to the body? Do the simple pleasures of life still hold it to this world? Is it ready to be torn from its flesh?"

Aleja, confused by the strangeness of Maran's speech, looked upward towards Taka.

Maran waved an almost transparent hand in front of her face. The veins in them shown like spider webs.

"You must look at me my dear, and do not fear to respond." Maran gave Taka a sideways glance. "After all, I am Taka's equal, and if I was charged with your care, you would not suffer such indignities as he has put you through. For Jin embraces the joy in this world, and, unlike the

Clay People who birthed you, or those who only gave gifts of potatoes in reed baskets, the city of Jin has gifts worthy of your sacrifice. Look upon them."

Maran held out his ghostly hands towards the contents of the chests. For the first time, thoughts of Ivo, Sara, and her own self-pity were driven far from Aleja's mind.

"The glory of Jin, for our Vessel, for her sacrifice."

The light from the jewelry reflecting into Aleja's eyes was almost blinding. Aleja smiled, and forgot herself as she rose slightly from her chair. Aleja never had a great fondness for ornaments, but the beauty, craftsmanship, and refinement of the works before her were breathtaking. Each was exquisitely unique, and even to wear one piece of them would have made her the envy of every Daughter in Corazon.

Kalim's loud, hacking cough brought Aleja back to her senses and she returned to her seat. Taka walked forward towards the delegation, gave them his thanks, and politely encouraged them to return the contents back into the chests.

He looked impatiently at Maran.

Maran smiled broadly back at Taka. He whispered into Aleja's ear.

"They please you, don't they my dear? I can see their light in your eyes. That light sets my heart on fire."

"They are beautiful." Aleja whispered.

"Yes, they are, my dear. Do they make you wonder?"

"Wonder what?"

"About those pleasures denied our people? The poisoned pleasures, those unknown to us, the ones these beautiful objects only hint at?"

"What do you mean?"

"Ahhh," Maran exclaimed, and again, his hands came uncomfortably close to Aleja's own. "She does wonder, this little treasure."

A chill coursed over Aleja's skin at the sound of Maran's tittering laugh. It scraped and skittered like stones thrown onto slate.

Maran looked towards the closing chests. He took notice of Taka glaring at him, and laughed.

"Look at these treasures, my dear, and understand there are wonders and pleasures in this world you will never know."

Maran turned to look directly into Aleja's eyes.

"It pleases me to see the small light they have burned in your beautiful eyes, and I will remember it when I look in your eyes for the final time," Aleja jerked away at the sensation of Maran's thin fingers grazing the side of her cheek, "and see the light extinguished."

The back of Aleja's head hit the mirror, and she felt a coldness where the arrow cut her on her first day with Arrowchaser.

Darkness filled the Syncronia, the air became as thick as water, and the walls glowed in an eerie green. Aleja's eyes adjusted to the watery blackness, and her nose filled with the pungent smell of the food and tea of the Room of Reflection. The audience before her changed into faceless, sallow figures with the sickly, translucent skin of rock grubs. They glowed in the green haze created by the walls. And where Maran stood before her, she instead saw the dried flesh of the dead-skin mask creature staring at her, its smile now a hungry, ravenous grin.

Other skin-masked creatures stood with him, one with pale blue eyes and an empty hole where its nose should be. In the middle of them stood a small, trembling child. Aleja could not tell if it was a boy or a girl, for the child's head was covered by a shroud. The creature standing in Maran's place held a knife before the child's covered face.

The ghostly crowd in the Syncronia cheered as the creature sunk the knife into the child's throat. The child went limp. Aleja turned away at the sight of it. It was then she saw a woman behind her, her body more shadow than flesh, with only lines of ash where her eyes, nose and mouth should be. The woman turned down towards Aleja.

She sees me. Even without eyes. She can see me!

The woman's lipless face spoke in a voice that cracked like ice.

"Your skin is mine."

Aleja screamed and fell from her chair.

The ghostly crowd disappeared in a flash of light. Aleja now found herself on the floor of the Syncronia, and heard the remnants of her own shout echoing in the hall. Those who did not avert their gaze simply stared at Aleja with confused looks on their faces. Only Maran, who stood in a half bow, smiled at her.

Kalim helped Aleja back to the chair, and looked at Maran with undisguised contempt.

"It is time for your delegation to take your leave, High Chamberlain Maran." Kalim said. "Thank you for your gifts." She said without a smile.

Maran smiled and bowed to Kalm in return.

"No gratitude is needed, High Emissary. After all, the delegation of Jin is here to serve the Queen."

Aleja noticed Maran glanced at the mirror on the chair at the mention of the Queen, as if somehow he hoped it received his compliment.

"And you do so with dignity." Taka walked up to Maran, bowed, and then made a subtle gesture towards the exit.

Maran and his delegation pulled away from Aleja with slow, reverential bows. The gossamer gowns and robes of the delegation covered their feet, giving the impression they were floating backwards on the air. Maran's bow towards Taka and Kalim was mocking in its exaggerated reverence, and, as all the other delegations stood waiting,

Maran's curved back straightened as he and his retinue walked boldly out of the Syncronia.

Aleja watched Maran leave. He turned and smiled at her just before exiting the room. For the first time she was happy to hear Taka order her to her chambers, and for Kalim to accompany her there.

CHAPTER 17

As the last light of the sun disappeared from the horizon a single, mournful cry called out from the High Temple. The voice was followed by another from the temple to the north, and then by one from the east, and then on to another until the entire city was filled with the sound.

Each voice, joined in a skittering harmony with the others, sung a lament about the world left behind. A world destroyed by war, disease, famine, and the source of all misfortune; humanity's capricious vanity and insatiable greed. As the final singer joined in the chorus the lament changed into a song of unity, of humanity's reprieve from extinction, and of gratitude towards the Queen who saved them.

The final stanza swelled through the city, vibrating through the stone walls and streets and filling everything, living or not, with the power of its sound.

"There is no light without a flame.
The Queen rules, so that Justice may reign."

Aleja listened with eyes closed as the final sustained note rang out.

Aleja heard the Song of Remembrance and Reprieve, known by most in Corazon as the Evening Song, every night of her life. But it never sounded as impossibly beautiful as it did now. It began faintly, like the sound of distant, crashing waves, then grew as each voice echoing through the light wells returned from the halls as a ghostly whisper to haunt the voice that followed.

"It's beautiful, is it not?" Ivo whispered. The touch of his breath tingled Aleja's ear, and she felt warmth build in her cheeks.

"Yes it is." Aleja replied as she stared at the waterfall of orange and red light cascading down the white walls of the light well.

They sat in silence during the song. People responded in different ways to the Evening Song. Some fell onto the ground and buried their faces in the dirt, others held out their hands as if to receive water, some bowed their heads, and then there were those who simply stood in awe no matter how many times they heard it.

But all were silent.

"Are you cold?" Ivo asked, "There are blankets, or perhaps I should take you to your palanquin."

"No, I'm fine." Aleja said. "I want to be here."

I choose to be here.

"Perhaps the High Emissary is expecting you?"

"Her palanquin is waiting outside, but she is not." Aleja said dreamily as she stared up at the sky. The few stars in Corazon's sky were breaking through the growing darkness like pinpricks in a satin cloth.

Aleja didn't care if Kalim was waiting for her or not. She figured it was Kalim who chose not to attend the practice sessions, for she did not hide her boredom at watching over Aleja, so it would be her fault if Aleja was late upon her return to the High Temple. Sara was taken from her, and Ulaa only accompanied her in the High Temple. Since this was Aleja's last training with Ivo, with the ceremony only a few days away, what more did she have to lose?

Aleja let out a laugh.

"Are you afraid of her, Ivo?" She asked.

"A guard's only fear in life is to lose honor." Ivo replied sternly.

Typical response from a Guardian.

"You know to admit fear takes courage as well." Aleja said.

"My only concern," Ivo's said, his words controlled, "is she may expect you to be at the High Temple by now. You will see all the delegations of Corazon tomorrow, and will need to be present at all the ceremonies and the feasts..."

"Tomorrow will take care of itself. I can stay a little longer."

Aleja stared into Ivo's eyes. They were like a lush, green field that glowed in a golden dawn. He did not turn away from her stare, but drew hesitantly closer to her. Before Aleja could even think to accept, or protest, their lips were locked in a long, lingering kiss.

They pulled away from each other slowly, and shared a laugh with foreheads pressed against one another.

Aleja drew into Ivo's arms and stared up at the sky in silence. The hilt of the knife Ivo kept at his side dug into her back and she jerked away from his embrace.

"I'm sorry." Ivo said as he hurriedly tried to remove the belt that held the knife. Aleja saw the silver lemniscate on the hilt of his dagger.

"You were sent to the Wastes." Aleja immediately regretted her bluntness.

Ivo slowly folded the belt around the knife.

"No one is sent to the Wastes. They choose to go, either by their own words, or by their own deeds."

"But a Judge decreed you go."

Ivo was silent for a time. Aleja could see the belt shaking slightly in his hands. Ivo's eyes were now focused on it, and not on her.

"Yes." Ivo said finally, then looked at her. "Did you ever make such a decree?"

"No. I could have. Once. But I did not utter the words."

"I know. The Caretaker who wanted death for the man who killed her son."

"You heard about it?"

"I don't know any in Mir who have not."

Aleja looked away from Ivo. She gazed at the open halls that intersected the room, as if by sight she could suddenly run down them and hide her shame. It would have been easy to end the conversation by requesting to take her leave, and yet Aleja found herself speaking.

"You must think me a fool." she said.

"I, of all people in Corazon, should never be the one to presume to judge you. But when I hear people speak of what you did, they say nothing of foolishness, they speak only of wisdom."

Aleja's laugh echoed up the light well.

"Wisdom was it? It was a childish trick, a dereliction of my duty to render judgment in the Queen's words. That is how I would speak of it. According to the High Chamberlain it is why I am to die for the Queen. Not to be punished, of course, but to be redeemed." Aleja said with a bitter laugh.

Aleja left Ivo on the seat and started towards the hallways. Ivo called out to her in a plaintive voice, stopping her in her tracks.

"When the Judge decreed I be sent from Corazon to the Stone Islands, I also protested the Queen's wisdom. The Judge's response to my heresy was quick. She ordered the Guardians to bind my arms, and a gag was placed into my mouth. Neither was removed until I was thrown into the dark hull of a ship headed to the Wastes. I don't begrudge her doing her duty, but, when I think about what you did, I sometimes wish she had at least listened to my words before giving judgment."

Aleja sat back down next to Ivo, and laid her hand on his shoulder.

"I am no longer a Judge, but I can listen to you now."

"What use would it be to speak of it?"

"I don't know. Maybe none. Have you spoken to anyone about your life in the Wastes? Or your life before it?"

Ivo shook his head.

"You don't have a life in the Wastes. Not your own, anyway. That is the first lesson you learn. Just before they abandon you on the shore, the Guardians give you a knife and say 'Use it for yourself, or for others.' Some choose it for themselves, whether that means taking their own lives with it, or venturing deep into the Wastes on their own. Neither ever make it back to Corazon. Only those who use the knife, and all their wits and luck for the benefit of others have any chance of making it out."

"I was one of twelve who walked into the Wastes, and when I made it to the Yamanashi I was one of three. In the end only two of us made it back into the Queen's embrace. But neither of us would have even made it through our first night in the Wastes if it weren't for the others. When I made my pledge to be a Guardian, to be one of many, to disregard the ego that led to my fall, I did it with my whole heart. I finally understood it was my deeds that sent me to the Wastes, not the Daughter who passed judgment upon me."

"What were your deeds? Unburden yourself from them, Ivo, with your own words. Not the words of those who accused you."

Ivo let out a deep exhale. He stared down at the knife in his hands.

"I attacked a Chamberlain, accused him of abhorrent sins, things I now understand to have been wrong, but wholly believed at the time. I was one of the many children of the Caretakers. There are many parentless children in Jin, they fill the streets like flies on a trash-barge."

"We ran wild in the streets. Those who treated us with kindness only did so in public. For a time I was apprenticed by a man, an iron worker who thought forging metal and raising a child were done the same way. So I left him. My only skill was to take from others. I was just a thief. But it was then I noticed children were disappearing from the streets. Caretakers told me the children left for the Stone Islands or wandered into the mountains to join the Yamanashi people. But I knew better. Someone was taking them, and when he did, they were never seen again. I confronted a Chamberlain in Jin about it. After he spit at me I swung at him, and in the blink of an eye was tied up and thrown before a Judge."

Ivo shook his head.

"I suppose if I listened to her Judgment without protest, I would be on the Stone Islands now with the friends I thought I lost."

"The children," Aleja spoke softly, her hand drawing up to Ivo's shoulder, "did they really go to the Stone Islands?"

"That is what I was told." Ivo said with eyes closed. "It is what I believe now."

Aleja put her arm around Ivo. The entire time he spoke Ivo was staring at his knife and squeezing it in his powerful, calloused hands. Aleja laid a gentle kiss on his temple.

Ivo broke from Aleja's embrace and stood up. He fashioned the belt back onto his chest.

"I shouldn't have done that."

"Done what?" Aleja stared up at Ivo. He looked away from her.

"Shared with you. Tied you to me. You are not just a Daughter of the Queen, you are her Vessel. It is not right for you to become close with anyone. By the light of the full moon you will..." Ivo trailed off.

Aleja stood up.

"I will what?"

Ivo walked towards one of the halls.

"Let me escort you to the palanquin." Ivo paused, for only a breath, then finished his request with the word, "Vessel."

Aleja felt her face grow flush.

"You don't know what you're talking about." Aleja rushed by Ivo.

"I'm sorry." Ivo called out as Aleja made her way to the hall. "It was not my place to speak to you like that."

Aleja stopped and turned around. She hated how one as strong as Ivo looked so weak and pathetic to her now.

"That's right. Your job is to train me. Not to tell me my purpose. I still decide what I want to do with my body. There are still more sunrises before the ceremony. So, until then, whether I decide to sit with you or slap you, the choice is mine, and mine alone."

"You may remove me from your service if it pleases you."

Ivo spoke in the detached tone of voice he first used to greet her, the voice of a Guardian addressing those they protect.

Aleja's laugh this time was neither warm nor pleasant. She wanted it to hurt him.

But it saddened Aleja just the same to see that it did.

"No, it does not please me." Aleja bunched her training clothes into her hands. "Would you have me explain all of this to Chamberlain Taka? You Guardians always talk about your bravery and honor. Daughters have honor to protect also. What you're asking would make me look like a fool. Honestly, asking the head of my guard to step down because of a little spat."

"It's not your guard." Ivo said. He raised his head up and stared at Aleja in the eyes.

"It's the Queen's guard."

Ivo didn't flinch as Aleja's training clothes flew from her hands and onto his face.

"To the Wastes with all you!" Aleja yelled. "Taka. Kalim. The whole lot of you!"

Aleja stormed through the empty halls towards the entrance of the training grounds. The other Guardians, who were waiting just outside the room, hurriedly followed her.

"I can make it by myself!" Aleja shouted back at them just before breaking into a run. Ivo's Guardians followed her, but the others she came across in the halls either averted their gaze or ducked into other passageways at the sight of her approach.

Once outside, Aleja quickly looked over the last of the palanquins left in front of the entrance.

The palanquin waiting to take her back to the High Temple was not hers, nor was it Kalim's.

It was Taka's.

CHAPTER 18

Taka's home was far larger than most, and overlooked the beautiful expanse of the Bay of Mir. Taka's servants greeted the palanquin with deep bows, then brought Aleja to his balcony without a word.

Taka, as usual when he called on Aleja, had his back to her when she entered the room. He was staring out at the water, a glass of wine in his hand. His stance was the same as when she first met him, his legs spread apart in a perfect triangle, as he watched the fisherman prepare their crystal lamps for the night's fishing.

In the silence of his room Aleja heard the mournful sound of durodon whales singing in the distance.

From Taka's balcony Aleja could see the wide bay that led to the open sea. Aleja watched the ships make their way out to sea. Their lanterns, glass orbs of yellow and red, dangled off long poles extending from their hulls. The lamps hung over the water to draw the squid closer to the surface, and made the ships look like birds with wings of light.

One of Taka's servants handed Aleja a glass of wine. Aleja felt compelled to follow Taka in a drink.

"Do you like the wine?" Taka asked without looking at Aleja.

"Yes, High Chamberlain."

"You know where it came from, of course?" Taka said, still without looking at her.

Aleja took in the smell of the wine. She did not need the full power of her memory to know its origin, for it was as familiar to her as her own skin.

"It's from the South." Aleja said. "The Korosh Hills, with water from the Biyule River."

"Where you were from." Taka replied after taking a drink. "Although, of course, you are not supposed to remember that."

"Yes, High Chamberlain."

"I myself have been there several times. Very rocky terrain. They say the Clay people are one with the land they walk on, and like it, are malleable. Yet I found the terrain there to have a stubborn harshness to it."

Taka looked down at the cup in his hand.

"I can taste it in the wine. But I suppose you feel differently. To you the taste must be a sweet memory of your homeland. For it is said one born to the taste of dirt will savor stale bread and bitter fruit."

Aleja took a quick drink of the wine. Her teeth clinked against the rim of the cup.

It was one thing to chastise her, Aleja felt, but another to demean the people and the land she came from.

"Bitterness and spice linger on the tongue to remind us of the essence one life gave to feed another," Aleja replied after her drink, "and therefore is the true taste of any food. Sweetness is pleasant but insubstantial and brief, and makes us forget the sacrifice a life gave to nourish us."

"Yes, but is not sweetness and richness of taste a reflection of the skill of those who prepared the food? Those who have given their time and effort to prepare something to give pleasure to another? Take this cup for instance," Taka looked at Aleja for the first time and held the glass up to her face, "finely crafted and invigorated with the purpose of the glassmaker. It shows none of the impurities or imperfections of your clay cup. Its beauty lies in its crystal clear purity."

Aleja gritted her teeth for fear her tongue would loosen. She forced a sweet smile to her face.

"As beautiful as the goblet is, it would have no purpose without the drink it holds." Aleja's voice was calm and measured. "A man dying of thirst would esteem a hole in driftwood if it could hold enough water to save him."

Taka smiled, finished his drink, and then took the wine from his servant and poured himself another glass.

"I have not brought you here to teach you old lessons." Taka said as the servant poured with head bowed. "Especially ones meant to instruct young Judges about their role in this world. For the girl I asked to relate the Parable of Thirst in the High Temple is no longer just one of the hundreds of judges in Mir, nor one of the thousands of Daughters in Corazon, but the Queen's Vessel," he held up the glass into the air, "the cup the Queen shall fill."

Taka took a drink before continuing. Unlike when Taka told her about Sara, Aleja stayed silent this time, hoping her deference would encourage him to end his sermon quickly.

"What matters to me is not the drink this glass holds." Taka said. "After all, it is a plain beverage. No more special than one grain of sand is from another. No, what matters to me, is the glass itself."

Taka stared at Aleja as he poured the drink out slowly onto the floor. Small drops of wine sprinkled Aleja's toes.

"The glass is to be kept safe, to be kept pristine, to be worthy of the next drink it will hold. A drink that will not only quench our thirst, but put a fire in our bellies, and instill a purpose in our souls."

Aleja looked down at the pool of wine at her feet as it ran towards the edge of the balcony floor.

"My servants know I cherish this glass, so it is only to be handled by myself. No other has the right to it, no matter where they may sit at my table as guest, friend, or counsel. If they were to do anything to endanger it, I would dismiss them."

Aleja continued to look down at the wine-stained floor, and silently cursed the tears she could feel welling up in her eyes. The harder she fought to contain them, the more they seemed compelled to free themselves. A single tear ran down her cheek. Another quickly followed, and fell to the floor where it mixed with the last of the wine draining down a small crack in the floor.

Aleja looked at Taka with stinging, bloodshot eyes.

"I thank you for your hospitality, High Chamberlain, and all your advice, but may I take my leave of you now?"

"You may." Taka replied with a nod. "I myself will turn in soon. For we all have a long day ahead of us. The first step in a thousand mile journey. But first I must ask you to try the wine I keep for special occasions, one almost as dear to me as this glass."

Aleja watched as Taka took another bottle of wine from one of his servants. The bottle was opened, and Taka poured a small amount into his glass. He brought his glass up to Aleja's lips.

"Drink." He said as he stared at her with his oceanic eyes.

The taste was sweet, complemented by the sensation of burning spice, and hints of berries and oak that revealed themselves as the liquid lingered on her tongue. Aleja could not deny this wine was finer than the wine of her people, and unlike anything she ever tasted.

"What do you think?" Taka asked as he held the glass close to his chest.

"Delicious, High Chamberlain." Aleja reluctantly admitted.

Taka nodded.

"We must not only protect the drink." He said. "But also the cup that holds it. And those who expose the cup to damage, must be kept from it."

"What do you mean?" Aleja said, suddenly fearing Taka found another who could be punished for her actions.

"You will never see the Guardian known as Ivo again. His carelessness with the Queen's Vessel is inexcusable. He had no right to keep you beyond the Song of Remembrance, and showed remarkable lack of wit by teaching you the forms. He will serve as a Guardian in Andrid where he will watch over the ships bound for the Wastes. He will reflect upon how his carelessness with you has taken him one step closer to being sent back to the Wastes for good."

"But he only took me to hear the Queen's song in the light wells." Aleja protested. "He did nothing to endanger this Vessel. There is no need to banish him from Mir. I beg of the High Chamberlain to speak to High Emissary Kalim. It was she who–"

"Who what?" Taka shouted. "Who had her trust in him, and you, betrayed? You have no say in this matter, and you will not speak of it to anyone else or they will face a similar fate as Commander Ivo. You should feel fortunate Sara will not be joining him."

"It's not his fault or hers! It's mine! Punish me if you want, not him!" Aleja shouted and threw the clay cup to the floor. Taka threw up his hands before his face to protect himself from the shards that flew upwards.

Taka stormed forward and grabbed Aleja by the arms. Aleja struggled to break free but the power in his grip was too much.

"You insolent child!" Taka shouted in her face. "How dare you question any of my decisions? Who do you think you are?"

Taka's attendants scurried from the room with heads cowed.

"You think I can't take more from you?" Taka shook Aleja. She stared at him with mouth agape. He was never shy about showing anger, but Aleja felt this was more like madness. "Arrowchaser? That horse will be food for dogs by morning! I'll send my Guardians to pull Bao from your room and cast her into the sewers! I'll make her clean waste pipes until her fingers are worn to bones!"

Aleja looked on in horror as Taka's face changed. She was no longer looking into his pale blue eyes, but instead empty holes with pinpoints of light. His face was like a skull covered in dried, cracking leather. It was one of the skin-masks of her nightmares.

"We can take more than your life!" The skin-mask screeched, its voice like daggers in Aleja's ears. "We can destroy everything you love!"

Taka threw Aleja to the floor. She gasped for breath, and felt the burning pain of a scream stillborn in her lungs for lack of air. It wasn't until one of the servants put her arms around Aleja that she felt safe enough to look up at him.

Taka stared down at her, his face still full of anger. But, to Aleja's relief, it was again a human face.

Taka took a breath to regain his composure. His attendants flittered around him, one wrapping Taka's hand in white linen that quickly turned red. Aleja looked at the floor. Taka's glass laid on it, broken in half by the base.

Taka pointed at Aleja with his bloodied hand.

"You will no longer ride Arrowchaser. And forget about getting any pleasure from tormenting Ulaa. Kalim will watch over you while you spend your last days in your room. Your servant Bao will remain, but only as a reminder there are consequences for your actions. And your words."

Taka signaled for his Guardians, a large stocky one named Ker and a female named Rhea, to take Aleja away.

Taka's attendant helped Aleja to her feet, but gave way to Ker and Rhea to take Aleja to the palanquin.

Just before the cover of the palanquin closed Ker called out to Aleja. He stood by the street with a smile on his face.

"Next time you want to disobey, remember what you saw, girl." Ker said with a wink. Aleja heard Ker and Rhea laugh after the curtain was closed.

What does he mean by that? What did I see? Am I living in a waking nightmare?

Aleja took a cloth to wipe Taka's blood from her arm. Her nose filled with the scent of the tea. Aleja threw the cloth from the palanquin and covered herself. Even though there was no chill in the air she still felt cold. Every time she closed her eyes she saw the skin-masked creatures staring back at her. She thought of the name the Queen gave them.

The lost children.

Could Taka be one of them?

Once back at the High Temple she was led quickly to her room. To her relief Bao was there. Bao let out a surprised shout as Aleja embraced her. Aleja saw how it made Ulaa and the Maidens uncomfortable, but she didn't care. Bao helped Aleja to bed, and shooed the Maidens out of the room. She sat by Aleja, and held her hand as she drifted off to sleep.

CHAPTER 19

"You're trapped, Aleja."

Kalim stared at Aleja from across the table in her room. A large game board of black and white stones lay between them. Kalim's white stones surrounded Aleja's black stones in many pockets on the oaken board.

"I must say the quality of your play has deteriorated over the past few days." Kalim said as she removed Aleja's stones from the board. Kalim gave Aleja the look she often did when she was just as annoyed to be in Aleja's company as Aleja was to be in hers.

Perhaps I'm Taka's punishment for her. She's too powerful to dishonor publicly, but not too powerful to inconvenience.

"Maybe you're just finally getting good at this." Aleja replied.

Aleja picked up a stone and held it over the board. The stones, smoothed by the waves of the southern sea, yet as supple as Aleja's own fingertips, made a satisfying clicking sound as Aleja placed them on the board. Kalim gave Aleja a disapproving look, placed a stone to complete the encirclement, and removed more of Aleja's stones from the board.

"Maybe both." Kalim said.

Aleja shrugged as she stared at the board, repeatedly rubbing one of the stones between her thumb and middle finger.

The basis of the game was simple, and yet, unlike Aleja's life at the High Temple, the possibilities of movement and action were countless. A grid was carved on the board and each player took a turn placing their stone on a point on the grid. If you managed to encircle your opponent's stones you removed them from the board and claimed them.

"Are you going to place your stone or grind it into dust?" Kalim said.

Aleja looked back at Kalim, who slumped back into her chair and crossed her arms in a most undignified pose. Aleja wondered how a woman of so many seasons could still pout like a child.

"Do you agree to end the game?" Aleja asked.

"No, I don't." Kalim said in a throaty rasp that had grown more pronounced over the past few days.

Kalim cleared her throat noisily.

"Then I need more time to think of my next move." Aleja said, and then jumped as Hermes let out a shriek. Aleja almost reflexively threw her stone at the bird, but held back. There were many things that irritated Aleja about being held captive with Kalim for her final days, but the obnoxious bird was by far the worst. It was only affectionate with Kalim, and once snapped so hard at Bao it bit through her tunic.

Aleja looked out the latticed window, and almost broke out in tears at the sight. There were more lights in the city of Mir than stars in the sky, and they shone in a myriad of colors.

"Time is something I have, my little dew petal." Kalim said. "I can't say the same for you."

Aleja glared at Kalim.

She won't get a rise out of me. No matter how much she tries.

"I have two more days left." Aleja replied calmly.

Kalim coughed.

"When was it ever 'your' day, Vessel? I must say it is shocking to hear one of our own speaking so vainly."

Aleja rubbed the stone harder, but her voice remained calm.

"I've heard the Yamanashi believe everyone lays claim to their own life, and to remain within the group is a choice." Aleja said. "For them, every day is their own."

"Well, we are not Yamanashi barbarians. Besides, who told you such nonsense?"

"A Mirish merchant who traded with them in Andrid."

"A merchant!" Kalim scoffed. "You'd trust the word of a person whose life depends on telling people something is more valuable than the price they themselves paid for it?"

Aleja shrugged.

Bao woke up with a loud snort.

"Do you need anything, Daughter?" Bao said with a yawn.

"Can't that simpleton call you Vessel? She hasn't done it once in all the time I've been here." Kalim snapped.

Aleja ignored Kalim's comment.

"No Bao, why don't you rest awhile?" She said. "There is still time before supper."

Kalim sighed as Bao quickly fell back to sleep.

"That oaf is as useful as a cart with no wheels. You could have any choice in servants, and yet you kept her."

Aleja looked at Bao, and thought of Taka's threats. The stones made grinding and scraping sounds in her fist.

"Is it really my choice? If Taka doesn't like her, he can just be rid of her."

"I'll be sure to share that with him."

Aleja threw a handful of stones at Kalim. Kalim did not move, and showed no shock as the stones pelted her chest. She only smiled, and then placed the stones back on the board.

The attendants, who stood stunned by Aleja's outburst, hustled in a panic towards Kalim.

"Perhaps he should," Kalim said after waving off the attendants, "for your sake. It would spare you more pain when the Queen takes control of your body. The less connected you are to your own life the better it will be for you when the day comes."

"What do you care what is good for me?" Aleja snapped back.

Kalim coughed again. Hermes, perched in the corner of the room, grew increasingly and noisily agitated as Kalim struggled through it. Aleja, much to her own surprise, felt a twinge of concern watching Kalim try to stop the coughing fit.

Kalim took a napkin, and with more dignity than she usually mustered in front of Aleja, wiped her mouth.

"Should I tell you a story perhaps," Kalim said brightly, "to ease your mind?"

"I doubt you know a story I haven't heard."

Aleja looked away from Kalim, and wedged a stone into the latticework.

"Probably not this one." Kalim replied, seemingly without offense. "It is an old one. Ancient really. And not about the Queen's children. It's about the Yamanashi."

Aleja paused. She turned towards Kalim and placed the stone in her hand back on the table.

"I might be interested." Aleja said in a voice desperate to hide how much she really was.

Kalim smiled when she saw the effect of her words on Aleja's attention.

Unlike Aleja's people, whose blood and traditions came from the Drowned World, the Yamanashi people believed they sprung from the seeds of the first flower to bloom on Mount Obake, the tallest mountain in the Yamanashi range. Many in Corazon were curious about the Yamanashi but, unlike most, Aleja always desired to see them with her own eyes.

It was rare for the people of Corazon to have any contact with them. Part of the reason was the terrain. The Yamanashi Mountains was a forbidding range with a few, precarious roads clinging tightly to steep, rocky cliffs. Another was the Yamanashi people themselves. They kept themselves hidden deep within the mountains, where few people in Corazon dared go.

"What's the story about?" Aleja asked.

"It's about how Corazon came to be."

Aleja placed her shoulder on the windowsill and her head on her hand.

"Tell me."

Kalim took a sip from the tea that cooled in her clay cup, sat up straight, and folded her hands onto her lap.

Then she began the tale.

CHAPTER 20

*"T*here was once a man who lived with two daughters in a small house on a meadow bordering a forest. As sunny and pleasant as the meadow was, the forest was dark and thick with trees that blocked out the sky. Inside the forest even a cloudless day would seem like night."*

"Every day the man would venture into the forest to cut wood, which he would sell to the villagers who lived far from the forest. The villagers themselves would not go into the forest, for they feared it, and believed it was the abode of unhappy and vengeful spirits. The daughters would wait for their father in the shade of a tree whose roots were in the black soil of the forest, yet the trunk curved outward and arched over the sunlit meadow. The girls would swing from the branches that dangled from the trunk as they waited for their father to return with his cart full of wood and mouth full of stories of the wondrous things he saw that day."

Aleja heard Bao breathe heavily. Bao was awake, her eyes wide as she listened to Kalim's story. Kalim did not turn to look, and seemed to be in a kind of trance as she told the tale, her voice hovering like a kite in high wind.

"But one day, when the girls were now young women, and the curved trunk of the tree was thick and strong, their father did not return. One of the sisters, who was diligent and respectful, believed they should wait for their father, and not venture into the forest to look for him, for this is what he told them to do every morning he left to chop wood."

"The other sister, who was fiery and difficult, wanted to search the forest that very night. The respectful sister tried to reason with the other, but it was not long before they quarreled, and neither was able to convince the other to join them, either in wait or in search."

"The respectful sister waited under the trunk of the tree as her sister went to search for their father. But he was never found. Every morning the sisters quarreled, and each day the fiery sister went into the woods while the other waited by the tree. For one cycle of the moon this ritual was repeated until finally the day came when the fiery sister did not return. Now the respectful sister waited under the tree for both her father and her sister all day and night, and did not take bread or water, and began to wither."

"The village people visited her and tried to convince her to stop waiting, to take care of herself and her home, and to take up a brave husband who would venture into the forest to cut the wood the villagers needed."

"But she would not listen. The villagers grew angry with her, and told her neither her father nor her sister actually vanished in the woods, but had abandoned her and were living happily without her. But she stayed, and when the villagers found her lifeless body, they buried her under the arch of the tree and took what they needed from her home."

Kalim stopped to listen to the thunder rumbling outside. It had a strange, cascading quality to it, as if the clouds were calling out to one another.

"You know my dear," Kalim spoke wistfully, "in the Yamanashi Mountains thunder echoes in every cavern and ravine, and sends the sound far. In some of the passageways that lead to their lands they say the sound of a single pebble dropped onto the ground lasts a lifetime."

"No, I didn't know that." Aleja said, startled by the gentleness in Kalim's voice.

"A simple belief of a simple people." Kalim said, then shook her head, as if she were waking from a dream. "Do you wish me to finish the story?"

"Yes." Aleja answered eagerly. She smiled at Bao, who stared fixedly at Kalim. Even Hermes, for once silent, appeared to be listening to the tale.

"A cycle of the Moon passed when the fiery daughter returned after wandering the forest in vain. She saw her sister was no longer there, and their home was barren and livestock gone. The sister went to the villagers and demanded they return what they took and to tell her what happened to her sister."

"At first the villagers protested, and did not believe she was the missing sister, for her time in the forest much changed her. Her hair was now matted and tangled as the forest underbrush, her eyes dark as its moonless night, and skin as crackled and grey as the bark that covered its trees. But when she showed them her father's axe, which she found entangled in the branches of a gnarled oak, they believed her at last. They returned what they took, and showed her where her sister was put to rest."

"When the fiery sister saw her sister was truly gone she wailed above her grave. Tears poured out of her eyes, ran down the cracks of her skin, and formed puddles by her feet. Her toes, which became shriveled and black during her journey, stretched out and took in the water from her tears, and became roots that drove themselves deep into the ground. Her feet and legs bound together, and her crackled skin became that of bark. Her father's axe splintered as her hands and arms turned into branches covered in beautiful flowers. Her hair reached up for the arc of the tree trunk under which they once waited for their father and became entangled with it, and grew like vines as it wrapped itself up the trunk of the tree until all that was human about the sister was gone."

"The sister and the tree from the forest now formed an archway, a bridge between the forest and meadow, and where the two trees met sprung a new trunk, one that grew higher and higher until it disappeared into the clouds. The tree grew so high it pierced the glass cover of the sky and entered into the blue waters of our world, where its tip broke through the surface of the sea and became Corazon. From this story we know the life in our world is born from the death of another."

"So the Yamanashi believe in another world?" Aleja asked.

"Not just another world." Kalim said after a drink. "Countless worlds. Each stacked upon each other like layers in a cake, and all of them rotating in the opposite direction from the other." Kalim laid one hand over the other and twisted them in opposing directions as she spoke. "That's how they explain night and day."

"How so?"

"When we are below the sea above us it is day. When we are under the earth it is night. The stars are the glitter of diamonds and other jewels buried deep in the earth above us."

"What of the sun?"

"What of it?"

"I mean, how do they explain it?"

"The Yamanashi believe at the top layer there is a God of Light, who is so bright and hot the ground is melted iron, and the seas are nothing more than steam. The God's light shines down through the layers until it ends in a world where there is no light at all. The Yamanashi believe in death a soul tries to find the link between the worlds, and is ever trying to get closer to the Sun God. In our world they believe Mount Obake is that link, and when you die you climb it to the top and either make it into the world above, or are cast down to the world below."

"What is a soul?" Aleja carefully pronounced the new and unfamiliar word.

Kalim paused, and looked unsure whether she should speak or not. It was as if she had suddenly caught herself saying too much.

"It is the life and memories of the body that lives on when the body dies." Kalim shifted in her chair.

"I don't understand. They don't believe in rebirth? How can there be life without the body?"

"The Queen lives on without her original body." Kalim responded quickly.

"Yes, but, she is a Goddess. So the Yamanashi won't join her embrace because of ego? Because they want their memories to last forever?"

"Well, they believe differently than us."

"It doesn't make sense."

"What doesn't?" Kalim's voice cracked. She drank quickly from the tea.

"I don't believe it. After all, even from here I can see the top of Mount Obake, and certainly it is not breaking into another world. Also, you said they believe in countless worlds, yet at some point they end where their Sun God is, and where he isn't."

Kalim launched into a coughing fit. She waved off the attendants and took a long drink after the fit subsided.

"Are you alright Kalim?" Aleja asked, then handed her a napkin. Kalim accepted it and put it to her face.

"Yes, yes. I always have a hard time when a new season approaches." Kalim said through the napkin. After cleaning her mouth Kalim took a deep breath and resumed her explanation.

"I said the worlds were countless, not infinite. And, according to the Yamanashi, the Mount Obake we see when we are alive is only half the height of the true size of the mountain. They believe our living senses are limited, and only a soul can perceive the true reality of the world."

Aleja thought for a moment. Only one moon ago she would have dismissed everything Kalim said as utter nonsense at best, heresy at worst. But after the visions of the past few days she thought it made some sense. Perhaps there was an unseen world, and the closer you came to death the more you were able to perceive it.

But where would the Queen fit in such a world?

"Fascinating." Aleja said. "Still, it's strange."

Aleja paused. She forced herself to sip from the tea Kalim brought for her. Usually Aleja dumped it into the nearest plant when Kalim wasn't looking. This kept her from drinking it, but unfortunately also encouraged Kalim to bring more.

"Interesting, yes," Aleja said after forcing the tea down, "interesting, but wrong."

"Well, certainly the Yamanashi feel the same about our beliefs. They don't understand why a Goddess needs to live among her people."

"To protect and guide us, of course." Aleja said. "Why would they want their God to be so distant?"

Kalim smiled.

"So they may no longer remain children in this world."

"What do you mean?"

Aleja waited for Kalim to answer, but she only stared at her, as if struggling to find the words. Aleja had never seen Kalim so serious, even when she was criticizing her. Aleja thought this may have been the first time she ever heard Kalim speak without a hint of mockery in her voice.

Instead of answering, Kalim launched into another hacking cough. She did not refuse the Maiden's help this time. They rubbed her back as the painful coughing continued. By the time she was finished it was clear Kalim was in no more mood for discussion.

"Now, enough talk." Kalim's voice was a throaty rumble. "Let's see how fast your lump of a servant can bring up more tea."

Kalim brushed off the Maidens help as she stood up and went over to Bao.

Aleja thought about the Yamanashi. She remembered a map of Corazon Sara once shared with her, and in her mind traced the jagged eastern ridge of the Yamanashi, a place called the Bonesaw, with peaks so pointed it looked as if they could spear clouds out of the sky.

Aleja imagined herself walking along the long, rolling foothills of the mountains, a land covered in a thick green blanket of grass and clover, where the people devoted themselves to breeding horses and herding sheep. In her mind's eye she saw the lush, dense forest that formed a wall between the plains and the Yamanashi Mountains. She imagined herself riding the wind that made waves in the emerald sea of evergreen trees, and hovering over waterfalls plunging from cloud covered mountains into deep valleys obscured by silver mist.

Aleja was so lost in her daydreams she did not hear Kalim slump to the floor, nor did she first register Bao calling out to her.

Hermes flittered above Kalim, who convulsed as she lay coughing on the floor. The attendants, who were busy setting the table, dropped their trays with a clatter and rushed to Kalim's side. Aleja got up with a shout, and knelt down beside the suddenly frail and fragile looking Kalim.

Aleja and the Maidens turned Kalim over carefully. There was blood in the spittle that sprayed out of her coughing mouth.

Kalim stared at Aleja with wild, terrified eyes.

Aleja could only make out one word in between the coughing. With one last gasp before she fell into unconsciousness, Aleja heard Kalim say a name.

"Sara."

What shocked Aleja the most was not to hear the name of her friend. For although it was Kalim's voice, and only Aleja seemed to hear it, the sound did not come from Kalim's mouth.

It came from the Queen's Mirror.

CHAPTER 21

It was the night before the procession, and Aleja sat up in her bed staring at the Queen's Mirror, thinking about the day and all that happened leading up to it. If she could not make sense of it, the mirror, if it had any power at all, could help her do so.

Aleja thought of Kalim.

Kalim was still breathing, haltingly and with effort, when the Maidens took her to one of the Sanctuary Rooms to see Taka. When Aleja woke the next day Bao told her Kalim was dead.

People did not spend much time mourning in Corazon. Kalim's body, like others, would be taken out of the city and interred in one of the large urns scattered throughout Corazon's farms and fields. As the sun warmed the urn, Kalim's flesh would melt off her bones, and drain out of the urn to replenish the soil.

Even her bones would be taken out of the urn to be ground up and thrown over the dirt.

It was a way each life repaid the debt it owed to the food it consumed. Every meal in Corazon began with the simple blessing "Thank you for giving me your life." Aleja understood it as a blessing for the food on her plate without thinking much about what it really meant. But when she sat at the final banquet held in her honor, she thought about all the lives given to bring so much food to the table.

Aleja had never seen such a splendid feast. After years of eating simple soups, rice, pickled vegetables and dried fish she never imagined there could be a meal so rich in variety of taste and color. Yet, despite the delight the feast promised for Aleja, all the spices and tastes fell dead upon her tongue. Aleja tried to work up an appetite for the food, but picked through it with little enthusiasm.

Two Guardians stood behind her the entire meal. It pained Aleja to think that, because of her, Ivo wasn't one of them.

Aleja shuffled uncomfortably in her bed at the thought of Ivo.

He was only a boy, Aleja chided herself, *one I barely knew. It was only a moment we shared, nothing more. It was nothing lasting.*

But as hard as Aleja tried to convince herself, such reasons to forget Ivo gave her no comfort. And thinking about their last words together made it even worse. Aleja wanted her words to hurt him, but it was she who now felt their sting.

At the time Aleja couldn't understand Ivo's reaction after he told her why he was sent to the Wastes. It was only when she laid awake in the darkness of night that it was clear to her.

Ivo thought his suffering in the Wastes cleansed him of his anger. As much as Aleja wanted to hear him, as much as she wanted to calm his heart, she only reopened a wound she hoped to heal. She now realized he was redeemed in the Queen's eyes, but not in his own.

Guardian's pride themselves on mastering their emotions, in not giving in to anger, even as those around them have lost all such control. But he was still angry, and still believed he was wronged, and the sudden realization pained him more than Aleja believed she could ever truly know.

But what of my own pain? What about the decisions that have brought me to this place?

A place of such great honor. Where I am no more than a living statue. I've given so much of my life to the Queen and her children, why did she need more of me?

I had to give up my home, my memories, my place in this world, and now even my own flesh.

Couldn't Ivo see how his words could cut me as well?

It was all too much for her. Ivo banished, Sara's company taken from her, and now Kalim was gone. Even though Aleja chafed at Kalim's coarse manner, and resented her company when she would have rather spent her last days with Sara, Aleja was surprised at the feeling that she missed her.

Was it all fate? Or was the Queen preparing me for loss?

Is there any meaning in any of this?

Aleja was seated with Taka at the feast, but thankfully not near High Chamberlain Maran. She didn't have to suffer his sickly voice or a touch from his trembling hands. If she did, Aleja would have lost control of the scream that nestled into her chest the moment she sat down.

Aleja wanted to be near Sara one last time. Whether it was because of Taka's orders or Sara's own choice, Aleja did not know, but Sara was seated far from Aleja and avoided eye contact for the entire meal. It was the first time Aleja saw her since the night on the balcony, and it was only from afar.

Perhaps she cut her attachment to me.

Aleja tossed in her bed. Her temples throbbed at the memory of Sara enjoying the company of the young men at her table, and not sparing a look for her friend.

Kalim was right. I should have done the same.

She was able to ignore such thoughts at the feast while Herdmaster Turik slurred the history of Corazon into her ear, but not now when all was quiet. When all was dark.

She remembered the feast in excruciating detail. But Aleja decided, if it would only help her sleep, it was better than remembering anything else.

Aleja remembered the way Turik scratched at the blue paint that framed his eyes as he spoke. His blinking was as incessant as his conversation. His hands, one with a cup full of wine, at times moved with less control than his mouth.

"Unlike so many others, I suspect," Turik said in a space of six quick blinks, "it does not surprise me the Queen has chosen a Clay girl for her Vessel, for their blood is the closest to the blood of the Drowned World, the blood of the ancients."

Turik stopped, perhaps waiting for Aleja to comment, but she simply nodded to him to continue as she held up her cup to be refilled.

"The Queen was careful to mix all the bloodlines when we first came to this island." Turik readjusted himself in his seat as he spoke. "This was most wise. A bloodline that runs long runs thin, the ancients once said. But as the population grew after several generations the Queen no longer dictated who could breed with whom. The power of the Herdmasters declined as a result, for we were not only responsible for maintaining the strength of the animals brought here, but of the people as well."

"In a city as central as Mir, it was only natural people should form relationships with others from all parts of Corazon. But for your people, isolated on that long stretch of barren land, there was not as much mixing of blood. That's why many Clay people, including your honorable self, have hair as black as night, while most in Corazon tend towards brown."

Turik reached up to touch what little of his hair remained. Whatever tinge of brown or black it once was, it was reduced to tufts of white now. Turik smiled as he saw Aleja's gaze following his hand.

"The Herdmasters once held great influence in Corazon." Turik said for what Aleja thought was the fortieth time this night. "They committed the lineage of every person and beast to memory. There was a time when a

Herdmaster could have told you if one of your ancestors ever rode the ancestor of your horse, Arrowchaser."

"With all due respect, Herdmaster Turik." Aleja said. "Arrowchaser is not my horse, nor is anything else I have been given. But I do take your meaning."

"I'm sorry if I offended, Vessel." Turik replied, too embarrassed or too drunk to notice Aleja's breach of protocol in referring to herself incorrectly. "He did choose you, though. That can't be taken away."

A lean, leather skinned man sitting across from Turik spoke up.

"Arrowchaser. It's an odd name isn't it? How did he come by it?"

The man was a mystery to many in the room. Aleja knew his name was Ricci, and that he was High Chamberlain of Andrid, a small, isolated harbor town far from Mir. But she didn't know why he sat so close to her.

It was an honor for anyone to sit close to the Vessel, even if the person was a High Chamberlain. But a dignitary from Andrid was a strange choice. For many, a post in Andrid usually meant a person was one mistake away from complete banishment.

A cloud Ivo now lived under. Aleja thought ruefully. *Taka must have sat Ricci here to remind me of Ivo. This man was given a place of honor out of spite.*

Even so, Aleja welcomed Ricci's company. He seemed a decent and intelligent man. A man of moderation who ate even less than he spoke.

"By his speed, High Chamberlain Ricci." Turik said.

In Turik's slurred speech "Ricci" came out more like "Rithi".

"No, not by his speed, High Chamberlain." Aleja delicately lowered Turik's raised hand with her own. "Although he is faster than any other in the Queen's stables."

"Please tell us how he came by it, Vessel." Ricci said as Turik stared in bleary eyed surprise for being corrected about one of the horses in his care.

"When he was a colt, already fiercely independent of his mother, boys would practice archery in the meadow next to his. As the boys shot their arrows into a tree Arrowchaser ran alongside the fence. At first the boys thought he was only there to beg for the apples they would eat as they practiced. But then they noticed he would ignore the apples in their satchels once they worked with their bows."

Aleja paused. She noticed the din of conversation in the room vanished into complete silence. All eyes, and ears, were now directed towards her. Aleja turned her attention back to High Chamberlain Ricci. He looked at her in a way that made her think of her father.

Perhaps he is kind. Like my father was. I hope so, for Ivo's sake.

Aleja cleared her throat, and spoke quickly, eager to lose the attention of the guests.

"Arrowchaser would watch the boys string their arrows, and at the first hint of release, would dash off the same distance as the tree they used for targeting. And then he'd come back to do it again. The boys swore Arrowchaser ran the length faster than the arrows did."

Silence held in the hall. Aleja's eyes darted nervously. She took up her cup, bowed to the crowd, and took a drink. Once the wine touched her lips the conversations in the room resumed.

Aleja drank the rest down. Her head began to spin, but she held out the cup for another.

The High Chamberlain of Andrid took the pitcher from the Maiden and, without a word, filled Aleja's cup and drank with her.

"My apologies, Vessel, but who told you that story?" Turik said in a drunken attempt at a whisper.

"You did of course, Herdmaster Turik. Don't you remember?"

Turik nodded heavily, his red face almost hitting the table.

"Apologies again, Vessel, but I don't even know the tale myself. Arrowchaser was just given to us that day to break. I didn't even think to learn much about him. He was too wild to be in the Queen's stable."

Aleja noticed High Chamberlain Ricci listening intently to their conversation as she slowly chewed on a small morsel of food.

"Perhaps one of your stablehands, then." Ricci offered.

Turik appeared to consider the possibility, then shook his head so vigorously it could've flown off his neck.

"No. None would dare speak so casually to the Vessel."

"Are you questioning the strength of my memory Herdmaster Turik?" Aleja said in a voice that channeled Kalim's sharpness.

Turik's eyes went wide.

"Oh, no, no. "Turik stammered. "You must be right. Someone shared the story with you. Forgive my arrogance at assuming to know all that happens in my stables."

Aleja held up her hand.

"Nothing to forgive, Herdmaster. Please, do not let this disturb your enjoyment of the evening."

High Chamberlain Ricci smiled at Aleja and nodded his head. Aleja returned with a bow, then sat back in her chair and sipped from her cup. Even though the next day would be her last, she had felt impatient for the evening to end soon.

But now, with the evening done and morning approaching, Aleja remembered Kalim's advice.

"Never wish a day to end before its time."

Aleja threw off her blankets and stood up. She saw the shadow of an attendant come forward, but waved her off. Aleja walked up to the mirror.

Speak to me. Comfort me.

Silence.

Why did you say Sara's name?

Aleja thought about the tale she told about Arrowchaser. The words seemed to come out without her control.

Turik spoke the truth.

No one told her the tale. But she knew it was true. Somehow, in a way Aleja struggled to comprehend, the story behind Arrowchaser's name was as vivid and as real to her as one of her own memories. The memories of her homeland and her Grape Mother. Of her father.

The memories of her dreams.

Are they my memories? Any of them?

There was no answer in the mirror. Only the dark of night.

Before the attendant could stop her, Aleja grabbed the mirror and held it up, intending to smash it onto the floor. The jagged edges cut into her hand, and before she could throw it, she collapsed unconscious.

CHAPTER 22

Aleja could not remember how she came to be in this place. The forest was dark, unfamiliar. Pale white trees, their limbless trunks towering like giant wooden spikes, pierced the starless night sky.

Aleja felt afraid. More than ever in her life.

The feeling crept into her slowly, like a chill that cuts through the skin and then buries itself deep into the bones. Aleja walked along a path with stumbling, uncertain steps.

The twigs under her feet looked like burned bones. Blots of red colored the leaves on the ground.

A strange, rumbling sound filled the forest. At first the sound was chaotic. But as Aleja walked deeper into the forest she detected a pulsing rhythm in it. The low rumble was joined by a halting, high pitched screech tearing through the forest like a knife ripping through flesh.

Aleja began to run, hands over her ears, hoping to somehow outrun the sound. The ground glowed in the distance. She ran towards the glow and came upon a canyon filled with light. She looked down into it, and saw the Syncronia. Instead of a mosaic of the Queen there was an enormous, bright mirror pulsing a strange, liquid light. The skin-masks were on the Syncronia stage, standing behind a child covered with a veil. As they held up the knife they would use to kill the child, the mirror's light intensified and reflected off the ghostly skin of the audience. Only one face in the crowd looked any different from the others. It was a man, looking up at the stage with tear-filled eyes.

My father!

Aleja watched helplessly as the child was killed, and covered her ears at the sound of her father's scream. The light from the mosaic went out, and the forest again filled with a terrifying noise. The forest was now filled with the ruins of an ancient city, one that looked like the decaying corpse of Mir. The buildings were torn apart by towering trees, the streets blocked by thorn bushes, and streets littered with rot and ash.

Aleja could not escape the forest, and got lost in the maze of trees and crumbling stone. The faster she tried to run, the slower her legs moved. She collapsed on a decrepit, crumbling wall, and felt a chill flow like a wave over her skin.

She was not alone.

There was another with her, in the forest. Someone, or some thing, that followed her out of the canyon. She felt it coming, and yet could not run away.

It was a woman. She walked towards Aleja with a strange, awkward gait. Her ankles twisted with every crooked step. The tatters of cloth that clung to her looked as black as pitch against the sallow milkiness of her skin. The woman's gnarled arms flailed wildly, and her thin, razor sharp fingers scratched the air.

Aleja opened her mouth to scream but nothing came out. The forest was now completely silent, as if the ground sucked all the sound out of the air.

Aleja knew the woman. She had seen her before, just for an instant, in the Syncronia the day Maran's icy finger grazed her skin. It was the Ash-faced woman.

The woman's flat, featureless face glowed in the darkness as she inched towards Aleja. Her fingers writhed like centipedes. The line of ash where her mouth should be curved upward into a smile.

The Ash-woman's voice carried through the stillness of the forest like the echo of water dripping in a cave.

"I see you."

Roots sprung up from the ground and wrapped around Aleja's legs. The Ash-Woman reached out for Aleja. Her fingers opened and closed like pairs of boney scissors.

"Give your skin to me."

The Ash-Woman's needle-like fingers pressed into Aleja's chest. Aleja screamed and tore the woman's fingers off her hand. The Ash-Woman laughed as new fingers grew from the stumps. The old ones crawled up from the ground and onto Aleja's legs. The fingers, looking like boney worms, crawled up to Aleja's chest. Aleja screamed as the fingers dug through her shoulders and arms and nailed themselves into the wall.

Despite the pain, she screamed defiantly into the Ash-Woman's grinning face.

"I won't let you take me!"

The trees burst into pillars of flame at the sound of Aleja's voice. The heat from the fires caught hold of the Ash-Woman, who showed no pain as it consumed her. The Ash-Woman's skin cracked and blistered. Charred flakes of it blew off her face like pieces of burning paper.

She continued to claw at Aleja as her own burning body crumpled to the ground.

Aleja screamed in agony as the Ash-Woman's burning fingers tore through her skin. The blood emptying from Aleja's wounds was a deep red color, but came out dry as powder. Aleja's flesh began to shrivel as the dust flew out of her body like sand from a cracked hourglass.

A wall of fire blew through the forest and the Ash-Woman exploded into a cloud of dust.

When the dust cleared Aleja saw her father Amedeo standing in front of her, the Queen's broken mirror in his hands.

Aleja pleaded with him to stop as he raised the mirror up to her face.

Aleja stared in horror at her reflection.

Her skin hung loosely from her skull like wax from a melting candle. The wounds on her body flapped open like curtains caught in a breeze.

Amedeo cut himself with the mirror, then picked up handfuls of ash and dirt and swirled it into his blood. The mixture drifted from his hands and into Aleja's wounds. Aleja's skin blackened as her body filled with earth.

Amedeo spoke to Aleja, his voice cold and distant.

"They have closed the door." Amedeo said.

Amedeo's face cracked and broke apart, and then he too turned to ash. Only his voice, and the mirror, remained.

"You must open it." Her father's voice echoed.

"What? What do you mean, father? I don't understand." Aleja's body shook as she spoke.

"Take from them, what I have given to you. You must give life to death."

Aleja saw her reflection in the mirror. At first it was in pieces, but it gradually came together. Aleja watched incredulously as it changed. Like the image of the Queen on the Syncronia mosaic, her hairless skin was black as a starless night and her eyes like the fire consuming the forest. But her features were her own. It was as if her face had joined with the Queen's.

Aleja's reflection spoke with the fragile voice of the Queen.

"Find your path, Aleja." The reflection said. "Run."

CHAPTER 23

There was a smell, slight at first, like one that slips up a person's nose at the taste of an almond. But it grew stronger. It burned into Aleja's nose and forced open her eyes.

Everything around her was cloaked in a fog. She saw lights flickering in the dim, and large swaths of color. Reds and yellows that became more vibrant as the milky haze in her eyes trickled away.

There were also faces. And voices. But Aleja could not tell if they were those of men or women.

"What of the procession?" whispered a garbled voice.

"It must be cancelled. The ceremony is the priority." Replied another voice, higher pitched than the first.

"But all the preparations? What will the people think?"

"Anything we tell them to think."

Aleja's vision cleared. Two shadowy figures turned towards her. Once closer, Aleja could see the figures were Taka and Maran.

"Are you with us, Vessel?" Taka said as he looked into Aleja's eyes.

"Yes." Aleja replied. Her own voice sounded removed, as if someone else in the room spoke for her.

Aleja was in her room at the High Temple. It was darker than it normally would be, for only a few lamps were lit. The images in the mosaics that decorated the room seemed to dance in the flickering light.

Aleja noticed a gleaming light in a corner of the room. It was the mirror. From what Aleja could tell, the mirror was not reflecting light, but shining its own.

Taka drew his face in close.

"Tell me where you are, Vessel."

"My room."

"What was the name you once had?"

"Aleja."

"And mine?"

"You are High Chamberlain Taka."

Taka appeared satisfied. The smile on his face gave Aleja chills.

"What happened, High Chamberlain? I remember falling, but nothing else."

"You fell, it's true. But you are safe in your room now."

Shadowy figures lurked in the corner of Aleja's eyes. Aleja did not turn her head towards them for fear of what she might see.

"What of its hands, Taka?" Maran said in his sickly, sweet voice.

What does he mean "its"?

Aleja looked down and saw her hands were bandaged. From the thickness of the bandages she thought the cuts were deep. But she felt no pain in her hands.

"It's of no concern." Taka turned away from Aleja.

Maran snorted.

"Is that so? The...Queen...may disagree." Maran laughed. "Perhaps you should confer with her first. Take a look at them. They are gouged to the bone. If we don't heal the girl first the Queen won't have hands, she'll have crippled claws."

Taka glared at Maran at the mention of the Queen. Aleja thought Maran's phrasing was odd, as if he referred to the Queen in jest.

Taka stood up to face Maran. To Aleja it seemed as if they were silently challenging one another.

Eventually, Maran moved past Taka and crept in close to Aleja.

"There must be no more delay, Maran." Taka said as Maran inspected Aleja with his jaundiced eyes. "All other conditions are right. The sky shares light and dark. The ceremony will proceed as we have planned."

Taka turned towards the shadows lurking in the corners of the room.

"Remove the bandages." Taka said to them, and then glared at Maran. "Let's see if the cuts are as bad as you say."

Maran sneered.

Bao came forward with another servant and knelt before Aleja. She gave Aleja an odd, but reassuring smile as the two servants unwrapped the bloodied bandages. Aleja was afraid to look down to see the cuts, but did so after Maran spoke.

"I don't believe it." He said with a gasp.

Aleja looked down at her hands. They were unblemished, no cuts, not even the stain of blood on them. Bao pressed her thumbs into Aleja's palms, smiled again, and skirted away with the bandages.

"Not as bad as you say, Maran." Taka replied with what seemed like a laugh. "And to think you mocked my methods to strengthen the Vessel."

"But you saw the blood. You know she must have been cut." Maran protested.

"I hope this is not one of your tricks, Maran. You must know by now I'm not easily amused." Taka scoffed.

As Taka spoke Maran knelt beside Aleja. His eyes slowly looked over Aleja's body.

"And what of its legs?" Maran pointed to the scrapes on Aleja's knees. "Surely the Queen wishes to suffer none of the pain of healing, and these are such nasty cuts."

Maran's hand drifted down onto Aleja's knee.

The instant Maran touched Aleja the room filled with a deafening cracking sound. Aleja was back in the garden, pulling herself through the vines as the man with the dead-skin mask grabbed her leg.

This time Aleja did not escape. The creature pulled her back into the room and Aleja fell onto the floor in the middle of a shaft of moonlight.

This vision was different. It was worse than the nightmares that plagued her nights. The brief flashes of the garden Aleja saw before were like memories of a distant dream. This time, she felt the coldness of the floor and heard the slumping, thudding steps of the creatures around her.

Dark, rotting forms surrounded Aleja. They pulled off their skin-masks with their putrid hands. They reached out greedily for her, and cried like a child alone and afraid in the night. Their breath fill the room with the stench of decay.

In the moonlight Aleja saw their pale, rotting faces, with looks of pitiful anguish in their drooping lips and sightless eyes.

They were horrible. Unlike anything she had ever seen.

And yet, among the crowd of shadowy faces, disfigured as they were, Aleja recognized some of them.

Taka. Maran.

She even recognized the face of one of Taka's Guardians, the thick, heavyset one named Ker.

As they were about to fall upon her, Aleja heard a woman hiss out a command to stop. The Ash-Woman appeared before Aleja.

Aleja screamed and tried to get up to run. Vines sprouted out of the floor and held her legs and arms to the ground.

The Ash-Woman's long, spindly nails came in close to Aleja's face, but did not touch. The Ash-Woman drew one of her fingers across the top of her own face, and cut the skin in two places. Blood poured out of the slits.

A pair of eyes, their irises a deep, oceanic blue, peered out from the gash.

The Ash-Woman made another cut across her face. The skin peeled back to reveal a grinning mouth full of long, yellow teeth.

The Ash-Woman's head twisted towards Taka.

"This body fights me so. Make it mine, Taka. Now."

Despite the hideous appearance of the Ash-Woman's mouth, her voice was more beautiful than any who sang the Queen's Evening Song.

The Taka-creature responded slowly, as if he struggled to understand the Ash-Woman. He lurched towards Aleja.

A child's voice shouted out from the corner of the room. It was the voice of a young girl. Aleja only saw her in shadows. The girl's face was covered in a veil.

A dagger, with one black blade and one white coming from opposite ends of the handle, dropped from the veiled girl's hands. It chimed as it hit the floor, and landed within Aleja's reach.

Aleja fumbled with the dagger. Her fear at the sight of the rotting Taka coming for her made her fingers as weak as blades of grass.

The Ash-Woman turned to face the veiled girl.

"No!" The Ash-Woman hissed. "Impossible! We killed you!"

The Ash-Woman shrieked and her fingers sliced at the girl. The girl vanished, and the Ash-Woman was left with only the veil in her hands.

Taka grabbed Aleja. Aleja's fingers grazed the hilt of the dagger, and she felt the symbol of the Queen, the silver lemniscate.

She thought of Sara and Ivo. Her anger over how they were taken from her coupled with regret for how their last moments together were spent. She wanted them all to feel it. Taka, Maran, the Ash-Woman and all those who wanted to take everything from her. Even the Queen.

Aleja gripped the dagger so hard the lemniscate on its handle bore into her palm. She tore free from the vines and jabbed the knife into Taka's gut. Taka shrieked and flailed on the floor. The others backed away.

Aleja stood up and slashed at Maran. Both he and Taka screamed and exploded into dust.

Aleja closed her eyes at the first stinging blast of dust. When she opened them again, she was standing in her room in the High Temple. A shocked Taka stared up at her from the floor.

He had been knocked backwards. Ker appeared out of a dark corner of the room and ran to his side to help him up.

Maran backed away from Aleja, but rather than help Taka, laughed nervously at the sight of him awkwardly getting up like a bird with a broken wing.

Before any in the room had a chance to say anything, Aleja shouted at Taka.

"What are you?"

Taka stared at her in silence.

Aleja backed away towards the balcony door. She grabbed a long, iron candlestick and held it up.

Ker was about to walk towards Aleja but Taka held him back. Taka neither said nor did anything to stop her retreat.

It was Maran who came forward to talk to Aleja.

"You must be calm, Vessel. The Queen is to take her place in your body tonight, and we cannot have you fight it. It would be difficult for her, and painful for you."

"I don't believe you!" Aleja screamed. Her hand went back for the handle to open the balcony door.

Maran smiled.

"What are you going to do? Grow wings and fly away? Please be calm. Ask us questions if you must, and we will answer what we can. But you must calm yourself. I understand your fear. I can help you with it."

Maran's voice was soothing. Aleja could feel a weariness take over her body. Her hand fumbled with the door handle and she lowered the candlestick.

Maran's reaction was fast, almost a blur. His arms seemed to grow as he reached out to grab Aleja. The sight of him coming towards her jarred Aleja out of her stupor and she swung the candlestick down at his hands.

Aleja didn't put all of her strength into the swing, but it was enough to crack the bones in Maran's withered hands.

Maran withdrew with a shriek.

"Ahhhh!" Maran screamed as he held his now crippled hands to his belly. "The pain, Taka! The pain!"

Despite her fear, Aleja laughed at the sight of Maran screaming like a child as he ran out of the room.

Taka and Ker stared at Aleja in silence. She raised the candlestick over her head, and readied her next swing.

Taka scoffed, and then led Ker out of Aleja's room. Once outside, Aleja heard Taka speak to someone in the hall.

"You must calm her." Taka said. "The Queen cannot take her in such a state." Aleja did not hear the other person's response, but watched warily as Taka took one last look at her and then walked out of sight.

A solitary figure entered the room, face shrouded by a hooded cloak, and holding a single candle.

The figure closed the door and faced Aleja. Aleja tightened her grip on the candlestick.

The figure lowered her hood, and held the candle up to her face.

Aleja's grip on the candlestick weakened. There was a ringing clang as Aleja let it fall to the floor.

It was Sara.

CHAPTER 24

Aleja fought back tears at the sight of her friend. Sara placed her candle down and embraced Aleja, then led her to the window seat where they had so many talks before.

The seat was under a large, latticed window decorated with carvings of dolphins and fish. The animals came to life on the walls when the full light of the moon shone through the carvings.

Once Sara dried Aleja's tears they watched as the light animals danced across the wall.

"There is not much I will miss about this room, but I will miss seeing that." Aleja said.

"The craftspeople who made this room were the best in Corazon." Sara replied. "You deserve this beauty in your life, for what you are about to do."

"Is it wrong that I want more of it, Sara? That I want more life? That I'm so angry and afraid?"

"No."

"I thought I wouldn't ever talk to you again. I'm sorry for what I did to you. I was afraid to die with you still angry with me."

Sara pulled Aleja close. Aleja's nose crinkled at the strength of the rose oil Sara now adorned herself with. Most people would have not noticed the difference, for it was slight, but for one with a memory as strong as Aleja's it was striking.

"You've changed your oils." Aleja said.

"Yes." Sara said with a hint of hesitation. "Do you like it?"

"I do. It's just…"

"What?"

"Nothing."

Sara drew back and looked at Aleja.

"Unburden yourself Aleja. Please, on this last night together. Hold nothing back. You must accept the Queen with an open heart. Why did you attack Maran and Taka?"

Sara's eyes were full of compassion, yet also with an insistence in them Aleja had never seen before.

Aleja opened her mouth but hesitated. She didn't quite know why, but felt the urge to hold back from Sara.

This is Sara, Daughter of the Queen, Maiden of the High Temple, performing her duties. Aleja found herself thinking. *Not my friend. That Sara has already moved on, to her I'm already dead.*

"I've missed you." Aleja said. She hoped Sara would say something to help quiet the thoughts that made Aleja reject her.

"But I've been here. We were at your feast together. I wasn't able to sit with you," Sara's hand grazed Aleja's cheek. "I've not forgotten about you."

Aleja nodded. She felt ashamed at her own selfishness. How could she have been so stupid to put Sara in a position to be punished by Taka?

Aleja felt trapped by all the feelings that swirled inside her. If this was to be her last time with Sara she wanted to share more, yet felt at this moment incapable of doing so. How could she express to Sara what seemed so unbelievable to herself? The visions, the nightmares. Was Sara right all along there was no difference between the dream world and the real?

Aleja turned towards the door at the sound of a forceful knock. Sara rubbed Aleja's head.

"Don't worry. It is Bao. I sent her to the kitchens so we could have one more meal together."

"Thank you, Sara." Aleja felt her throat constrict at the words. "I missed you."

Sara stood up and smiled. She touched one finger to her temple, and another to Aleja's.

"We will always be together, Aleja."

Aleja watched as Sara went to the door and let Bao in. Bao nodded hesitantly towards the Guardians who stood outside the door and made her way into the room with a large tray of cakes and a pot of tea. Bao walked in the room hunched over like a whipped dog, and did not look at Sara as she walked towards Aleja and set the tray down before her.

It was only a glance, but as she prepared the cups Aleja could see apprehension in Bao's eyes.

Once Bao poured the tea from the iron kettle into the clay cups the scent of the tea filled the air.

The scent was so strong it almost sent Aleja into a swoon.

It was the tea from the Room of Reflection, only with an odor even stronger than before. The mere smell of it made Aleja's eyes feel heavy, but the rush of fear it instilled in her kept her senses sharp.

Sara sat beside her, took a cup, and held it up to Aleja.

Aleja looked into Sara's large, warm brown eyes. It was brief, just a glimmer, maybe a trick of the light, but for a moment, Aleja saw another person staring out from them.

"Don't make me hold the cup any longer, Aleja." Sara said with a playful laugh. "It's burning my fingers."

"You said you'd never offer me this tea again. I don't like it, remember?"

"What? You drink it all the–" Sara's smile disappeared from her face. She set the cup down calmly and turned away from Aleja. "Of course, I forgot, you don't like it. I'm sorry, it has been a long day for me as well."

Aleja stared at Sara. Her smell, even her embrace, felt…wrong. But she had to believe her eyes. It was Sara that looked back at her. It was Sara's voice she heard. But why did it feel so different? How could she not remember the tea?

"Tell me Aleja, what caused you to lash out at Taka and Maran?" Sara said as she put aside the cup.

"The visions, Sara."

Sara nodded quickly.

"Yes, the visions. Of course. Are they still troubling you?

Aleja stared at Sara, suddenly unable to speak. She saw her silence made Sara uncomfortable.

"Please, Aleja." Sara gripped Aleja gently by the arms. "You must release yourself of all worries and anger if you are to be receptive to the Queen. I don't know much about the ceremony, but if the Vessel is not ready, I've heard it can be difficult."

Aleja took a deep breath.

"The visions scare me Sara. They always have. But they never felt as real as now."

"You've had more than one today?"

"Yes. When I fainted, and when Maran and Taka were in the room. I see them in the visions, but they are like monsters. And there is another with them, a woman with a face white and smooth like marble, but covered in ash. In the visions she comes for me. She wants to take control of my body."

"She's the Queen?"

"No."

Aleja looked into Sara's eyes and saw uncertainty, not the care and love she had come to expect.

"What if it's true, Sara? What if it is not the Queen who will claim me, but this monster that haunts me?"

Sara broke Aleja's gaze and embraced her.

"It is natural to be afraid, Aleja. We all will be, when we know our life's journey is at an end. But we must trust in the Queen, she has a plan for us all, and we must all do our part to see it through. Your memory will live on in her. In a way, you will live in this world longer than anyone who will see the sun rise tomorrow. This is not the end for you, it is only the beginning. Your name will be as eternal as the sea."

Aleja looked at the steam lifting out from the tea as she listened to Sara speak.

"Can I ask you one more thing about the visions?" Aleja said as she turned back to her friend.

"Yes, of course." Sara replied warmly.

"How do you know about them? I never told you."

Aleja backed away from her friend.

"Who are you?" Aleja fumbled at the candlestick behind her.

"What are you talking about, Aleja?" Sara replied sweetly.

"Sara never would have given me this tea. She knew I hated it."

"Please, Aleja. You're afraid. Stop with this nonsense."

Aleja looked up at Bao. Bao looked back and forth nervously between the two of them.

"What is it, Bao?" Aleja said. "What do you know?"

Before Bao could speak Sara stood up in front of her.

"What use is it to ask her? What's wrong with you? You must calm yourself, drink from the tea and you will see this is just fear clouding your eyes."

"No. Something is in the tea. I won't drink it. And if you were really Sara you would understand why."

"What are you talking about? How could you say such things about your friend?" Sara's eyes filled with tears. She held her arms out to Aleja. "Forget about the tea. I just want to see you at ease. I'm failing in my purpose, and it hurts me so."

Sara turned away and covered her face. She wept loudly.

"You're breaking my heart, Aleja. Remember how bad it felt to part with such harsh words. I don't want that for us."

Aleja supposed she should have felt guilt seeing Sara weep. But she felt nothing. Something about it was wrong. It was not the way someone would cry, but more like a mockery of it. Like a parody of an emotion.

Then Aleja saw it. A small, tuft of a white feather in Sara's hair. Sara self-consciously ran her hand through her hair. The feather fell from her head and drifted slowly to the floor.

Could it be from Hermes?

Aleja felt as if all the breath in her body was suddenly pulled out.

"Kalim?" Aleja said as she backed away.

Sara turned around to face Aleja. Her eyes showed no trace of tears, and there was a smirking grin on her face.

Aleja saw it now.

You can wear a mask, but the eyes cannot be hidden.

Aleja stared at Sara wide eyed. Sara looked down at the feather now lying on the floor. She smiled.

"It's you, Kalim. Isn't it?"

"Don't be foolish." Sara said with a laugh.

Sara reached out to embrace Aleja, but she jerked out of her grasp. Sara lowered her arms, and stared at Aleja coldly.

"How?" Aleja asked in a shocked whisper.

"You ask how?" Sara laughed. Not in the loving way Aleja was used to, but in the mocking fashion she heard so often from Kalim.

"You are not the only Vessel in Corazon my dear. After all, a Queen needs a court, those who can serve her in the way she is accustomed. We can't expect those who only know one lifetime to understand. Now drink the tea, Aleja. The Queen will not wait much longer for you. And if you will not give, she can, and will, take."

Sara's smile was bittersweet.

"Believe me, for once. You don't want that."

Aleja felt no fear as she looked at her friend, whose body was no longer her own. Aleja only felt anger. She reached over for the tray, picked it up, and threw it against the wall.

"No! I won't! Let her take me if she can!"

Sara looked wearily over at the tray. She clicked her tongue against her teeth and reached into the long sleeve of her gown.

"Stubborn Clay girls, and a Judge at that." Sara shook her head. "I told them we would have this problem choosing you. I was the only one to think your face miraculously appearing on the Syncronia walls was more menacing than promising. But even though they need me, they never listen to me. Pity. It would have been easier if they did."

"Who?" Aleja called out.

Sara ignored Aleja's question. She calmly pulled a long needle with a strange glass handle from her sleeve. The point of the needle caught the light, and Aleja saw a small drop of a green liquid drip from the tip.

"If only you listened. It would have been easier for you, too." Sara held the point of the needle in Aleja's direction, and then lunged at her.

Aleja tripped on the small table as she dodged Sara's thrust. Sara leapt on Aleja and pinned her to the floor with an effortless quickness.

Aleja held out her one free hand to block the needle. She struggled to break free. Sara's legs were threaded tightly under Aleja's knees. Sara kept Aleja from pushing off and rolling her over the way Ivo taught her.

Sara grabbed Aleja by the throat with her free hand. Aleja gagged at the pressure on her windpipe. Sara's grip on Aleja varied from strong to weak, as if she didn't know how to control her own hands, but it wasn't long before Aleja felt dizzy and her grip on Sara's wrist weakened.

"Don't fight it, Aleja." Sara pinned Aleja's arms to her chest with her body. Sara drew in close and held the needle to Aleja's throat. "Just a little sting to make you slee–"

From the corner of her eye Aleja saw a black object swing towards the back of Sara's head. It made contact with a thud.

Sara looked up to see Bao standing over her, a large iron pan in her hands. Dazed, Sara touched her head, stared at the blood now dripping down her finger, and collapsed unconscious to the floor.

The glass handle of the needle clattered on to the stone floor. Bao kicked it away and pulled Aleja up.

Outside, the Guardian's banged furiously on the door. Aleja heard them shouting for the keys.

Bao pulled the keys from her pocket and dangled them in front of Aleja.

"We go now, Daughter. I packed for us. We must leave."

Bao helped Aleja up and led her to the small, servant quarters.

"But how?" Aleja said. "The Guardians are at the door. How will we escape?"

Bao held up a candle to the image of the Queen on her wall, and then covered the Queen's angry, red eyes with her hand.

"Queen help us." Bao said.

There was a slight click, and once Bao withdrew her hand, the image of the Queen split in two.

Aleja closed her nose at the rush of rank, stale air that filled the room.

Behind the image of the Queen was a short passageway leading to a ladder.

Aleja stared in disbelief at the ladder. It extended both upwards and downwards into impenetrable darkness.

"How did you know about this place?"

Bao shut the door behind them just as the Guardians managed to break into Aleja's room. She rushed back in front of Aleja and pulled off a lantern hanging on one of the wet, gleaming walls.

Bao placed a pack on Aleja's back and pushed her towards the ladder.

"Bao," Aleja protested, "who told you?"

Bao stopped. She lowered her head as if thinking deeply about Aleja's question, then pointed back to the door. There was another relief of the Queen carved into it. This one kind, motherly.

"She tell me." Bao said, "Our Queen."

CHAPTER 25

"What do you mean the Queen told you?" Aleja tried to catch her breath.

Bao pushed Aleja ahead and lit the candle inside the lantern. A green crystal inside the lantern drank in the light, and began to glow.

"Not important now. Where we go is."

"Where are we going?"

"Up."

"Up? I thought we were trying to get out of here."

Bao climbed up the ladder, lantern still in her hand, and looked back at Aleja.

"Up is out. Hurry, Daughter, Guardians come soon."

"What?" Aleja walked up to the ledge and looked down. Her heart raced at the thought of getting a bad grip on the ladder and falling into the abyss.

Muffled shouting could be heard from behind the wall. If the Guardians couldn't figure out where they went, Aleja was certain Taka could. Any moment now they would be found.

Despite her best efforts to control it, Aleja could feel the first twinges of panic starting to set in.

Bao got off the ladder, placed her thumbs into Aleja's palms, and pulled Aleja to the ladder. Aleja slowly gripped the cool iron bars and found her footing.

"Trust." Bao said with a smile. "Up."

Aleja nodded, and began to climb.

The ladder went up a shaft barely wide enough for even Aleja's slender frame and pack to fit through. For Bao it was even worse. And yet, it was Bao who was pushing Aleja to move faster.

For as long as Aleja knew her servant she had never seen Bao move with such speed. She was a short, stocky woman who looked twice as old as Aleja. It took her ages to perform the simplest task, but Aleja had always found a strange comfort in her. Bao never appeared to be under pressure to do anything, and this attitude helped Aleja relax, especially during her first days in the High Temple.

But now Bao was pressing Aleja to climb with more and more speed and urgency. It was as if Bao was under the control of another master, a far more demanding and decisive one than Aleja ever was.

"Faster, faster Daughter. They come soon." Bao would hiss anytime Aleja's tempo slowed.

There seemed to be no end to the heights they were climbing. Aleja wondered if once they reached the top of the ladder they would have gone to the top of the High Temple to see the Queen herself.

If there really is a Queen.

Eventually the shaft came to a tiny room connected by four intersecting corridors. Bao told Aleja to step off the ladder.

The air was stale, as if not a single breath had been taken in the halls since the High Temple was made. In the dim light Aleja could see small creatures running along the floors. Aleja jumped and let out a shout at the sensation of tiny clawed feet scurrying over the top of hers.

"Shhh," Bao said with her finger to her lips, "Maybe others here."

"Where is here, Bao?" Aleja demanded. As much as Aleja wanted to flee from this place, her annoyance at being ordered around by her servant was beginning to nag at her.

"Here is High Temple." Bao said after what Aleja assumed was, for Bao, a thoughtful pause.

"Yes, I know that, Bao," Aleja hissed, "but these halls, where do they go?"

"Out."

Aleja took a deep breath at Bao's answer, and for a moment wished she still had the candlestick so she could give Bao a knock on the head.

Bao turned down one of the halls and gestured for Aleja to follow. Aleja grabbed Bao by the sleeve.

"Bao, tell me, how did you know about these halls?"

Bao did not remove Aleja's hand. She looked up at Aleja, her face twitching, as if the words were trying to sneak their way out of her mouth.

"Queen showed me. When I sleep, I hear your mirror. The Queen lives there. She tells me you in danger."

"What do you mean? I was the Queen's Vessel. She was going to claim my body for herself. What kind of danger could I be in?"

"No, No." Bao vigorously shook her head. "Queen not take people. Queen not take Sara."

Aleja let go of Bao's sleeve. The mention of Sara's name felt like a punch in the stomach.

Bao pulled on Aleja's arm.

"Must go now."

Aleja stopped Bao from leading her on down the hall. She wasn't going to take one more step unless she had some answers, even if it were from someone as simple as Bao.

"Bao, tell me, who took Sara? Did the Queen tell you?"

Bao nodded yes, the fear on her face shone brighter than the light from the lamp.

"Who took Sara?"

Who was going to take me?

Bao's lips trembled.

"Demons."

The word came out as a whisper, yet echoed down the empty corridors as if it were also trying to find a way to escape the High Temple.

Aleja stared at Bao in shock. Aleja did not believe in such creatures from the Drowned World, for the Queen was the only thing eternal.

How could Bao still believe in anything used just to frighten children into behaving?

Aleja was about to chide Bao for her foolishness but stopped herself at the sound of a stone door opening in the hallway. Bao gasped and gave the lantern a twist. The flame extinguished. The crystal glowed a soft, green light that was only visible to them.

Bao took Aleja's hand and placed it on her shoulder.

"No question now. Go."

Aleja did so, then turned back just in time to see a shaft of light fill the hallway behind them. She heard voices and the sound of footsteps closing in. Aleja ran quickly without Bao's prodding. Each passage seemed narrower than the last, as if the walls were fingers of a fist closing its grip around them.

Aleja only let go of Bao's shirt twice to climb up two shorter ladders that led to other hallways. The air in these halls was cool, almost damp. In them, Aleja thought she could hear the sound of rushing water.

Bao stopped in the middle of the hall and knelt down by the floor. Aleja noticed the gleam of metal on the floor, and saw in place of one of the stones was an iron panel.

"Help me." Bao began to pry the panel open.

Aleja knelt down to open the panel, and cringed at the sound of the creaking hinges. She thought she heard the footsteps stop at the sound.

Once the panel was opened the sound of rushing water was louder, almost deafening. Bao twisted the lantern and the green glow of the crystal grew brighter.

Aleja realized at once how Bao intended for them to escape.

"There has to be another way." Aleja whispered to Bao.

Bao shook her head.

"No. This is way."

Aleja climbed down into a tunnel with an arched ceiling so low she had to stoop down to walk in it. Water rushed down the middle of the tunnel in a copper half pipe, and all that was separating Aleja from falling into it and being swept away was a stone walkway barely wider than her own feet.

Aleja heard the iron panel slam down, followed by noises that sounded like Bao was trying to wedge something into it to keep anyone from following them.

Not that Aleja could imagine anyone trying to do so. The walkway was so cramped, the water deafening, and the darkness could drive anyone to madness.

Bao handed Aleja the lamp and pointed towards the tunnel they were about to walk into. Aleja looked at the water rushing by their feet, and then stared at Bao in disbelief. Bao smiled in return.

"Don't fall," she said.

CHAPTER 26

Aleja and Bao walked the slight incline of the water shaft with each foot carefully placed before the other. The stones were slippery, wet with a watery glaze gleaming in the green light of the crystal lantern.

Both Aleja and Bao walked hunched under the low ceiling. Aleja fought the feeling that the farther she walked through the passageway, the tighter it became.

"How much farther?" Aleja shouted back to Bao, her voice barely cutting through the din of rushing water.

"Not much. Get out soon."

Aleja's head grazed the curved ceiling. The desire to stand erect was becoming overpowering.

"When is soon?" Aleja made no attempt to hide the irritation in her voice.

"After now." Bao shouted back.

Aleja cringed.

Was that a joke? Is this really Bao walking with me?

Aleja heard a loud snap, like the crack of a whip. It wasn't long after the sound that Aleja felt water rushing over her toes.

"Go faster." Bao shouted.

"What's happening?" Aleja turned to shout back but stopped when her forehead hit a wall.

"More water coming."

"How will we get out of here?"

"You go faster, you get out."

Aleja suddenly had the urge to swing the lantern at Bao's head.

The water was now up to her ankles. Aleja knew she wouldn't be able to go forward once it hit her waist. Maybe even before that.

There was another series of snaps, followed by long squeaking sounds.

Aleja thought back to the grating sound of the hinges on the floor panel. She figured somewhere ahead a panel was being lifted and the water from other pipes was now coming into this one.

All the water is being diverted into here, Aleja thought with growing horror, *someone's trying to flush us out.*

Aleja yelled in frustration as the water reached her knees. Each step in the rushing water was like trudging through a muddy field. But in a field the only danger was losing a sandal. In the water shaft, any sandal that slipped off Aleja's feet was likely to be followed by Aleja herself.

Aleja heard Bao yell. At first she thought Bao slipped and was now plunging into the depths.

Aleja let out a sigh of relief when she felt Bao grab onto her shoulder.

Bao pointed up to something hanging from the center of the archway.

"There!" Bao yelled, her mouth almost at Aleja's ear. "There! Grab it!"

A ladder hanging from the center of the ceiling led upwards into a small chute. It was almost out of reach for people as short as Aleja or Bao. Worse, to climb it meant dangling in the air over the rushing water.

There would be no room for mistakes.

Aleja stared back at Bao in disbelief.

Was this part of your plan?

Bao gave Aleja's cheek a smack. Then nodded, as if apologizing, and pointed again at the ladder.

Despite being slightly dazed from the shock of being struck by her servant, Aleja reached out to grab the iron handle. She strained to grab hold, and felt her toes reach the edge of the walkway now submerged under water that was almost waist high.

Bao took the lantern from Aleja to free her other hand and hooked it through the straps of her pack.

Summoning all her strength, Aleja reached out to the bars, then let out a yell as her foot slipped off the edge. She fell, but was caught by Bao, who was holding onto the wall.

"Jump, Daughter."

"But I'll fall!" Aleja wailed.

"Water take you down. Go now!" Bao yelled back.

Aleja stretched out her hands. The tips of her fingers grazed the first bar of the ladder. With a scream she pushed off the walkway and wrapped her hands around the ladder.

The rush of water on her legs almost pulled Aleja down. Her arms burning from the strain, Aleja reached for the next bar and began to pull herself up. Despite how much pain she felt as the iron ground into her palms, or how her own weight tore at her shoulders, Aleja managed to pull herself high enough to get her footing. Aleja couldn't believe the training she received gave her the strength to do this. It had to be coming from somewhere else.

Aleja saw Bao struggling to reach the ladder.

Bao's fingers were locked into shallow grooves of the stone wall. Bao would make a tentative reach for the bars, but the force of the rising water threatened to knock her off her feet, and her hand quickly went back to the wall.

The water level now reached higher than Bao's waist. Aleja could see her steadily being pushed backwards.

For the first time, Aleja saw fear in Bao's eyes.

"Go Daughter! You leave me!"

Bao was losing her grip on the stone. Aleja crouched at the foot of the ladder, locked an elbow around the bar and reached out for her.

"Take my hand! Do it now!"

Bao hesitated.

"Now, Bao. I order you!"

Bao reached out with both hands. Aleja grabbed hold and pulled with all her strength. Bao's weight and the pull of the water tore at her arm. She felt like it was about to be ripped off her body.

Eyes closed in pain, Aleja swung her arm towards the ladder. For a moment, Bao felt suddenly lighter, and Aleja, her eyes still closed from the strain, thought she lost her.

But when she opened her eyes Aleja saw Bao wrap her hand around one of the bars. Aleja pulled on Bao's other hand to help her lift herself out of the water.

Aleja's arms burned as she climbed to make room for Bao.

With one final, exhausted groan, Bao managed to free her legs from the water and prop herself underneath Aleja.

"No time rest, Daughter." Bao said between gasping breaths. "Go."

Aleja nodded and reached for the next step in the ladder. They climbed up for what felt like an eternity until, with the green light of her lantern sparkling against the wet stone walls, Aleja saw the metal door that led to the way out.

CHAPTER 27

A beam of moonlight, thin as a thread hanging from a needle, shone through a slight crack in the panel. The thought to ask where they were going next didn't cross Aleja's mind. All she cared about now was they were getting out.

Aleja's arms screamed for rest as she made it up the ladder. The panel did not open easily, and after the first unsuccessful attempt Aleja felt a panic coming on. But with some calming words from Bao she located the small lock that held the door shut. Aleja pulled the pin free and groaned as she pushed up the heavy panel door.

Aleja rolled her body out of the narrow chute and stared up at the night sky. The air was cool, and Aleja shivered as a breeze blew over her soaked clothes. Aleja helped Bao out of the tunnel, and then let the panel door slam shut. Countless birds of all colors and sizes, nestled among the statues decorating the edges of the aqueduct, scattered noisily at the sound of the slamming door.

It took Aleja a moment to realize they were on one of the towering aqueducts that fed into the High Temple. Aleja knew you could walk in a straight line out of the city on the top of the aqueduct and figured that was Bao's plan. The only problem with the plan was if there were Guardians in the way there was no going forward. Aleja didn't have to look over the edge of the aqueduct to know going over the sides wasn't an option.

Bao rested by Aleja's side, her chest heaving as she took heavy breaths. Aleja blinked as she stared into the night sky. After the dark of the tunnels the light of the full moon seemed as blinding as the sun.

Bao got up with a groan. Aleja couldn't fathom how Bao was able to stand when it hurt Aleja to even sit up.

"Get up, Daughter. We walk out Mir now." Bao's breath was heavy.

"Just a little more rest."

"It is night. We need leave before sun comes."

"What difference does it make? They could see us in this moonlight anyway."

"People walk here when sun rises. They will stop us."

"How do you know this, Bao?" Aleja looked up at her skeptically. She had gotten them this far, but Aleja couldn't shake the feeling that somehow, it was not Bao who was leading her out of the High Temple to an unknown destination, but someone else.

Is someone manipulating her? Like how Taka and Kalim manipulated me?

Bao sat down and pulled off her pack. She pulled out a large object wrapped in colorfully dyed linen. Bao unwrapped layer after layer of the linen, and pulled out a thin, dark object. Aleja noticed she was careful not to handle the object without the linen.

Bao held it out to Aleja.

The jagged edges and gleaming surface of the mirror were unmistakable. Aleja saw her reflection, almost translucent in the moonlight, and turned away.

"You took it from the room. Why?"

"It help you."

"How?" Aleja's anger gave her the strength to sit up. "It has done nothing for me but fill my mind with nightmares."

"Because you don't listen, Daughter."

Bao held the mirror out towards Aleja.

Aleja recoiled. She felt the urge to grab the mirror from Bao's hands and fling it over the edge.

"You only hear demons. Demons use mirror's power to speak to you. Don't listen. Listen to Queen."

"There are no demons, Bao. Don't be a child."

The birds tiptoeing around Aleja rustled their feathers at the sound of her voice.

Bao's face reddened.

"Demons took Sara. Demons in your dreams."

Bao shoved the mirror into Aleja's hands.

"Don't want demons take you."

Aleja looked into the mirror and stared at her shadowy reflection. Her hands grazed along the sharpness of its edge. She felt the pain of a cut, yet when she looked at her hands the skin was still smooth and untouched.

"Mirror help you on journey, Daughter." Bao said.

"What journey? To where?"

"Out of Mir."

Aleja's looked out over the city beyond the gardens. The lights of the city twinkled like stars, and from the top of the aqueduct, seemed just as distant.

"Bao, listen to me, don't you understand it may all be a lie? Even the Queen! Whoever told you this, they could be leading us into a trap."

"No. Queen take you out of trap."

"Even so, Bao, we have to be careful about trusting anyone."

Aleja wrapped the mirror and placed it in her pack.

"Or anything. Now let's get–"

Aleja stopped abruptly. Several birds walked among them, their claws rapping on the stone, but one stood out from the rest. Most were crows, others smaller birds, but all sleek with unadorned crowns. Aleja spotted a large bird, its pale body glowed, and its feathered crest standing out like the beautiful sails of a Queen's ship amongst humble fishing boats.

The bird's head tilted as it watched them. It let out a squawk and spread its wings.

"Bad girl." The bird said with an ear piercing shriek.

"Hermes." Aleja called out soothingly. She held out her hands as if offering the bird some seeds. "Come here. It's your friend, Aleja."

"Bad girl." Hermes squawked in reply.

"No, Hermes. It's your friend. Come here."

Aleja moved closer, with Bao circling behind the bird. Hermes let out a squawk, then unfurled its wings and began to back away.

"Must tell mother." Hermes said as it flapped its wings.

Aleja lunged at Hermes. She felt a whip of air as Hermes launched itself out of the way. Bao leapt into the air after the bird, and was almost sent spinning off the edge as Hermes' claws dug into the top her head. Aleja pushed herself up and swung at Hermes, who let go of Bao and off towards the High Temple shrieking all the way.

"Bad girl! Bad girl! Must tell mother! Bad girl!"

Blood dripped down the side of Bao's face. Aleja cleaned up as much as she could with a cloth from her pack.

"They'll know where we are now Bao. Where do we go?"

Bao, still holding the cloth to her bleeding head, rummaged through her pack. She pulled out a long rope with an iron hook at its end and held it up for Aleja to see.

"We go down."

CHAPTER 28

"This place good."

Bao knelt down by a statue of a stone eagle perched over the edge of the aqueduct.

Aleja stopped reluctantly. They only walked a few paces before finding it, and were still above the High Temple Gardens. The lights of Mir were still far. But the sight of them made Aleja anxious to get as far as possible from the High Temple.

Maybe if we just ran. Fast.

But the drop from where they were on the aqueduct to the next highest building was far too high to even think about jumping. Aleja supposed since they would still have to lower themselves down to one of the lower levels of the aqueduct, this place was as good as any.

Aleja held her arms close to her chest. The night air of Mir was usually cold, but it was made worse by the stiff wind that wrapped the wet linen of Aleja's torn peplos close to her skin.

"Climb down." Bao hunched by the eagle and held the rope out to Aleja.

Aleja cautiously peered over the edge of the aqueduct. The aqueduct was as wide as any road in Corazon, and walking on the middle of it, it was easy to pretend there wasn't a drop on each side. But the illusion vanished the moment Aleja looked down and saw the tops of the large trees of the Temple Garden.

They look like bushes.

"No." Aleja came back from the edge shaking her head. "I can't do it. Let's run. It is still night. We could make it to the wall before anyone else got up here."

Bao fixed the iron hook in-between the wing and head of the eagle. She gave it a sharp tug.

"Guardians be here soon, Daughter. You saw bird. We be catched. Demons take you."

Aleja huffed. She didn't feel like hearing about "death by demons" anymore, especially when falling to her death seemed the more likely possibility.

Bao threw the rope over. Aleja didn't have to look over to know it didn't even go halfway down to the ground.

"We can't climb all the way, Bao."

"No." Bao tightened the straps of her pack, and then did the same for Aleja. "Just half. Then run. Get to houses and can jump on roofs."

Bao pointed to the silhouetted rooftops of Mir in the distance.

"Jump off?" Aleja scoffed. "First we almost drown, now we're going to leap? I thought you were trying to save me Bao, not kill me."

Bao stood up and walked right up to Aleja. The look in Bao's eyes alone could've thrown Aleja off the ledge. Aleja stepped back. Bao picked up Aleja's pack and thrust it into her chest.

"No. I not save you. You save you."

Aleja nodded her head after a pause, then put the pack on.

"We go now." Bao crouched by the eagle. "I be first. Show it safe."

Bao reached around the eagle, grabbed hold of the rope, and swung herself over the edge. The iron hook scraped against the stone as the rope bore Bao's weight.

Aleja knelt down behind the statue, placed a hand on each of the outstretched wings, and watched Bao climb down. The rope made a terrifying stretching sound with each of Bao's lurching steps, but showed no sign of tearing.

Aleja closed her eyes and rested her head against the cool, smooth statue. Her hands reached out tentatively for the rope.

She took a deep breath.

There has to be another way.

She readied herself, and gripped the rope so tight it burned. Rather than look down, Aleja's gaze held at the line of eagles that decorated the edge of the aqueduct. A shadow raced from behind one statue and then just as quickly hid behind another.

Aleja placed her hand to her mouth. From behind the statue Aleja heard a sharp, whistling sound, almost like a bird's, and then saw three other figures emerge and rush towards her.

Guardians.

Aleja flung herself over the edge. The rope swayed, and for a brief terrifying moment Aleja thought she lost her grip. The rope twisted as Aleja struggled to find her footing.

Guardians shouted overhead as Bao shouted at Aleja from below.

"Watch out, Daughter!"

Aleja looked up just in time to see a Guardian reach down to grab at her arm. Aleja ripped her arm from his grasp, but her hand slipped and she slid down the rope. Just as she was about to lose the rope entirely her foot landed on a small ledge, which stopped her slide just enough for Aleja to regain her grip.

Aleja winced at the burn she felt in her palms, then pulled herself back to the wall and looked up.

A Guardian's face, now looking paler than the moon, stared down at Aleja. He reached out for her.

"I'm sorry for my rashness, Vessel," the Guardian yelled down at her, "I will not try that again. Please, take my hand. We wish for no harm to come to you."

Other Guardians joined him, all calling out for Aleja to climb back up.

"Don't listen, Daughter." Bao shouted up at her. "Come down now!"

Aleja tentatively looked down below. Bao was no longer on the rope. Aleja cringed at the sight of the large, white rocks lining a stream in the garden below. She could not help picturing her own body lying broken on those rocks, staining the pure, white stones with her blood.

Aleja looked up at the crowd of Guardians above her. Their outstretched hands were so comfortingly close, while the ground below was so dangerously far.

"Yes, yes, Vessel. Give me your hand."

Just go back. This is all foolishness. Just accept your fate.

Aleja took her hand from the rope and held it up. The Guardian climbed over the edge of the aqueduct. He held on to the eagle's wing and reached out towards Aleja.

Even so, his fingertips only managed to graze hers.

"Just a little more, Vessel." The Guardian called out to her, his voice calm and full of compassion. "I'll bring you back to safety. Just reach a little more."

Aleja placed her feet onto the wall and pushed herself towards the Guardian. She was about to grip the Guardian's hand but stopped at the sound of a familiar voice.

"Reach a little more, Guardian. Where is your courage? Lean out!"

Aleja couldn't see him, but heard enough to know the voice belonged to Ker. Aleja dropped her hand lower down the rope and took a hurried step down.

The young Guardian, his grip on the eagle's wing already strained, lunged out for Aleja. Aleja heard a scream, and then saw a flash of a body plummeting past her, the force of its descent almost knocking her from the rope.

Aleja looked down just in time to see the body of the Guardian bounce off the side of the wall and then crash onto the stones below with a sickening thud.

There was no sound from above. The Guardians were still, their faces frozen in horror. One still held his arm out, as if he thought there was a chance to pull his fallen comrade from the ground.

Tears welled in Aleja's eyes.

"I'm sorry." Aleja mouthed the words, but knew it would do nothing to give them any comfort.

There was no forgiveness in the Guardians' eyes. They looked at her with such anger Aleja thought they may throw themselves down upon her just to knock her to the ground.

"I don't care if she does fall!" Ker screamed at the Guardians who hesitated. "Pull her up!"

The rope lurched upwards. Aleja let out a yelp as the first pull slammed her into the wall. Bao shouted at her from below. Aleja looked down and saw her head sticking out from beneath one of the archways.

"Jump! Jump!" Bao pointed frantically at one of the reliefs that decorated the walls. It was the Queen, holding out her arms to caress the sick laying at her feet. The statue was beside her, but only Aleja's fear kept her from leaping towards it.

Aleja tried to slow the Guardians by wedging her feet against the wall and pulling back, but it only served to drag her toes painfully along the stone.

"Jump!" Bao screamed. "Now, Daughter! Now!"

The Guardians pulled with such strength and speed the statue was a full body length below Aleja now. One more tug, and all chance of escape would be lost.

Aleja pushed herself off the wall and flew into the air. Aleja's feet fell into the waiting arms of the Queen, but she slipped, and saw no pity in the Queen's cold, stone eyes as she fell from her embrace.

Just as Aleja was about to join the body of the Guardian below she managed to grab one of the Queen's arms. Dangling from the Queen's wrist, Aleja let out a yell as she pulled herself up and placed her feet on the heads of the bodies resting in the Queen's lap.

Aleja looked down for another foothold.

At Ker's barking order the Guardians were now descending the rope. Aleja also saw other Guardians using their own ropes to chase her down.

The Guardians moved downward quickly, as if they were in a controlled fall.

Aleja climbed down the body of the Queen, her eyes searching for the quickest way to get down to Bao.

Suddenly, a Guardian swung at her from the side. He tried to reach his arm around Aleja's waist, but just as he did Aleja leapt down onto another statue. Aleja's foothold on the statue was good, but rather than grab hold and look for the next step, Aleja leapt down again.

Aleja felt no control over her body as she leapt from perch to perch down to the archway. It was only when she took her last step, from a stone waterspout pouring water from the mouth of a sea creature, that Aleja thought about what she was doing. Her foot hit the spout awkwardly, but it was enough to launch herself through the archway opening and crash into Bao.

Bao wrapped her arms around Aleja as they fell to the floor.

It was another waterway, this one uncovered. A steady stream of water flowed by them in a large, copper half pipe.

They were on the walkway that brought rainwater from all over Mir into the Water Hall. Aleja could tell it was indeed beautiful as Sara said, even in the dark shadows that now encased it.

But there was little time to admire its beauty.

Aleja and Bao landed only a hair's width from the pipe. The pipe was smooth, and the water flowed fast and deep. Only one slip further and they would have been swept back into the High Temple.

Aleja groaned and rubbed her head as she got up. Bao lay dazed on the floor.

Aleja held out her hand. To her relief, Bao came to her senses and took it.

"Are you alright?" Aleja said once she helped her servant up.

Bao, her eyes blinking, gave an unsteady nod.

A Guardian launch himself off his rope and onto the floor. Taka's female Guardian Rhea followed quickly after. Unlike Aleja and Boa, the Guardians landed gracefully. They approached Aleja slowly and confidently.

Rhea held a whip in her tightly clenched hands.

Holding Bao's hand, and ready to run, Aleja turned from the Guardians only to see another pair land in front of her. Once to their feet these Guardians also walked calmly towards Aleja and Bao, as if they already had them in their hands.

After climbing down Bao's rope, Ker landed with a dull thud onto the stone floor. His hand fell to the hilt of his knife.

"How about we make this easy, Vessel?" Ker said with a wink.

Aleja and Boa looked at each other. With Guardians on their sides and the water to their backs, there was no escape.

They were trapped.

CHAPTER 29

The Guardians, their feet spread wide and hands held out in a grappling stance, stood a few paces from Aleja and Bao. All had ropes tied to their waists and one was armed with a Bo staff.

Aleja held on to Bao, and her heels clung to the edge of the walkway.

"Careful Vessel," Ker said, "we wouldn't want to lose you down that pipe."

Aleja steadied herself. She moved her feet forward into the guard position Ivo taught her.

"You didn't seem to mind before when you almost drowned us." Aleja said.

Ker grinned.

"We thought you were in the lower tunnels. No one imagined you'd be so foolish to try to escape through the water tunnels, especially when they are flushed at night."

Ker motioned to the Guardians. They formed themselves into a semi-circle and moved in.

"Careful with the Vessel." Ker said in a confident, almost bored, tone. "But don't worry yourself with the servant."

Aleja stood back to back with Bao. Her servant whispered to her in a voice that cut through the sound of the rushing water like a razor.

"We fight them, Daughter."

Aleja thought by now there was nothing more Bao could have said or done to surprise her. Aleja stared at Bao's clenched fists in disbelief.

"There is no point in resisting Vessel." Ker said in response, as if he heard Bao's words. Ker removed his hand from the hilt of his dagger, and held his thick arms wide as he moved towards Aleja.

"Even if you could get past us, there is nowhere for you to run to, no place to hide. You won't make it past the walls of Mir. Every Guardian will know your face. They will curse you for abandoning your purpose, and causing the death of one of their own in doing so. No one in all of Corazon will come to your aid…." Ker let out a mocking laugh, "…not even your beloved Ivo."

Aleja tensed up. She wished Ker's smug face was close enough to give it a quick punch. Someone as sure of his strength as Ker probably wouldn't expect it. Ker, and the other Guardians, were in close but appeared careful not to force Aleja back any further towards the water.

They weren't as careful with Bao. In a flash Bao was flailing in the arms of a tall Guardian who looked as if he was going to dump her into the water.

"Tie the servant up, Rhea." Ker called out as Bao screamed.

Rhea pulled at Bao's arms to tie them, and then doubled over after Bao gave her a quick kick in the gut. Bao then butted the back of her head into the mouth of the Guardian who held her. He let out a spitting curse and dropped Bao onto the floor.

Ker's large, meaty hands reached out for Aleja. But distracted by Bao's sudden attack, he hesitated.

Aleja saw the rope dangling behind him.

The Guardians to Aleja's side grabbed at her, but only managed to catch a few strands of hair as she ducked to avoid them. Ker was too slow, and almost fell on his face trying to tackle Aleja as she ran to the edge of the aqueduct. Aleja's momentum carried her to the edge of the aqueduct and, rather than falling to her death, she jumped onto the rope at full speed.

As she launched herself into the air, Aleja let out a yell that was more triumphant than fearful. Aleja swung so high she felt like she could crash into the moon.

Aleja tried to swing herself over to the next archway but her momentum slowed. Aleja hovered just for moment before careening back towards the archway where she jumped.

The Guardians let out panicked shouts the moment she disappeared behind the curtain of ivy that covered much of the archway. Just as she was about to land back on the walkway Aleja saw Ker run to the edge and look down.

They thought I fell. Aleja realized just before she swung back.

But although Aleja saw him, Ker apparently didn't see her.

Aleja swung her legs toward him and kicked his face with both feet.

Propelled by the force of her swing, Aleja's kick was devastating.

Ker was sent spiraling backwards. His large body slammed into the other Guardians, knocking one of them into the water pipe. The other was crushed to the floor by Ker's now unconscious bulk.

Aleja was just above the waterway when the rope suddenly jerked back, causing her to flip and land on her side, with her legs dangling precariously over the water.

Blinding waves of pain shot through Aleja's shoulder as she pushed herself up.

The Guardian pinned under Ker tried to pull Aleja back down. Aleja clawed downwards onto his hand with her nails.

Aleja's stomach turned at the sensation of bits of skin and flesh pack under her fingernails. The Guardian, his legs still pinned under Ker's body, let go with a bloodcurdling scream.

Aleja stood up and kept her back to the water. She wasn't worried about falling in so much as letting one of the Guardians get behind her.

Bao, her back near the edge of the aqueduct, was still fighting with two guards. She clawed and kicked at them like a street cat cornered by a pair of dogs, but the fight was running out of her.

The tall Guardian gave Bao a kick to the chest. Bao flew backwards towards the edge of the walkway and dropped out of sight.

Aleja stared at the empty night sky behind the Guardians. It seemed so unreal. There was not even a sound, not a yell or scream. Bao was there one moment, and in the next, she wasn't.

"Murderers! How could you? How could you?" Aleja screamed at the Guardians.

The tall Guardian stood mouth agape. Rhea stared at him, and then slammed a fist into his chest.

"You were not to kill her." Reah shouted. "We don't seek vengeance."

"I'm sorry. In my anger…I forgot myself." The Guardian looked over at Aleja, the shock in his face mirroring hers.

Aleja didn't notice the Guardian pinned by Ker's body was now free. He rushed at Aleja and slammed into her. The world around Aleja spun as they both fell into the water. There was a loud cracking sound, and suddenly Aleja's arm was wrapped in pain.

Aleja closed her eyes and mouth against the rush of water. She did not hear or see the Guardian get swept down into the High Temple. Aleja could only think about the stinging pain in her arm keeping her from joining the Guardian down into the water tunnels.

It felt like her arm was wrapped in knives. Aleja clawed at her arm to free herself from whatever it was that was clinging to her, and felt the tight leather of a whip.

Rhea, helped by the tall Guardian, called out to Aleja.

"Don't fight it, Vessel, let us pull you up."

Aleja cringed with every tug of the whip as the pair pulled her back to the edge. The tall Guardian reached out for Aleja's hand as Rhea held on to the whip. Aleja pushed away his hand and placed her own on the ridge, then summoned the strength to push up and take the whip from her arm. Once freed from the whip her arm was covered in a spiral of red lines.

The Guardians reached out to pull Aleja out of the water. Aleja angrily pushed their arms away and slipped backwards. Reah quickly caught her, and had no trouble pulling Aleja out of the water on her own.

Once she was out of the water the Guardians stared at Aleja warily. Rhea wrapped up her whip while the tall Guardian prepared the rope tie Aleja up.

Suddenly the tall Guardian was sent flying over Aleja and into the water. It happened so fast Aleja barely had time to duck out of the way. As the Guardian was swept away Aleja looked up, and to her amazement saw Bao standing with a large bo staff in hand.

Rhea swung around and went for her whip.

She was fast, but not fast enough.

Bao charged at Rhea and cracked her in the ribs with the bo staff. In a blur Rhea was sent reeling backwards into the water after her comrade.

Bao dropped the staff and rushed to Aleja, who looked up at her servant with disbelieving eyes.

"I thought you'd fallen."

Bao nodded her head.

"I did." Bao said as she helped Aleja to her feet.

"But…you should be dead."

"My clothes caught stone." Bao pulled up a part of her gown. There was a large tear up the side. More disturbing to Aleja, the skin beneath was covered in a large bruise. Bao led Aleja to the ledge and showed her the relief where her fall was stopped.

"I climb up." Bao said as if it were the most natural thing in the world.

Aleja laughed through her tears.

"I thought I'd lost you."

Bao smiled.

"Not yet."

Aleja looked over at Ker, who still lay unconscious on the stone floor. The thought crossed her mind to dump him into the water as well.

"What should we do with him?" Aleja asked.

Bao walked behind Aleja, pulled the mirror out of her pack, and then motioned for Aleja to unwrap it.

"You know demons took Sara?" Bao asked.

Aleja sighed. She couldn't be sure what to believe.

Even though Aleja was going to have her body taken over, somehow the idea Kalim transferred her spirit into Sara's body was difficult to accept. Aleja, like all the people of Corazon, was taught since birth to transfer a spirit was the power of a Goddess, not of a frail human with no life outside their physical form.

"I don't know, Bao." Aleja said wearily. She closed her eyes. Right now she would have gladly taken rest over the answers to all her questions.

Bao frowned. Aleja reluctantly unwrapped the mirror. Bao motioned for her to hold the mirror in front of Ker's face.

"You know he is demon?"

"I don't believe in demons, Bao." Aleja replied wearily.

Bao pulled at Aleja's arms, and positioned the mirror over Ker's face.

"Look." Bao pointed to the mirror.

Aleja hesitated. Fear grew in her heart. Fear that Bao was right. Because then, there would be no turning back from this. If everything she knew was a lie, where would she have to go to find the truth? Did she even want to find it? The choice would be hers, and hers alone. Now that it came to a decision, to believe or not, Aleja found the prospect of a life of uncertainty and doubt terrifying.

Aleja wanted nothing more than to close her eyes and find herself back in her bed. Back to the comfort of her little room, eating cakes with Sara while watching the light make shadows of playful dolphins on the walls. She wanted to wake up with the sun, eat a simple meal, serve her people, and retire for the night with the knowledge she would be doing the same thing the next day.

"Look!" Bao cried, "That took Sara!"

Aleja let out a deep breath and looked into the mirror.

Even though it was covered by the mirror, Ker's face was visible in its black, liquid surface. It was as if what Aleja held in her hands was not a mirror at all, but rather the thin surface of water.

"It's just Ker. Nothing more, Bao."

"Look closer, Daughter."

Aleja moved her face closer to the mirror.

Ker's face changed. Not just once, but countless times.

Each face, some of men, some of women, peeled from the next like layers of an onion. The first faces were those of Corazon's people. Brown skin, full lips and noses, with dark hair and eyes. But as Aleja drew closer the faces began to show more variety. Some were monstrously pale, others dark as night. Their hair was dark and curly, thin and yellow, or even red like a flame.

Underneath all the faces, looking through all the eyes, was the person she knew as Ker.

Aleja knelt beside Bao. They looked down together at the face in the mirror, that of a lovely woman with raven black hair and bronze skin much like Aleja's own.

Impossible. It can't be.

"You see, Daughter?"

Aleja shook her head.

"Yes, Bao. Yes, I do. But she looks nothing like a demon. She could be one of our own people."

"She is, Daughter. They all are. But not Ker."

"What do you mean?"

Bao took a deep breath then winced. Her elbow clenched to her bruised side. Aleja could hear a strained, whistling quality to Bao's breath.

"Listen to me, Daughter. Never lose mirror. It is light in dark. It is song in silence. It protect you. Queen protect you."

"But Bao, that makes no sense. The Queen wants to take control of me. That's why these people are after me."

Bao shook her head. She looked upward towards the High Temple.

"Woman up there. She not Queen. She like him."

Bao looked down at Ker. The mirror hovered just above his head. Bao took another deep, painful breath, then looked back at Aleja.

"She like this."

Bao pushed Aleja's hands down so the mirror covered Ker's head.

Aleja's ears filled with shrieks. It was as if all the birds in Corazon suddenly screamed in unison. But the sound came from the mirror, not from the flocks perched on the aqueducts above.

Aleja stared in horror at the sight of Ker's featureless face. His skin was dry and cracked, the nose and ears formless masses of withered flesh. The creature's hollow eye sockets were lit by tiny pinpoints of light that looked like stars trembling in a deep, impenetrable abyss.

It was the face she saw in her visions.

I can't believe it.

Unlike the other faces in the mirror, this one was alive. It looked over at Aleja, and the thin line it had for lips tore open. A sound came from the shredded skin, like wind blowing through a cave, and Aleja's nose filled with the smell of decay.

"Skin. You're just skin." The creature croaked.

The creature's laugh sounded like the skittering legs of beetles. Aleja ripped the mirror from the face, and the laughter stopped.

Ker's face was visible again. Even for all the gruff menace it exuded, it seemed like the face of a child in comparison to what was underneath.

"What are demons, Bao?"

"Spirits. Live forever. But need bodies." Bao pointed to the mirror. "They stole Queen's power, use it to take bodies. Queen is broken, weak. You make her strong again."

"How will I do that?"

Bao looked confused.

"You not know how?"

Aleja shook her head. She didn't even know where to run to, much less what to do when she got there. Help the Queen? Aleja didn't think she could even help herself.

Ker grunted, but did not wake. Whatever Ker was, dumping him into the water might kill him, and Aleja couldn't bear the thought of another dying because of her, even if it was a monster. They decided to leave him where he was.

Aleja wrapped the mirror quickly, and placed it carefully back into her pack. Without another word, they started towards the city. The light of the sun was beginning to show itself, and the red tiled roofs of Mir glowed in the morning light. Aleja could see the misty outline of the Yamanashi Mountains in the distance. It looked like a dark blue stain on the pale haze of the morning sky.

Once Aleja and Bao made it to the rooftops, and the sun rose over the horizon, the mountains took shape in the light of dawn. They looked as solid and real as the roof she stood upon.

Before leaving the rooftops and dropping to the street below, Aleja took a moment to admire their beauty. She thought of the story Kalim told her about the Yamanashi, and of how the true height of Mount Obake could only be seen when you die.

It's like the mountains are spirits at night, and only in the light become bodies of soil and stone.

CHAPTER 30

"Forgive me, Daughter. We must stop."

Bao took her arm from around Aleja's shoulders and doubled over. Ever since they made it down to the ground, after leaping from the aqueduct onto a roof, then climbing down into the first of many alleyways they kept to, Bao's condition gradually worsened.

Aleja almost carried Bao through the last few narrow passageways. So far they escaped notice, but it wouldn't be long before someone would stop to help them. And that kind of well-meaning attention would bring notice by Caretakers, or worse, Daughters or Guardians.

As Bao sat on the ground, her back to one of the many unremarkable white walled homes, Aleja looked up into the sky. The sun pulled itself from its bed in the mountains, and the clattering din from the stone streets nearby grew louder. It was far too risky to walk anymore through the streets.

Two women in tattered, muddied clothes, one barely able to stand while the other with the tattoos of a snake running down her arm, wouldn't make it halfway through any of the busy streets of Mir without being stopped, much less make it past the city walls.

Aleja scanned the nearby alleyways for anything she could use as a disguise. She only saw a pile of firewood and some discarded clay pots, most broken, some with leafy green plants growing out of them. Most of the houses in this part of the city only had windows on the second floor, so there was nothing Aleja could quickly snatch from any of them. But there was one window in climbing distance from the woodpile.

"Wait here Bao. If anyone comes, pretend you're asleep." Aleja said.

Aleja took a short run, one foot leaping on to the wood pile, the other on to the wall, and grabbed hold of the windowsill. Breathing out through her nose to keep herself quiet, she pulled herself up and peered in.

The room held little more than a bed and a small table.

A servant's room Aleja thought with relief.

No one was inside, and the sight of the white sheet the covered the bed gave Aleja an idea.

Aleja stifled a grunt as she pulled herself into the room. Too exhausted for stealth, Aleja fell to the floor with a thud. The floors were made from thick planks of timber, rough but sturdy, and Aleja hoped they would muffle the sound of her fall.

She listened for a sound from downstairs, but heard nothing. Aleja grabbed some unwashed laundry from a wicker basket, pulled the sheet from the bed, and hurried back out the window.

Once she was back on the ground Aleja rooted through the pile of timber until she found a stick long enough to pass for a cane.

By the time Aleja was finished Bao was almost asleep. The sound of her labored breathing pained Aleja's own chest. She wanted nothing more than to let her servant rest, but knew Bao may never wake up if she did.

Aleja quickly changed into the peplos she found in the basket, folded it only once around her waist. It was a servant's peplos, plain except for a geometrical pattern at the hemline around her neck and ankles. It was an acceptable disguise, but the sleeveless gown left the distinction on her arm exposed.

Taking a knife from Bao's pack, Aleja cut the wide, white sheet in half. It was now in the rectangular shape of a palla, a simple garment women used to cover themselves when the weather turned cold.

The makeshift palla covered the entirety of Aleja's distinction. The white fabric was thin, and Aleja knew in full light the darkness of her tattoos would show through, but it was enough to disguise them if they kept moving.

Bao groaned as Aleja nudged her by the shoulder.

"Get up, Bao, get up!" Aleja whispered.

Aleja looked up at the sound of a group of men talking about the day's celebrations. From what she could tell they were not far off. It would not do to be found this way, Aleja thought. They had to move now.

"There will be no procession!" One of the men complained. "All those preparations for nothing."

"I don't give a whit about the procession." Another replied through what sounded like a mouthful of food. "As long as there is wine."

"More than you need! And games too!" Replied a third voice, "Enough to take your mind off the Vessel."

"Still..." The first man replied as Aleja tried to pick up Bao. "...it would have been a once in a lifetime event to see her."

"Bah!" Spat out the man with the mouthful of food. "So you don't get to stand on a rooftop just to see a speck in the crowd pass you by. It's no loss. Anyway, there'll be plenty of other women to see today. And they'll be close enough to touch! Let one of them tell you she's the Vessel. It'd be all the same to you!"

The three men laughed in unison. Aleja could tell they were just around the corner and coming her way.

Aleja pulled her nearly unconscious servant up. Bao cringed and let out a sharp cry of pain. There was a pause in the men's laughter.

Bao, now fully awake, held on to Aleja. It looked as if she was going to cry out again.

"You must be quiet." Aleja whispered. She placed the stick in Bao's trembling hands and threw the rest of the blanket over Bao's shoulders.

Like Aleja's servant disguise, the look of a Master wasn't perfect, but would be enough to blend in the crowded streets.

Aleja took her side by Bao like a servant helping a feeble master, and listened for the voices.

Aleja smiled at the men as they turned a corner and walked towards her. The men, now drunkenly trying to look respectable before entering a busy street, paid them little mind as they passed by.

Aleja made sure Bao had a steady grip on the cane, and put her arm around her servant.

"Walk with me," Aleja said, "and keep your head low."

Aleja guided Bao out of the alleyways and onto the street. The stick appeared to help Bao, and they moved faster than before. Not at a fast enough pace to ease Aleja's worries, but good enough to keep up with the throngs of people crowding the street.

Aleja knew they were not far from the Wheel. Beyond would be the familiar streets of Aleja's old home, where she would have little trouble finding her way. Perhaps she could find shelter there.

If only this were a normal day in Mir.

But it wasn't.

The din of the crowded street was echoed by the thousands of others all throughout Mir. Everywhere around Aleja, faces and fingers pointed upwards towards the High Temple. Aleja let herself look up. Even Bao, her eyes flittering and head bobbing, was roused enough by the commotion to look as well.

Pillars of red smoke poured out of the High Temple.

"It's a fire?" Bao said in a dazed, weary tone.

"No, Bao," Aleja whispered, her voice close to Bao's ear. "It's a sign. They are telling the people the Queen has transferred her soul to the Vessel's body. Now the celebrations can begin."

"But it not happen."

Aleja hushed her companion. Even amidst this revelry, there could be prying ears and eyes.

"It did happen, Bao. Remember that."

That Taka didn't want the people to know the ceremony did not occur was no surprise to Aleja, but she didn't realize till now how it may make escaping the city easier.

Despite Ker's threat every Guardian in Corazon would know to look for her, Aleja gambled that Taka would not risk discovery the Queen had not transferred by spreading the word of Aleja's escape to all Guardians in the city, much less the entire island. Over time, perhaps, if a suitable story could be concocted for people not to lose faith in the Queen. Aleja felt sure this day, and perhaps the next, only a small group of Taka's most trusted Guardians would be looking for her.

That Aleja heard none of the town criers offer any explanation for cancelling the procession, but instead announce more free wine, food and games to celebrate was also telling. Taka either thought people were too stupid to question it, or planned to get them too drunk to care. Either way, it would make crossing the Wheel easier.

Still, the question of what to do about Bao gnawed at Aleja as they made their way through the city. Bao's breathing was getting noticeably worse. And even though it might mean capture, Aleja couldn't bear to leave her behind.

As much as Aleja feared Bao would be captured and punished, she also feared she may have to continue her journey alone. The realization of that fear shamed Aleja, and she tried to keep her worries from her mind and focus on the problem at hand.

The celebration slowed the crowd. People embraced, danced, and shared drinks. Aleja tried to get off the jammed street where people were filing into to an amphitheater to see one of Mir's greatest attractions, that of its famed acrobats performing the most incredible feats. Not the least of which was to grab the horns of charging bulls and leap over them.

Aleja politely but urgently pushed through the crowd. Some moved for her, but increasingly, Aleja saw puzzled stares looking back at her as she went by.

Bao's labored breathing became louder and more noticeable. More than once Aleja waved off offers of assistance.

I have to get off this street.

Aleja admired Bao's strength, even envied her for it. A weaker person like herself would have stopped and demanded rest. But Bao kept going, following Aleja's lead without question even though Aleja herself was full of them. Where to go being the first and foremost one in her mind.

There was no obvious place to stop on this street. It was too packed with people, and lined with merchants who would most likely shoo away an old woman sitting to rest by their wares. If Bao was unhurt they could have continued down the web of alleyways. Aleja decided Bao's only hope was to take this street past the Wheel and find a place to rest somewhere along the barren, dusty streets in the poor part of the city. Aleja knew her old home was out of the question, but maybe she could stay one night with the stable girl who secretly let her ride horses. If not there, then maybe a warehouse, or even under the roof of a walkway. Anywhere other than a Sanctuary House or Temple, where they could not escape notice.

But how to get beyond the city walls? Disguise themselves further and hope to leave undetected among the crowds going home after the celebrations? Climb up one of the aqueducts and make a run for it? Or somehow stumble across one of the much whispered about, but most likely mythic, tunnels under the wall?

None of the possibilities sounded promising. But Aleja figured she could save questions for the night.

The crowd came to an abrupt stop. Aleja slammed into the back of a large and rather jovial man, who was raising his cup in toast with others. Drops of red wine from their cups dropped on Aleja's head like rain. Her attempts to thread her way through the mass drew only annoyed and helpless looks from the crowd around her.

"Please, my master is sick, let us through." Aleja pleaded repeatedly. Few took notice of her. Aleja's voice, weary and high pitched, was drowned out by the sound of a deep, resonant voice calling out behind her.

"MAKE WAY! MAKE WAY!"

Aleja did not have to look back to know who called out.

"Guardians" Aleja whispered urgently to Bao, "We must hurry."

Aleja's heart raced at the sight of the Guardian's bo sticks weaving through the sea of people like shark fins.

Rather than making way, the crowd pushed towards Aleja and knocked Bao to the ground. Aleja thrust out her hands to stall the crowd, to keep them from walking on top of her. But there were so many people, and there was so little strength left in her.

"Stop! Stop!" Aleja screamed as she beat on the backs of the people drifting backwards. Bao lay on the ground helpless, unable to get up, her hands clutching at her side.

"Stop, you fools! Stop!"

Aleja couldn't reach down to help Bao up and hold back the crowd. Aleja swung at the face of a finely dressed man who stepped on Bao's ankle. The man, his eyes red and heavy lidded, stared back at Aleja with bleary incomprehension that changed quickly into red faced anger. He slurred out a response Aleja ignored, her attention on the backs of the people threating to collapse on Bao.

Aleja didn't see the man's shove coming. It knocked her sideways, and away from Bao. Aleja yelled in frustration as Bao disappeared from her sight.

The side of her head throbbed as Aleja fought and clawed to get back to Bao. It was no use. The force of the crowd continued to separate them. The harder she fought, the more Aleja seemed to get pushed back.

"Bao! Bao!" Aleja screamed, no longer worrying about maintaining the ruse she was servant and Bao the master.

Amidst the shouts of revelry and drunken laughter Aleja thought she heard Bao's voice, faint and weak, calling back.

"I'm safe, Daughter, I'm safe. You go."

Aleja, struggling against the momentum of the crowd, began to be pulled down by it. Bobbing heads hovered over her. It was like she was back in the tunnels, only this time swept away by a mass of humanity more suffocating than all the water in the High Temple.

Two, large meaty hands suddenly separated the bodies threatening to crush her. A large, burly man pushed his way towards Aleja. Without a word he lifted Aleja up from the ground and carried her through the crowd. Now resting with her belly on his shoulder, Aleja saw the telltale signs of wine droplets on his back.

It was the man she bumped into just before losing Bao.

Aleja squirmed at the sight of the Guardians coming up behind her. She caught sight of Rhea, the female Guardian who they fought on the aqueduct. The others were with her, but they did not notice Aleja as they tried to force their way through the crowd.

The burly man grabbed on tighter as Aleja squirmed. Some gleeful onlookers, mostly young men, cheered at the sight of him carrying off a young servant as if she were a freshly caught tuna.

"Shut it, you gutter carp!" The burly man gruffly shouted, and then, more soothingly to Aleja, "Careful, girl. Just getting you to your master."

"Is she well?" Aleja responded breathlessly.

"She's not trampled. But injured. We'll help you to a Sanctuary House. My men are already taking her there."

No. We can't go there.

Sorry Bao, I've failed you.

Aleja looked anxiously over at the Guardians still trying to push their way through the crowd. The crowd responded to their efforts more with confused, helpless stares than moving feet. The burly man had no such trouble getting through.

He walked briskly through the crowd as if it were no more than a field of wheat. Aleja saw faces in the crowd filled with an awed reverence as he passed them by.

"You have a name, girl?" the burly man called out. Before Aleja could answer her savior, he yelled at another "gutter carp", and then doubled a man over with a knee into his gut.

Aleja didn't think to say "no". It would have been an acceptable answer in Mir, for most servants came from the countryside, where the multitude of children resulted in many receiving a number from their parents rather than a name.

Aleja called out the first thing that came to her mind.

"Grape Child."

The burly man's laugh was interrupted by a pained shout from another unfortunate drunk in his path.

"Odd name for a servant here. Your master from the Clay lands?"

"Yes," Aleja replied without hesitation, fearing another clumsy lie would expose her. "We came for the ceremony. My master is old, and wanted to see the Vessel before she left this world."

"Too bad she didn't get her wish." The burly man responded. "Still, she must be proud. To have a Clay girl be a Vessel for the Queen."

"Yes, she is very proud." Aleja's voice cracked.

"Aren't we all?" The man said with a laugh. "Just goes to show even as low as dirt is, it still touches the sky."

Aleja looked in the direction of the Guardians, who were now little more than sticks stuck in the mud. Just before the burly man took her into an alley Aleja saw Rhea's eyes squint.

Cursing her stupidity, Aleja ducked her head down and hoped she escaped notice.

Her hopes were dashed at the sound of Rhea's voice ringing out through the noise of clanging bells, beating drums, and full throated singing.

"STOP THAT MAN!"

CHAPTER 31

Once they left the main road, and slipped through a series of alleys, the burly man set Aleja down in front of the Sanctuary House. Several sick and injured people milled outside the dilapidated building. A single Caretaker, her eyes puffed and weary, attended to the people with little more than kind words and a sympathetic ear.

All of the Queen's children were supposed to receive the same care, but Aleja now saw it was not true. It was instantly apparent to her some places suffered more than others, and unfortunately, the people suffered for it. In Aleja's carefully sheltered life, both as Judge and Vessel, she heard stories of such realities yet never had to face it. Now that she did, the hypocrisy of Taka's world angered Aleja to her core.

The burly man looked at Aleja, then up at the building. His nearly toothless smile stretched to ears swollen and wrinkled as cabbages.

"It's not much to look at, but your master will be treated well here." He said. "We'll make sure of it."

Aleja was about to ask who "we" actually was when a group of ragged looking men approached her.

The men, their scarred skin as tanned and stretched as leather, bowed to the burly man with great reverence. The burly man returned with a curt nod but said nothing.

One of the men, a stick of a man with matted hair and tattoos that looked like a child had drawn them on his skin, approached Aleja.

"Your master's inside. She's got a bed, and a Caretaker is with her."

The man's voice was dry and cracked as the ground.

"Thank you." Aleja replied with a deep bow. She fought every urge to look over her shoulder to see if the Guardians were behind her. These people helped her, and she must show respect, but Aleja was eager to get inside. She could feel the Guardians getting closer.

"How's the old woman?" The burly man asked.

The Stick-man paused. His feet pawed at the dirt like a child fearing punishment from a parent.

"She'll feel no pain."

The burly man nodded, and then turned towards Aleja.

"We have someone who needs to say something to you." He said.

Confused, and growing more anxious to leave the streets, Aleja looked at the burly man, smiled and bowed.

"Thank you for your kindness. But I am duty bound to check on my master. May I take your name, then speak to this person after I see my master?"

Aleja tried hard not to sound rushed. The urge to turn around and check for Guardians caused Aleja's fingers to twitch.

The burly man smiled as if he were unused to such polite conversation.

"I'm the Shepherd." The burly man replied. "Your master is in good hands, and you'll see her soon. Indulge me, Grape Child."

Aleja nodded and forced a smile.

"Yes, my apologies Shepherd. I thank you again for your help."

The Shepherd clicked his teeth at his men, who promptly dumped a man at Aleja's feet. It took a moment for Aleja to recognize him. His fine robes were reduced to muddied tatters, his hair a gnarled mess, and the paint on his swollen face smudged and smeared.

Aleja felt a pain in her jaw at the sight of him, and realized it was the man who pushed her.

The man swayed unsteadily on his knees.

"What do you have to say to her?" The Shepherd demanded with a sharp kick to his side.

The man let out a grunt, then looked up groggily at Aleja. He smiled. Blood traced the edges of his teeth.

"Sorry I kept you from your Master."

"Wrong." The Shepherd's voice was calm, with no warning of the smack he subsequently gave the man's face. The people around them looked away as if the act of violence, delivered so coldly and quickly, had not occurred. Even the Caretaker pretended not to notice.

Only Aleja showed any shock at the act. She grabbed the Shepherd's arm before he could strike the man again.

"Stop this. This is not what I want. Even if this man hurt me, I won't see anyone hurt in my name."

The Shepherd stared at Aleja, then to her hand on his arm. Aleja let go of him, and hung her head.

"I apologize, Shepherd. I thank you for trying to correct the wrong you saw. But I must be with my Master, and this man has suffered enough for his offense."

"Maybe." The Shepherd lowered his hand, then turned to the man and pointed to Aleja.

"You are in this girl's debt. And she is in mine. When I come to call on you, for whatever reason, you will open your door to me."

The man nodded his head vigorously. The Shepherd's men pulled him up and dragged him away.

The Shepherd looked at Aleja.

"You must have a good master. Most servants wouldn't be so shocked to see a slap in the face."

"Yes, I have a good master." Aleja spoke hurriedly, and could no longer resist taking quick looks behind her, "and I wish to see her now."

The Shepherd came in close. His large frame blotted out the sun.

"I'm a good master too. You can ask my men. When most people would stand dumb as sheep, I saw you fight. I like fighters. If you are in need of a new master, you need not go back the Clay lands, just come back here, and ask for me."

Aleja nodded her head.

"Alright then, Grape Child…" The Shepherd looked down the length of Aleja's arm where her tattoo lay thinly hidden beneath her palla.

The Shepherd smiled. The look of it sent shivers down Aleja's spine.

"…you can go to your master now."

"Thank you." Aleja rushed towards the Sanctuary House, bowing profusely as she did so. The Shepherd's men returned her bows with half nods. The Shepherd just stood with arms crossed and stared at Aleja, with the same unnerving smile never leaving his face.

CHAPTER 32

leja took one step into the Sanctuary House and immediately covered her nose at the smell. It was more a house for dying than for healing. Beds overflowed with the frail, yellowed bodies of the sick and old. Caretakers stepped carefully over floors crowded with emaciated bodies staring back at them with haunted eyes.

Despite the sights and smells, small groups of children ran past Aleja to grab food from trays carried by novices. The Caretakers chastised the children as they slipped through the room like eels through a fisherman's net, but could do little to stop them, busy as they were with attending to the old and sick.

Aleja felt the sting of her last words with Ivo again at the sight of a group of Sanctuary children gleefully scurrying up a stairwell with scraps of food in their little hands.

It must have been hard to grow up in a place like this.

The more Aleja wandered through the crowded room the pain of every judgment she ever gave weighed on her heart. She always felt so right in her decisions, that she knew what was best for every person who stood in judgment before her. But now Aleja felt she knew nothing about her people. Nothing of the pain and suffering that drove them to act out with such pettiness against their brothers and sisters.

How could Ivo, Bao, or anyone be cared for in such a place?

A Caretaker, pitchers of water in both hands, approached Aleja. Her voice was weary but polite.

"How may this Caretaker help you?"

"The Shepherd's men brought my master here. I would like to see her."

The Caretaker almost let the pitchers slip at the mention of the Shepherd. She cast an anxious look towards the door.

Aleja turned back and saw the Shepherd's Stick-man watching her. He stood with arms crossed, stared directly at Aleja, and made no attempt to hide from her.

"Come this way." The Caretaker said, and then led Aleja up to the roof of the building. As they walked up the stairs Aleja heard footsteps behind them. She did not need to turn around to know the Shepherd's man was following her.

The roof was covered in green. Large cisterns at every corner emptied rainwater into trenches that fed the plants on the roof. With a bittersweet smile, Aleja thought of the grape groves of the Clay lands, and how she once played among them, just like the children now darting under the small orange trees and pink flowered hibiscus that made a labyrinth of the roof.

Bao laid near the wall overlooking the street in front of the Sanctuary House. There were others with her, more finely dressed than those lying on the floors below, but just as close to death.

Bao was sleeping. Her chest was moving slowly but without rhythm. The Caretakers gave her lotus to ease her pain, but because of the slight whine to her breathing, Aleja knew Bao still suffered.

Aleja knelt beside Bao and took her hand. The Caretaker, still holding the pitchers, looked anxious to leave Bao's side.

"How is she?" Aleja asked.

"She feels little pain now." The Caretaker hesitated. "By the morning...all pain will be gone."

Aleja nodded her head and let the Caretaker take her leave. Through eyes blurry with tears, Aleja saw the outline of the Stick-man just beyond a wall of hibiscus.

Aleja gently brushed away a wisp of hair from Bao's eyes.

Bao opened her eyes at Aleja's touch.

"Daughter." Bao said with a smile.

"Bao," Aleja held tight onto Bao's hands, "you are without pain?"

Bao closed her eyes and nodded her head.

"Can you stand?"

"No. Daughter. You leave me."

Bao's voice was sharp. She held Aleja's face in her hands and looked into her eyes.

"I cannot." Aleja shook her head. "The Guardians will find you here. I fear for you. I can help you leave."

Bao shook her head. She wiped away Aleja's tears.

"I leave now, Daughter." Bao said with a weary smile.

Aleja burst into fresh tears at the sight of Bao's sweet, sad smile. She pressed her forehead to Bao's.

I can't go alone. I don't know what to do.

There was a great commotion on the street below. Aleja looked over the ledge and saw the Guardians on the street yelling for the Shepherd's men to leave. The Shepherd's men did so slowly. The Guardians were delayed but Aleja knew they would soon enter the Sanctuary House.

Aleja looked back at Bao.

"They here." Bao swallowed hard. Her face tightened. "You go. Now."

Aleja nodded. She laid a kiss on Bao's forehead.

"You good master Aleja. Don't want demons take you. Like take Pallas."

Aleja stared at Bao.

"Pallas?"

"She is Vessel. Before you."

Aleja wondered if the lotus dulled Bao's senses. But her servant stared back at Aleja with eyes as clear as a blue sky.

"You knew her?"

Bao took a short breath.

"When I was child. But demons took her. I don't let demons take you."

"Why didn't you ever tell me about this?"

"You not believe. You must see."

Bao lifted her head slightly and looked hard at Aleja.

"Aleja." She whispered. "You can't see Queen. But, believe in her."

"I don't know if I do anymore, Bao." Aleja said as she wiped her eyes. Bao smiled.

"It's alright. She believe in you."

Bao closed her eyes and rested her head against the pillow as if the effort of speaking exhausted her. She pushed against Aleja.

"Go now."

Aleja took one last look at Bao. She saw her chest lift, then rest, but did not lift again. Aleja wiped away her tears, then turned and walked away.

Aleja peered at the stairway through the leaves of a large hibiscus. A small flock of birds, startled by Guardians charging up the stairs, flew into the sky with shrieking cries. There were two Guardians, both of them from the group that tried to stop her on the aqueduct.

As the Guardians stopped to survey the rooftop, Aleja ducked behind a hedgerow and moved quickly towards the opposite end of the roof. She knew every Sanctuary House had multiple entrances and exits. If she could just make it to one before the Guardians did, and if there were no others waiting for her on the other side, she just might be able to slip out.

The hedgerow formed a path along the side of the roof that turned into the center of the courtyard. Aleja's side of the roof was a straight drop down to the street, but there were houses as tall as the Sanctuary House on the other side of the roof. Once Aleja got to the center she would have to creep among the potted plants to get to the other side unnoticed.

Carefully watching through the leaves for the Guardians, Aleja made it to the end of the hedgerow when she felt a hand on her shoulder.

"Leaving your master?"

Aleja turned to face the Stick-man. For one so skinny, his grip was strong.

"The Shepherd wants to see you."

Aleja twisted out of his grip. Through the bushes she saw the Guardians walk in her direction.

She had to rid herself of the Stick-man. Quickly.

"I'm getting her water. Let me take my leave."

"You're sneaking around to get her water?" The man scoffed. He grabbed Aleja's arm. Razor slices of pain vibrated where Rhea's whip had caught her. Aleja buckled but with her free hand laid a blow to the Stick-man's chest. The Stick-man took the blow with a laugh and grabbed on to her other arm.

Aleja tried to pull away but each tug sent shockwaves of pain up her arm. She remembered the move Ivo taught her the first day they met, but couldn't summon the strength to place one of her hands on the other as the Stick-man painfully twisted her arms.

"You got some fight for a Daughter, don't you?" The Stick-man said at the sight of Aleja's now exposed distinction.

Just as the man was about to take Aleja towards the stairs a Guardian appeared behind them.

"Help, Guardian! Help me!" Aleja screamed at the Guardian just as she caught sight of him turning the corner towards her.

The Stick-man turned around and dropped Aleja's hands at the sight of the Guardian charging at them. Aleja pushed him off and ran down the row of bushes. The Guardian pushed the Stick-man aside and leapt at Aleja. He missed her by a hair's length before crashing to the floor, his legs entangled with the Stick-man's.

Upon seeing another Guardian in the central courtyard, Aleja dashed to the stairs.

A pair of Guardians were at the bottom of the stairs. They charged up at the sight of Aleja. Aleja slammed herself into one of the cisterns, sending it crashing down the stairs onto the Guardians in an avalanche of clay, dirt, and rainwater.

The Guardians, dazed and on their backs, feebly reached out for Aleja as she leapt over them.

Aleja raced down the stairs and was followed by the thunder of the other Guardian's footsteps.

Aleja rounded the second floor corner when she found her way blocked by Rhea and three other Guardians at the foot of the next set of stairs.

As she weaved her way through the beds of the sickroom, Aleja searched for another way out.

In the dimness of the far end of the room she saw thin beams of sunlight coming from the cracks in a wooden door.

Aleja sent Caretakers spinning in her wake as she ran for the door. The Guardians trailing Aleja were even less considerate, one of them even pushing over a Caretaker who got in his way.

Aleja slammed into the door. The door, badly hung and decrepit, scraped against the clay floor, and moved only enough for Aleja to slip through the opening.

Once in the room, Aleja cursed her stupidity. It was a storage room, its walls lined with shelves packed to the brim with herbs and poultices. But no exit.

The light came from a long, thin crack near the ceiling.

Aleja slammed the door behind her and wedged a piece of wood between the door and its frame. It was enough to slow the Guardians, but wouldn't hold for long.

Aleja quickly scanned the room for anything she might have missed. She looked again at the crack in the wall. In frustration she threw a large container at it. Rather than bounce back down at her, the container smashed through the thin, flaky clay and disappeared through the wall.

Sunlight poured onto Aleja's face.

It was a window. Aleja realized. *One they covered to make this a storage room.*

It was obvious the job was a shoddy one, little more than sticks covered in clay. It would have angered Aleja to hear of such lazy work when she was a Judge, but now she could have kissed the workman to thank him for his indolence.

Aleja sent clay jars shattering on the floor as she scrambled up the shelves towards the hole.

Her feet still on the middle part of the shelves, Aleja smashed the rest of the patchwork wall with a glass jar. She then wedged her head and shoulders into the opening with one arm outstretched. Her other hand was close to her chest, and her fingers dug into the clay as she pushed up with her feet.

Aleja heard the wooden wedge in the door snap as she pulled herself through the opening, followed by shouts as the Guardians ran over the shards of glass and clay on the floor.

Aleja looked down at the alley below. Not as high as the Aqueduct, but a fall here would be just as final. But there was a balcony directly above her, with support beams just in reach. Aleja turned herself around, sat up, and grabbed a beam. Flailing hands rubbed against her ankles as she pulled her legs out.

Aleja readied her drop to a balcony across from her. The buildings of Mir, especially in the most crowded areas of the city, were built close together. Some alleys were so narrow people joked they were only made for cats.

Just as she was about to swing over, a hand grabbed Aleja's ankle. She kicked it off easily, but the effort sent her into a leap she was not ready for. Her silent fall ended in a loud crash.

Aleja landed on top of the plants and clay pots that littered the balcony. From the sound, and the pain of the landing, Aleja thought her own bones had broken. But the pots took most of the damage, and although the plant's limbs were broken Aleja was spared the same fate.

Aleja got up slowly and looked back at the opening. She saw the frustration on the face of the Guardian as he tried to wedge himself through. Finally he gave up and yelled to his comrades.

"She's in the building next door!"

Instead of running through the house and down to the street, Aleja propped herself up on to an adjacent window and used it to climb onto the roof. Aleja didn't wait to see the Guardians charge out of the Sanctuary House, nor did she notice the Shepherd and his men watching her leap from roof to roof as the Guardians climbed up the walls of the house to chase her.

Aleja only noticed one thing as her feet glided over tiles warmed by the midday sun.

A way out of Mir.

CHAPTER 33

A large network of scaffolding covered several blocks of the wall surrounding Mir. Just before she leapt down from a roof and scrambled through the crowded street below, Aleja saw the telltale posts of ladders scattered beyond the scaffolds.

From the number of men and women Aleja saw on top of the wall, the workers going back and forth over it with little supervision, it seemed likely she could find her way across.

Guardians stopped everyone at the gates to ask their business. Even if it was only a formality in most cases, Aleja didn't want to chance it.

But the work area, it had possibilities.

Aleja just needed to get there.

Once Aleja made it to a busy street, she wrapped herself in Bao's palla and tried to orient herself.

It was difficult, for she was not yet in her old district. The street, like many in this quarter, was narrow and crowded. Aleja was barely able to see over people's heads much less figure out exactly where she was. It helped her hide among a crowd, but she wouldn't be able to spot a Guardian sneaking up on her either.

Rather than wait for a telltale sign that she was pointed in the right direction, Aleja decided it was wiser to keep on the move rather than stopping to think.

As fast as Aleja moved, her pace was often slowed by large groups of people celebrating the day. Whenever she slowed to a stop Aleja looked out for any Guardians still on the rooftops or coming up behind her.

Eventually the street opened up into a large, crowded market square. Throngs of people danced and celebrated around a fountain in its center. Music and singing filled the air.

Worried a Guardian may be standing watch at the entrance to the square, Aleja snuck into the market in the middle of a large crowd. Once she slipped from the crowd Aleja was immediately greeted with the braying mouth of a donkey harnessed to a stinking cart of food waste.

Aleja pinched her nose and quickly moved deeper into the square. Once the donkey and cart were out of sight she let go of her nose and breathed in deep.

The smell of food, fresh and foul, drifted throughout the market. Aleja felt a stabbing pain building in her stomach, and a great weariness in her legs and arms. Her mouth was parched.

I have to eat. I've haven't had anything all day.

Even if the Guardians never caught up to her, Aleja knew her hunger would. If she didn't find some food or drink, she would not have the strength to make it to the wall, much less over it.

But Aleja had no money to buy food, and to wait in the long lines of the Sanctuary Houses for a bowl of rice would surely risk capture.

Shouts and laughter filled the market. People danced in the fountain in the center of the square. Some sat passed out face down on the tables. Aleja walked through the tables and picked half eaten food off the drunkard's plates and bowls.

Aleja grabbed an empty bowl from the lap of a vomit covered man passed out by a storefront. After checking the bowl for any bits of food the man may have given back to it, she held it out to the storeowner and asked for water. The storeowner, clearly annoyed by the chaos of the square, turned his empty pitchers upside down and yelled at Aleja to leave.

Not wanting to risk any more attention to herself, Aleja wandered into the crowd by the center of the square. She danced along with the others and held out her bowl. Some filled it with water, others with wine. They playfully placed bits of fruit in her mouth, sometimes sharing pieces from their mouths to hers.

Her hunger quieted, Aleja shared a toast, drank quickly, and moved towards one of the streets that led out of the square.

Aleja was almost away from the fountain when a woman called out to her.

"Sister! Sister! Stay! Dance with us!"

The woman, drink in one hand, and clothes drenched from the fountain, reached out and grabbed at Aleja's palla.

There was a loud tearing sound as Aleja pulled away from the woman. The woman's bleary eyes focused on the tattoos showing through the tear. She sloppily fell to her knees and began loudly proclaiming her apologies.

"I'm sorry, Daughter! I didn't know! Please forgive me! Please forgive!"

Aleja knelt down by the woman and placed her hands on her head. Aleja's eyes nervously darted around the growing, curious crowd of onlookers surrounding her.

"I forgive you! I forgive you. Please, quiet yourself." She spoke sharply into the woman's ear.

Despite Aleja's attempts to calm the woman she called out even louder.

"You are kind, Daughter! So kind! A million blessings to you who serves the Queen!"

The crowd stared at Aleja, and slowly, one by one, they began to fall knee to wobbly knee before her.

Aleja saw figures on the rooftops pointing her way. She quickly got up, gave the crowd a hushed blessing, and then sprinted away from the group towards one of the streets intersecting the square.

Almost upon the street, Aleja looked back at the rooftops. Only one figure remained. He stared down into the crowd, one hand to his forehead to block out the glare of the sun, and the other on the hilt of the knife dangling from his belt.

At the sight of a pair of Guardians standing at the entrance of the street, Aleja quickly turned around and walked away. Her head lowered and no longer daring to expose herself by looking up at the rooftops, Aleja wove through the crowd towards the other streets, only to find Guardians at each one.

Did all the Guardians here know to look for her? Or were some just manning a post? There was no way to tell.

What was worse, Aleja noticed some of the people at the fountain spotted her again. Now more curious than reverential, they approached her with drinks held high.

"Daughter! Daughter!" They shouted out. "Give us your blessing on this happy day!"

Aleja hurriedly bowed to them with hands folded by her chest, backing away from the crowd as she did so.

She saw the drunken woman from the fountain talking to Rhea. Before she could turn away their eyes locked. Rhea called out to the other Guardians, and then charged at Aleja.

Aleja scrambled onto a tabletop, sending food and drink scattering onto the laps of the stunned revelers. Aleja leapt from table to table with the grace of a dancer. Shouts and barking dogs followed her every step, as did the sounds of the Guardians barging through the crowd.

A tower of crates were stacked carelessly in the shape of a steep, treacherous staircase by one of the stores. If Aleja could get to the top of them, she thought there was a chance she could get back onto the roofs.

Aleja leapt off the table and ran towards the crates. The Guardian still on the roof seemed to anticipate this move and leapt down in front of her. Aleja would have jumped right into his arms were it not for a drunken woman in her path. After colliding with the woman, Aleja was sent spiraling sideways to the ground and rolled under a rumbling donkey cart.

Aleja didn't see the cart but she heard the creak of its wooden wheels as they ground against the dirt. She felt a pinch as the wheels caught her hair and pulled some from her head.

The cart stopped with Aleja still under it. A crowd quickly formed around the cart, eager to see if Aleja had been accidently crushed. From under the cart Aleja saw a thin, wooden door in the back of one of the shops that led into a narrow alleyway. She quickly crawled out from under the cart and scurried towards it through the legs of the crowd.

The Guardians, their path to the alleyway blocked by the crowd and the cart, screamed at everyone to move.

The passageway was dark, hidden from the sun by the tall walls of the surrounding buildings. Like many such alleyways in Mir, it was part of a labyrinth of intersecting passageways used to store waste before it was collected onto the carts.

Aleja didn't stop to think about the soft, mushy ground, or concern herself with the smell. She just ran.

Aleja took a sharp turn down a passageway which reeked of garbage. Just before the Guardians turned the corner to see her, Aleja ran gasping through an open door. She entered a room, a large empty kitchen, and slammed the door behind her.

Once inside, Aleja found herself face to face with an old woman. The woman, carrying bags of rice, stopped in her tracks at the sight of Aleja and dropped to her knees. The bags burst open and rice sprayed across the room.

"Forgive me." The woman said as her head hit the stone floor.

Aleja's jaw dropped open at the sight of the woman kneeling before her. The memory of the Caretaker doing the same on the grounds of the amphitheater, pleading for vengeance, flashed in Aleja's mind like a spark in the darkness.

Aleja grabbed hold of the Caretaker. She pulled up her face and looked deep into the eyes that once were so full of hate and anger, and now only saw tears.

There was a loud clattering somewhere from the front of the building. Aleja couldn't know if it was other servants or Guardians entering the Caretaker's house. Either way, she couldn't take the chance.

The desperation clear in her voice, Aleja whispered into the Caretaker's ear.

"Hide me."

Without hesitation, the Caretaker grabbed Aleja by the hand and led her into a small storage room. After pushing aside some clay jars, the Caretaker opened a part of the wooden floor and guided Aleja into a shallow hole underneath. The space was small, meant only to keep food cool in the earth. Aleja supposed at first it was lucky so much of it had been eaten today, to allow her enough space to squeeze inside.

Aleja wedged herself between piles of cabbages and radish leaves. The Caretaker closed the door, and Aleja heard scraping sounds as she put the jars back in place. Aleja's body sunk into the wet, coolness of the vegetables underneath her, her face and hands pressed up against the door.

The darkness of the enclosure was almost as suffocating as the thinness of the air. It wasn't long before Aleja began to tremble.

She took long, slow breaths to calm herself but the air was not enough to fill her lungs, only enough to give a taste of it on her tongue. A hunger built in her to take a deep breath, then release it with a scream.

Aleja heard the faint, muffled sounds of someone walking in a nearby room, occasionally interrupted by the sound of metal crashing to the floor. The fear of discovery refocused her for a time. But when the noises stopped, and all Aleja could hear in the darkness were her quick, shuddering breaths and the sound of her nails scratching against the door, the suffocating feeling returned.

Aleja would have pounded on the door if she could just stretch out her arms. She incessantly tapped her forehead on it. Her nails dug into the wood. Splinters speared the soft flesh underneath.

There was a stabbing pain in her back. It felt like the jagged edge of the mirror was digging in to her body.

She feared she was forgotten. One thought repeated incessantly in her mind.

Please oh please come back for me…please oh please come back…come back …come back…come back…

Aleja opened her mouth to scream. The mirror shook violently in the pack, and an inky blackness poured out of it and covered her face, drowning out the sound. Her mind went blank. She felt like she was falling deep into a void.

Aleja wasn't aware of the creak of the hinges as the door finally opened. Her eyes, now uncovered, adjusted to the cool, blue light of evening. She felt her face, expecting to feel the wet blackness of the mirror, but there was no trace of it on her skin.

CHAPTER 34

Once out of the hole, Aleja sat up with a loud gasp and began to sob. The Caretaker embraced Aleja, and ran her hand gently over her head.

"I'm so sorry, Daughter. It was the only place to hide you. The Guardians were here longer than I thought they would be."

After Aleja became calm she gently broke from the Caretaker's embrace.

"They are gone then?" Aleja said as she accepted a cup of water from the Caretaker.

"I only know they are gone from here. They came inside and saw the mess. I told them a girl ran through the kitchen, knocked me down, then ran outside. One of them ran out into the street, but the other stayed in case you doubled back. He asked me some questions, but left once a female Guardian shouted that they spotted you in another alleyway."

The Caretaker smiled.

"Lucky for you. Even so, I had to keep you hidden in case they came back."

Aleja pulled herself out of the hole and finished her water. As the Caretaker filled her cup Aleja looked back at her hiding place.

"How long was I under there?"

The Caretaker pursed her lips, as if she fought telling Aleja the truth.

"A long time. Long enough that I feared for you. But you were strong." The Caretaker smiled. "Like I knew you would be."

Aleja tried to return the Caretaker's smile, but found she could not.

"Why did you hide me?"

The Caretaker took a rag and wiped Aleja's face.

"Because you asked me."

Aleja held the Caretaker's hand and pulled it from her face.

"But you know who I am. You know I should not be here."

The Caretaker hesitated. She folded the rag and placed it into a pocket by her lap.

"Yes. And it would be a lie to say I don't have questions. But we must leave. I can take you to my home. You will be safe there for the night."

"Why don't we stay here?"

"This is a Caretaker's house, Daughter. Others will surely come. Please trust me. You will be safe in my home."

Aleja thought about the offer. Aleja reasoned if the Caretaker meant to lead her to the Guardians, she wouldn't have bothered to hide her. Anyway, what other choice did she have? To run from Rhea and the others all night until she reached the wall?

After everything she went through, trusting the Caretaker sounded worth the risk.

Aleja held out her hand to help the Caretaker up.

"How are you named?" Aleja asked.

"Opal."

"Opal." Aleja said with a smile. "Please call me Aleja."

Opal looked surprised at the mention of Aleja's name. She nodded uncomfortably at the informality, but did not protest.

Aleja looked to the front of the house. The street outside glowed in the orange light of the torches staked into the ground.

"How do we know there isn't someone outside waiting for us?" Aleja said.

Opal smiled.

"It doesn't matter." Opal took Aleja's hand and led her to the back stairwell. "We're not going out there."

They went to one of the rooms on the upper floor, a storehouse with shelves covered more with dust than food. Opal went to the corner of the room and pulled at one of the bottom shelves.

A small, hidden door, only high enough to crouch through, opened in the wall.

Opal beckoned Aleja to follow her through the door. Although the door was well hidden from a distance, upon closer inspection the crude hinges were visible.

This secret door was not made by the masters who made such passageways in the High Temple. But after her experience almost drowning in one such passageway, Aleja was thankful for it.

The passage to the next building was hardly wider than the width of the walls. Aleja crawled through the opening on her belly into a room much narrower than the one she just left.

The room had no windows or doors. Narrow shelves, these filled with jars and bags of rice, lined the walls.

"How many of these are there?" Aleja said in wonder as Opal shut the door behind them.

"Only a few. Only some of the Caretaker's homes have such rooms."

"But why?"

"Sometimes Caretakers wish to pass without notice. There is much done in Mir without the knowledge of Judges and Guardians."

"But don't all people know about these passageways?"

Opal shook her head and dusted herself off.

"Perhaps some know of them. But these rooms are reserved for Caretakers, who must protect the stores of the Queen. One of the stores is on the other side of this wall. It also has a hidden door. We've had to use them from time to time to move food when someone demands more than their share, or is not patient enough to wait for the Queen's blessings to be bestowed upon them."

"Who would do such a thing?"

"Mostly groups of young street people. Those raised by Caretakers who think hands are for slapping, not holding. What is worse is some of our people look to the street youths for the justice you and the Guardians should provide."

"Why?"

"We have a saying around here. The High Temple is far, the fist is near." Opal sighed. "I supposed not every part of the city has such leeches, but unfortunately this is one of those places. Our leech is called the Shepherd."

Opal spit on the floor at the mention of his name. Aleja was shocked into silence by the gesture.

Opal went to the far end of the room and placed her hands on the floor.

"We must be silent from now on. We will go down a ladder into a tunnel that begins under this house. We must not say or do anything that could be heard by those who live above."

So there are tunnels below Mir! Maybe there is one that goes under the wall!

Aleja's amazement was tempered by the knowledge she would now have to walk through one. The memory of Sara, and the land she described to her as they looked over a map of Corazon, crossed Aleja's mind.

The open plains of the Horselands sound enticing. Now more than ever.

The thought gave Aleja a renewed courage and resolve to make it out of Mir to see them for herself.

Opal opened the door slowly. Aleja only saw the first few handles of a ladder that descended into complete darkness.

"Go slowly." Opal whispered. "Find your footing quietly. When I close this door behind us it will be completely dark. Once underground, I will light a lamp."

Aleja did as Opal instructed, and felt little fear even as she waited a few moments at the bottom for Opal to take a lantern off the walls and light their way. Once underground, Aleja thought she could feel the mirror vibrating in her pack, as if the darkness and decay in the soil brought it to life.

The tunnel was long, too long for the feeble light from the lantern to reach the end of it. Opal directed Aleja to grab the back of her gown as they went through the passageway.

They walked quickly, and despite the length of the tunnel, soon emerged from it into a large underground storage room. They went upstairs after Opal checked for any others in the building. Finding none, Opal gave Aleja a fresh palla to cover herself with and a loaded sack to carry. Now above ground, Aleja breathed a sigh of relief as the mirror ceased to shake.

"No one notices a burdened Caretaker." Opal said as she threw a sack over her own shoulder. "Just keep your head low, and keep moving."

Opal opened the door and went into the street. Aleja followed her, then anxiously awaited as Opal locked up. The street was not crowded, just a few groups of drunken revelers milling about in taverns. Aleja could hear the fading echoes of music and celebration.

Opal was right about no one taking any notice of them. Aleja followed Opal, watching her footsteps as she moved with swift confidence through the city.

After a day of crawling through passages and running on rooftops, Aleja wondered if she should have hidden in plain sight from the beginning. After all, how many people would actually be able to recognize her face?

Children greeted Opal at the entrance of Opal's small home. The children, their faces dirty, their clothes little more than rags, walked up to Aleja and pulled on her dress.

"Who is she, Mother?" The children asked.

"My novice." Opal said without hesitation.

"Will she take care of us too?"

"Yes, she will." Opal said, and then, to Aleja's surprise, sat down and told the children all about how Aleja will cook their rice, mend their clothes, and play games with them.

The children, excited at first, gradually left her to play in front of the Sanctuary house further down the street.

"Sometimes, the best way to stop too many questions," Opal said to Aleja as she opened the door to her home, "is to give too many answers."

CHAPTER 35

Opal's house was much like the one Aleja once lived in. Small but clean, with a simple wooden table and furniture pressed up against walls decorated with faded frescos of sea animals.

Like many of the older homes of the city, there were no windows on the first floor. Opal lit a few candles as she moved about her home. Aleja sat on one of the wooden chairs which wobbled slightly as she took a seat.

Opal warmed a pot over the embers of a dying fire. Aleja's stomach growled as the scent of onions, potatoes and kelp soup filled her nose. A shiver ran through her body, more out of hunger than cold, and Aleja wrapped her palla tight.

"Are you cold?" Opal asked as she stirred the soup.

"A little."

"These embers are not enough to warm the house. My son should return soon with more wood."

"Your son?" Aleja said as Opal handed her a clay cup full of soup. Aleja savored the salty taste of the fermented bean paste that colored the soup a murky brown.

A slight dribble of soup went down Aleja's chin. Opal took a cloth and wiped it off for her.

"You've met him before." Opal sat down across from Aleja.

"Oh, of course. How stupid of me. It's not that I forgot. It's just that so much has happened since."

"I understand."

Opal took a long drink of the soup.

"Has he been a good son?"

Opal nodded.

"Yes."

"Does your son–" Aleja stopped herself, "-excuse me, how is he named?"

"Wren."

"Wren," Aleja said with a nod, "does Wren live with you?"

"Of course. He is my son after all." Opal laughed. "Thanks to you."

Aleja blushed.

"Usually he arrives in the evening to start the fire and warm the meal. We share it together. He sleeps down by the hearth."

"I'm glad Wren has become a good son for you." Aleja said. "But I must ask, can he be trusted to see me?"

Opal took Aleja's cup and walked back to the pot. To Aleja's relief, she didn't need to ask for it to be filled again. Opal spoke as she poured the soup into the cup in long, steady streams.

"Can I be trusted?" Opal asked.

"You have helped me so far."

"Don't you wonder why?"

"Yes." Aleja replied quickly, too tired to hide her true thoughts. She watched as chunks of potato slid out of Opal's ladle and disappeared into the broth.

"Truthfully, I don't know why. The sight of you shocked me. I almost didn't believe it was you. Perhaps it was just a dream, I thought, and maybe you would be gone when I opened the door. It was only when I still saw you there that I had to face the choice of truly helping you."

"So why did you?"

"Because you saved me."

"I don't understand."

Opal handed Aleja the soup and then sat back down.

"It shames me now, how much hate I had the day I stood before you. For Wren, for you, for our people. When my son died, it was as if all the love in me died with him. I couldn't forgive Wren, and to see this girl masquerading as a woman laying judgment on me was like a dagger in my heart. Others said it was wisdom what you did. I only saw a cruel trick. A joke to make me look like a fool."

"I've thought the same." Aleja said. "I'm sorry."

"No. You were right. You didn't make me look like a fool. I was one. And if it weren't for you, I would have been a dead fool."

"What do you mean?" Aleja put down her cup.

"Wren saved my life. I was ready to cast him aside. I didn't want him to repay his debt. But he persisted. One day as I attended my duties a cart broke free from the donkey that pulled it. I had no idea it was heading towards me. Wren leapt in front of it and pushed me out of the way."

Opal's eyes filled with tears. She nodded towards Aleja.

"It was then I finally understood the gift you gave me." Opal wiped her eyes. "You showed me what my hate would have done to me. Love filled my heart again, and it was then I forgave Wren, and took him into my home."

Opal finished her soup as Aleja looked at her in silence.

"So, yes, we can trust him. And it is he who will lead you out of the city."

"How?"

"Wren is one of those working on the walls. Surely you noticed the work going on?"

Aleja nodded her head.

"He can lead you across."

Aleja stopped Opal from getting up and pouring her more soup. She held on to Opal's withered hands and looked into her eyes.

"You're putting yourself in great danger. Do you want me to tell you why I am here, and not in the High Temple?"

"I'm not sure. Perhaps it's best not for me to know."

"I don't know if I should tell. What has happened to me has filled me with such doubt. I fear what I know, if it were to get out, may create doubt in our people's hearts."

"About what?"

"The Queen."

Much to Aleja's surprise, Opal laughed.

"Daughter. You who claim to guide us through the night are blinder than we. You fear our faith in the Queen will be shaken…"

Opal smiled wanly.

"…you're assuming everyone in Mir believes in the Queen as you want us to do. We are not as simple as you think. And not all of the beliefs of the Drowned World remain at the bottom of the sea."

Aleja stared at Opal in silence. The old woman smiled.

"Never mind me. It's your belly that needs filling now, not your head." Ladle in hand, Opal headed towards the pot.

Aleja jumped at the sound of the front door opening. Wren entered the house with an armful of wood for the fire, all of which he dropped at the sight of Aleja. It took some coaxing from Opal to get him to sit down.

When he did, Wren took his cup of soup, and never took his eyes off Aleja as he drank it.

After the meal Opal explained to Wren how he was to help Aleja. He seemed nervous, uncertain about the plan, but agreed to it nonetheless.

He spoke little, and kept his distance from Aleja. After the meal was cleared Wren sat alone to tend to the fire.

"Are you sure he will help me?" Aleja whispered to Opal as she laid out a thin mattress for her on the floor.

"I am certain. I also was shaken when I first saw you. He will be calm tomorrow."

Aleja laid down while Opal recounted the plan.

They were to make for the wall together. Caretakers often took food for the workers and no one would question Opal bringing along help. Aleja would then hide by one of the work sheds, where Wren would get her and take her across the wall.

"She can bring food for the workers." Opal said to Wren. "After the Caretakers feed a few Guardians, there will be opportunities to slip away."

"Don't worry." Opal reassured Aleja. "Wren will find a way to get you across without notice."

Aleja looked at Wren. He gave her an uncertain nod.

He looks more nervous than I feel. Maybe I should just chance it on my own.

Aleja considered slipping away once Opal went to bed, but the lure of sleep was too strong. She lifted her head with a smile as Opal placed a pillow underneath it, trying to show no hint of the worry she felt in her heart. Aleja listened for the soft murmur of Wren's breathing as he slept by the hearth, and hoped any change in it would wake her.

Aleja spoke softly to Opal.

"Thank you for all your help."

Opal caressed Aleja's cheek.

"Think nothing of it. Sleep now. You need your rest."

Aleja nodded, and then closed her eyes.

When she opened them again, almost everything in the room was gone.

Everything except for the mirror, and a shadow holding it in its hands.

CHAPTER 36

Aleja knew it was a dream, for now Opal's home had a window that flooded the room with a metallic blue light. But somehow, knowing it was a dream made her feel even more afraid.

The figure, the mirror held tight in its skeletal hands, sat looking out the window. A whistling wind blew outside.

There was the sound of rattling chains as it turned towards Aleja. She could not see its face for it was hidden under the darkness of its hood. The figure made no move towards Aleja. It was shackled to the floor at its ankles by long chains.

"Aleja."

Tears formed in Aleja's eyes at the sound of the voice.

"Sara." Aleja called out to the figure.

"Aleja, you must wake. They are coming."

"I can't run anymore. I need your help."

"This is your journey, Aleja. You must do it alone."

"I don't want to be alone."

Aleja walked towards Sara. She wanted so much to see her again. The sight of her sitting by the window reminded her of those meals they shared with Bao at the High Temple. The smell of incense, the shafts of light filtered through the latticed window. Her laugh.

Sara recoiled. She did not remove her hood.

"You must go alone. Any who go with you will suffer for it."

Aleja reached out for her friend.

"I want to see you. One last time. I miss you."

"You will. But you must be patient."

Aleja walked forward.

"Please, Sara."

Aleja pulled down Sara's hood and screamed.

Her once beautiful face was now decayed.

Just before she turned away, Aleja caught sight of the chains. They were not made of iron after all, but links of insects all crawling upward into Sara's flesh to consume her.

Sara stood. The chain of insects broke and scattered over the floor. In their place were thousands of shards of black glass.

Mirrors.

A different image was in each mirror. Some of the images filled Aleja's heart with joy, others with dread.

She saw Ivo, staring at the sea from Andrid's shore. There was Taka and Kalim arguing furiously in the High Temple while standing over Bao's lifeless body. Aleja saw her father, a broken piece of a clay cup in his hand, which he used to cut his skin just before cutting hers.

There were other images. Places and people Aleja had never seen before. She saw a strange girl with blood-red hair and the eyes of a wolf running through a shrieking tunnel of iron. There was a girl with the tattooed face of the Stone Island people. A face that was a mix of tears and blood as she walked through the remains of her burned village.

In one mirror a terrifying skeletal figure stared back at Aleja from its seat on a wooden throne. In another, a beautiful woman with iridescent skin giving life to people who seemed more animal than human.

Some images were not of people, but of places all over Corazon. But in the background of each, Aleja saw the faint outline of the Yamanashi Mountains.

Aleja saw the Queen, her red eyes changed into black, and filled with countless stars.

Just as Aleja thought she would fall into those eyes Sara spoke.

"Make her whole, Aleja."

The sound of Sara's voice was now as decayed as her lips.

"Make her whole."

Aleja backed up to the wall at the sight of her friend.

"What do you mean? Make who whole?"

"The Queen."

"I don't understand."

Sara said nothing more. She held out her boney hand as if to caress Aleja, but instead slashed her fingers across Aleja's throat.

Blood spilled over the floor. Aleja fell choking to her knees.

Aleja watched as her blood seeped into the pieces of the mirror. Some were silver, some black, but the colors joined as Aleja's blood connected them until they melted into one.

The mirror, now one piece but still liquid, stretched out over Aleja's arms and legs and then washed over Aleja's chest and face. Aleja opened her mouth to scream. The liquid mirror filled her mouth and the gash in her throat. Sara's decayed fingers cut through the liquid and pried open Aleja's eyes.

Sara's body began to crumble into dust. Her voice seemed to come from every corner of the room.

"Make her whole, Aleja. Give life to death."

Aleja's eyes went wide as she choked on the liquid mirror. Sara's body gradually disappeared into a cloud of black ash until all that remained was a voice reverberating in the walls.

"Death is a door. Only you can open it."

After the last of the mirror disappeared inside Aleja, she found she could breathe again. She felt a strange sense of peace. Her skin glowed an electric blue, and flicks of lightning shot from her hands. The wind in the streets became a storm so strong it ripped apart Opal's home. The walls now rubble at her feet, Aleja could see dark figures approaching her.

Sara's voice called out to her. It roared like thunder.

"Daughter of Light. Wake."

CHAPTER 37

Aleja rolled off her mat and groped blindly in the darkness for her pack, and to her relief, found it quickly with the mirror still inside. Aleja then looked towards the hearth.

Wren was not there.

Aleja ran up the stairs towards Opal's room.

Aleja did not wake Opal as she crept up to the only window that faced the street outside.

The street, dimly lit by the few remaining torches, was clear of people. Aleja breathed a sigh of relief and looked over at Opal. The old woman was sleeping soundlessly, a sweet smile on her lips. She remembered Sara's words from her dream.

"You must go alone. Any that go with you will suffer for it."

Aleja looked out the window again. Now she saw figures walking boldly out of the shadows and towards the house.

They were not Guardians.

A large man walked in front of the group. Even in the dim light Aleja could make out the face of the Shepherd.

A man cowered next to him. The Shepherd grabbed the man by the neck and pointed to Opal's door.

The cowering figure nodded and then looked up. Aleja caught his face in the light.

It was Wren.

The Shepherd pointed his men towards the door.

Aleja woke Opal.

"We have to go."

"What…why?" Opal rubbed her eyes.

"The Shepherd." Aleja said. "The Shepherd is coming for me."

Opal jumped out of her bed. She took Aleja to a small back room and opened a window that led to an alley below.

"Go to the wall." Opal said as she helped Aleja through the window. "Where we talked about last night."

Aleja nodded.

"I will find you." Opal said.

"Come with me now. You're not safe here." Aleja said as she dangled over the edge of the window, the balls of her feet set against the walls.

Opal frowned.

"I'm sorry. I was hoping I wouldn't have to do this."

Opal let go of Aleja's hands. Aleja fell to the ground in a heap.

"I have to stall them." Opal called out to her in a whisper. Just as she closed the window Aleja heard the Shepherd's men barge into the house.

Aleja heard shouting from the house as she ran down the alley.

In the shadows ahead Aleja saw the Shepherd's men coming toward her. They walked towards Aleja calmly and without haste.

Aleja turned around and saw another group coming at her from behind. One of them held a rope which he carelessly swung back and forth.

The Shepherd called out to Aleja from Opal's window. He held Opal by the hair. Aleja winced at the sight of the pain on her face.

"We're not those idiot Guardians, Vessel. So don't bother with the rooftops, or running into a garbage alley."

Aleja looked up and saw men standing on the rooftops on both sides of the alley.

"We just want to take you back to the High Temple." The Shepherd said. "I promise no harm will come to you."

"What if I don't want to go back?"

"Now why would that be?"

"I have my reasons."

The Shepherd grinned.

"Well then, let me give you a reason to change your mind."

The Shepherd pulled Opal's arm behind her back. Opal screamed in pain.

"Go, Aleja!" Opal gasped through her pain. "Leave!"

"Stop!" Aleja yelled at the Shepherd. "That's enough! I'll go with you."

Aleja walked towards the Shepherd's men.

"Don't trust him, Aleja!" Opal pleaded.

The Shepherd let go of Opal's arm and threw her to the floor.

"That's a good girl." He said to Aleja.

The Shepherd's men formed a circle around Aleja. They gave threatening looks to any people who tried to watch them from the windows above as they tied Aleja's hands.

Aleja was taken to a covered cart with Opal and Wren. Their hands were also tied. Aleja stared at Wren, who tried to avoid her gaze.

"I was trying to help you." Wren said weakly to Opal. "If the Guardians caught you with her–"

"Don't you speak." Opal hissed. "Don't you dare."

"Family problems?" The Shepherd said with a laugh as he entered the cart. The wood creaked loudly as he took his seat beside Aleja. The Stick-man who tried to stop Aleja in the Sanctuary House placed blindfolds over Opal and Wren's eyes.

The Shepherd took a blindfold from his man, and held it up to Aleja. He looked almost apologetic about it.

"We're not going to the High Temple, are we?" Aleja said with a huff.

"No. Trust me, I don't like to lie, but it's necessary sometimes. Too many ears around."

"Trust a man with a blindfold?" Aleja laughed. "Is it really necessary anyway? We are in a covered cart, and I don't plan to stick my head out for the view."

"I can't have someone with a memory like yours seeing where we're headed."

"So are you asking permission to place that over my eyes?" Aleja held up her tied wrists. "I'm not in any position to say no."

"I'm not all threats and intimidation, Vessel." The Shepherd said as he placed the blindfold over Aleja's eyes. "And I think it would be better if you and I get along from now on. After all, shouldn't those who share enemies, also share friendship?"

⟨HAPT⟨R 38

Aleja had only sounds and smells to help her know where the Shepherd was taking her.

Sound provided a few clues, or rather, the lack of it did. Wherever they were the streets were largely empty.

Unusual for a night of celebration.

Smell told more of a story to Aleja. The smells of wood and spice that once filled the air gave way to a fetid stench.

Even though Aleja had never been to this part of Mir, the strength of the stench told her all she needed to know.

They were in the waste quarter of the city, where barges loaded with trash left the city to empty their rotting cargo outside the city gates.

If there was a perfect place for a deviant like the Shepherd to hide his prize, Aleja thought, this was it. Almost all the people of Corazon avoided waste and defilement. Even the bravest and most honorable Guardian did everything they could to avoid exposure to uncleanliness and decay.

But someone had to do the work no one else would. Those who did were treated as outcasts. Even though their work was celebrated in ceremonial speeches, on the streets they were ridiculed when they weren't simply avoided.

Most of the waste workers lived in the area, and made it largely self-sustaining, so as to avoid much contact with the rest of Mir's citizens. The Shepherd must have known he would receive little interference from them. As long as he left the people living by the waste canals alone, they would leave him alone.

As they moved deeper into the waste quarter the smell grew so strong it made Aleja sick. Perhaps noticing her discomfort, someone rubbed a mint cream under Aleja's nose. She breathed it in deeply and welcomed the burn in her sinuses.

"We are here." The Shepherd said as the wagon jerked to a halt.

The Shepherd did not remove Aleja's blindfold or the ties around her wrists. Two of his men took Aleja by the arms and helped her out of the wagon. She heard a door unlatch, and was led into what she thought was a musty smelling room.

The Shepherd's men held on to Aleja as they urged her forward. Aleja felt the familiar knotted hands of the Stick-man around one of her arms.

"Watch your step," the Stick-man said in his dusty rasp, "we're going down now."

Aleja tried to peer from under her blindfold as she descended the stairs, which were wide but steep.

At the end of the stairs Aleja was led through what seemed to be a maze of corridors. The floor was made of stone, but worn and uneven. Aleja felt the heat of torches.

The men stopped Aleja suddenly. There was the sound of another door being opened. This time, once Aleja was led inside, the blindfold was removed.

A man with the head of a wolf stared back at her.

Aleja stared back at the creature's yellow eyes, her mouth open wide, but unable to scream, to gasp, or even to breathe.

The man held up a torch in his hand. The wolf's grinning mouth seemed to snarl in the flickering light. He was dressed only in a cloth wrapped around his waist. His bare feet stood on human bones embedded in the stone floor.

The creature spoke to Aleja, his voice muffled, yet still unmistakable. It was the Stick-man.

The wolf head. It's a mask.

"Follow me, Vessel." The Stick-man said.

The others guiding Aleja down the hall also wore crudely made masks of different kinds of animal heads. Yet as strange and terrifying as the sight of the Shepherd's comrades was, it paled in comparison to the horrors buried in the tunnel.

The walls and floors of the tunnel were lined with the bones of the dead, embedded in the very rock the tunnel was carved in. Skeletal faces, their jaws open in deathless screams, seemed to watch Aleja as she walked by. Their hands pressed against the walls, as if the dead were trying to push their way out of their stone prison. Aleja felt the mirror vibrating in her pack, and under the humming sound only she seemed to hear, was the whisper of a thousand voices speaking as one.

"Set us free, Daughter!"

Aleja, thinking the voice was one of the Shepherd's men, stopped and looked behind her.

"What did you say?" She said to a man with a bear's head.

"I said move it!" The bear head growled back at her.

The Shepherd looked back towards the man and shook his head, then moved next to Aleja and pointed to the walls.

"You see the paradise your Queen brought us to." The Shepherd spoke solemnly, his voice clear. He alone wore no mask.

Aleja stopped and looked around. The dead even covered the ceiling.

The Shepherd moved behind Aleja, placed his hand on her shoulder, and urged her forward.

"What is this place?" Aleja asked.

"Don't you know it?" The Shepherd replied. "It is your home."

Aleja scoffed.

"This is not my home. I have never seen any place such as this."

"Few have. It's what has been kept hidden from you. From all the people who cower under the protection of Taka's false Queen."

Aleja shifted to the side of the hall to avoid stepping on the bones. The Shepherd's henchmen showed no such respect.

"What happened here?" Aleja asked.

"That is not the question you should concern yourself with."

Aleja turned to face the Shepherd. Slightly behind him were Opal and Wren. They were still blindfolded, and were being led by two men with the heads of hawks.

"And what question should I concern myself with?"

"Not what *happened* here…" The Shepherd's grip tightened on Aleja's shoulder. "…but what *will* happen here."

Aleja stopped short. She nodded in the direction of Opal and Wren.

"What will happen to them?"

"That depends on you."

Aleja turned away from the Shepherd and walked forward.

"You tricked Wren into giving me up didn't you?"

"Hardly. He feared for Opal knowing she harbored the Vessel. He didn't dare have her get caught by Guardians. He thought maybe we could be a go-between. He's a nice boy, but not too bright, like a lot on this island. Just the way Taka wants them."

"You did trick him." Aleja said flatly.

The Shepherd scoffed.

"Do you really think they would have been treated well if you were returned to the High Temple?" The Shepherd clicked his teeth, "No. They would have been choking on the sands of the Wastes before the next moon."

"I wouldn't allow it." Aleja said with a confidence she did not feel.

"Foolish girl. The dead allow everything."

"What do you mean?" Aleja replied angrily.

"We're walking on them right now, and what do they do about it? If I walked on your face I'm sure you would have something to say, but only because you still draw breath. If Taka finds you he will kill you, let whatever diseased soul he is keeping possess you, and there would be nothing you could do to protect any you care about."

Before Aleja could reply the Shepherd's men parted in front of her, and the sight before her shocked her into silence. It was a door, like those in the High Temple, and covered in a carving of the Queen.

The Shepherd stood beside Aleja.

"Know where you are now, don't you?"

"How can it be?"

"Well, it's not the one you lived in exactly. But if it feels like home, it must be home, yes?"

The Shepherd walked past Aleja and held his hands up to the image of the Queen carved on the stone door. His large fingers covered the glow of her red eyes.

The door slid open. The Shepherd led Aleja inside a large hall.

They stood together on a stage before hundreds of people. Some wore masks, but most were dressed in the clothes that defined them. Aleja saw merchants, fishermen, bargemen, clay workers, pillow maidens, and street cleaners among the crowd. People from all walks of life in Mir. The low and the high. But none who served the Queen.

The crowd before her did not kneel. Some stared at Aleja questioningly, others indifferent, some with hostility.

But any who looked at the wall behind her, looked in fear.

"Welcome home, Vessel." The Shepherd said with a mocking bow. "Welcome to the Low Temple." The Shepherd let out a short laugh at what Aleja thought was a joke, but he then grew serious. He held his arms out to the expanse of the hall. His voice echoed through it. "The temple of the true Queen."

Aleja looked around the room. Although smaller than the Syncronia in the High Temple, the resemblance was unmistakable.

It even had a mosaic on the wall behind her.

But the face that dominated the center of it was not Aleja's, nor was it the Queen's.

It was a woman's face, one with a cold beauty, and glittering, iridescent skin. The images surrounding the face were enmeshed not in hair, but in the webbed, almost translucent pattern of a butterfly's wings.

The eyes did not have the dark almond shape like the eyes of Corazon's people, nor were they like the fiery red eyes of the Queen.

They were the eyes of a wasp.

CHAPTER 39

"See how they have lied to us, my brothers and sisters."

The Shepherd called out to the crowd from the forefront of the stage. His men stood in the wings with Aleja. Wren and Opal were both tied to a large stone pillar on the center of the stage.

"See how those who preach the truth deal only in falsehood."

The Shepherd held his hands out towards Aleja as he spoke. Aleja stood straight, and refused to look the Shepherd in the eyes. She stared forward towards the opposite wall, where a group of the Shepherd's masked men stood before a large, wooden double door.

"This once great hall, swallowed by the earth, was supposed to be forgotten. Even now as they tear down the city walls to build new ones, they plan for the people of Mir to forget the old wall as well. They wish us to see the city as forever unchanged. But we who know this place know the truth."

The Shepherd pointed up towards the face on the mosaic.

"Just as the Vessel's image now graces the walls of the Syncronia rather than the Queen's, we have witnessed this image of the Queen transformed into the Goddess who now looks down upon you."

Aleja could not resist looking back at the mural. She was curious at how the Shepherd could revere such a monstrous image.

It was the same image as before, but the wasp eyes were gone, replaced by beautiful green ones.

Why did it look different to me before?

"We are but a small ship in a mighty sea." The Shepherd moved towards the pillar. Wren kept his head low in shame, but Opal held her head up and looked at the Shepherd with defiance.

"A storm is coming to Corazon, my brothers and sisters. Join us, and none of you will be swept away by the waves."

Although there were several in the audience captivated by the Shepherd's speech, Aleja could see not all were swayed.

He is gambling on something here, and needs me to play a part in it to succeed.

Aleja saw the man who struck her on the street. Now sober, and surrounded by other merchants like him, he did not seem intimidated by the Shepherd or impressed by the ceremony. He stood with arms crossed, and watched skeptically as the Shepherd paced the stage.

The Shepherd walked towards Aleja with his arms extended.

I won't play your game so easily. Aleja thought as he approached.

"Look what I bring before you now. One of our Daughters, who was to be sacrificed to sustain the lie. The one you knew as the Vessel of the Queen."

The Shepherd's men pushed Aleja forward out of the deep shadows of the back of the stage. There was a collective gasp at the sight of Aleja. Even the merchant seemed fazed.

But only for a moment.

"A fraud, Shepherd!" The merchant called out. "I've seen this girl, she is just a servant you picked up off the streets!"

"I'm surprised you remember her that well," the Shepherd replied with a leering smile, "as drunk as you were. If only I had known at the time it was the Vessel you struck, I may have turned her in just to watch you be taken to the Wastes in chains."

The merchant's companions looked anxiously at him. He waved off their concerns as he approached the stage.

"And what proof do we have of your assertions? Any of them? That there is no Queen? That those abandoned to the Drowned World will come to Corazon." The merchant looked over at Aleja and pointed at her. "That this frightened little girl is the Vessel."

The sound of the Shepherd's laugh bounced eerily off the walls, as if the very stones joined in his mockery of the merchant.

"You ask for proof? What proof has the High Chamberlain given you that you hold on so strongly to his lies?"

The merchant smiled.

"Life and prosperity are all the proof I need, Shepherd. The Queen's gifts may be meager for some, but all of Corazon share in them."

The merchant turned to address the crowd.

"Who among you can say the Queen has never given what she promised? Who here has not received the blessings of food, home, and the company of their brothers and sisters? That some may have filled their plate more than others at her banquet is true, but I see nothing to suggest it is all a lie."

There was a murmur in the crowd. The Shepherd was silent. Aleja could see the merchant's words were having an effect.

The merchant walked closer to the stage. He pointed towards the mural behind Aleja.

"Are we really to kneel to some creature with the pale skin of the dead? What are the promises of this fraudulent mockery of our Queen?"

"Life, merchant." The Shepherd replied coldly. "She promises a life without end. And when she returns to the land that is rightfully hers, you will drop to your knees if you want to keep it."

The merchant stopped and stared at the Shepherd.

"You dare to threaten us with death?"

"It is no threat. It is what we all share in. Life or death. We have been worshipping a false Goddess, one who rules through fear and denial of our spirit. Only a Goddess of Death holds power over the living." The Shepherd pointed upwards towards the face on the mosaic. "She is the Goddess of Life, and she will share its power with us."

The merchant looked towards Aleja. As much as he tried to hide it, she could see doubt growing in his eyes.

"What proof do you have that she is the Vessel?" The merchant said. "And don't say the tattoos. I know many a merchant who has helped smuggle an errant Daughter to the Stone Islands. Finding a Daughter to play a role in this mockery is not so difficult."

The Shepherd turned towards Aleja.

"What say you?" The Shepherd said. "Should you tell them who you are? Why you fled the High Temple?"

Aleja stared at the Shepherd and shook her head.

The Shepherd seemed neither surprised nor disappointed.

The Shepherd walked over to the post where Wren and Opal were tied up. He pulled off both of their hoods. Aleja noticed on the post there were carvings similar to ones she saw in the Room of Reflection, but worn down and chipped. She noticed a small drain by Opal's feet, close to where the stone floor was worn and indented, as if it suffered the wear and tear of feet rubbing against it for thousands of seasons.

The Shepherd lifted Wren's head up while the Stick-man lifted up Opal's. They forced both to look out at the crowd.

"Who among you recognize these two?"

There were sporadic shouts in the crowd. Some acknowledged they knew Wren, others Opal, and a few both.

"Then you know these two were judged by the Daughter known as Aleja, who was later chosen to be Vessel. So what say you, Wren? Is this the Daughter who judged you? Is she the Vessel?"

Tears in his eyes, Wren shook his head yes. The Shepherd smiled triumphantly at the crowd. Aleja looked at the merchant. He crossed his arms and shook his head to his companions.

"What of the woman? What of Opal?" Several in the crowd shouted out.

The Shepherd nodded towards Opal. The Stick-man pushed her face towards Aleja and commanded her to speak.

But Opal only laughed.

"Why, she is just a servant girl, Shepherd."

The Stick-man slapped Opal across the face. She bit her lip, and spit a trail of blood into the drain by her feet. Then she smiled and called out to the crowd.

"You are fools if you believe this blasphemy. May you all choke on the sands of the Wastes if you harm a hair on her head–"

The Stick-man gagged Opal at the Shepherd's signal.

Aleja saw anger burn in the Shepherd's face. He had not intimidated Opal as much as he thought. The merchant jumped upon the opportunity the Shepherd's miscalculation provided.

"So which of the Shepherd's witnesses are we to believe?" the merchant said with a renewed confidence. "The one who supports this farce or the one who repudiates it? I have heard nothing from those who claim to have seen the Vessel with their own eyes. Why don't I bring my own witnesses, Shepherd? Now that yours have said their piece."

The Shepherd glared at the merchant, but did nothing to restrain him as he walked onto the stage.

"So, any of you who have seen the Vessel, speak up now. Let's put this story to rest, because the night is long, and my bed calls upon me to do the same."

After the laughter in the room died a woman spoke up from the crowd.

"I know these two, and I was present at their trial." She said as she pointed to Wren and Opal." I do believe this girl resembles the Daughter, Aleja. I've heard her voice. If you wish to prove it to me, Shepherd, let me hear her voice."

Slowly, even among those who had expressed doubts, the crowd began to call out for Aleja to speak.

The Shepherd came close, as if his presence alone would compel her. But Aleja stood silently, and stared through the Shepherd to the wall across from her.

"She will do more than that, my brothers and sisters." The Shepherd stared into Aleja's eyes and smiled. "For she has brought the proof with her."

"And what would that be? A servant's cup from the High Temple?" The merchant said with a laugh few shared.

The Shepherd walked up to the merchant, who was now standing on the stage, and placed his arm around him. The merchant tried to pull free but the Shepherd held him tight. The merchant looked unafraid, but did not share in the Shepherd's smile.

"Those of you who think you've been summoned just to accept what I say, know that I asked this man to come here because I knew he would doubt me. I value his doubt. I am not like the Chamberlains who only desire obedience."

There were audible gasps as the Shepherd produced a shining blade from his tunic and held it up to the now squirming merchant. Aleja stared transfixed by the blade. It was not made of metal, but a silver, glass-like material. Aleja saw her eyes reflected in its jagged edges.

A mirror.

It was then Aleja noticed the mosaic was made of small pieces of the same material as the knife. The woman's eyes seemed to follow the motion of the Shepherd's blade as he held it out to the crowd. The mirror in Aleja's pack quivered so violently she thought it was going to leap out.

"Let this man believe in lies."

The merchant's legs buckled as he tried to slide out of the Shepherd's grip. He called out to his companions, who only looked on in disbelief.

"You, my brothers and sisters," the Shepherd pointed the blade towards the crowd, "will believe in miracles."

There was a collective scream as the Shepherd flipped the blade around and jabbed it into both of the merchant's eyes. Aleja, so close to the sight of the man's eyes being ground into jelly, covered her face and doubled over. The merchant's high pitched shriek tore through Aleja's ears.

But then it stopped. Aleja uncovered her face, expecting to see the merchant dead upon the floor. But he stood, his face now radiant and unbloodied, and turned towards the mosaic with a look of awe. He looked upon the face with both of his eyes whole.

"Yes, Yes!" The merchant cried. "I see it now! Her beauty!"

The crowd moved closer to the stage. All were silent, most with hands over their mouths.

They fell to their knees before the Shepherd's Goddess.

The Shepherd moved in close to Aleja. Aleja could feel the heat of the Shepherd's labored breath. Her nose filled with the scent of garlic. His men tore the pack from Aleja's back and thrust it into her hands. Aleja saw the Queen's mirror gleaming inside.

"Take it out." The Shepherd pointed at it with the knife.

"Take it out. Show it to them. Or Opal will not see another dawn."

Aleja's nostrils flared as she stared back at the Shepherd.

"Surely you noticed the drains at the base of the pillar?" The Shepherd said with a smile. "The stone around it is stained red. Long ago, it was not only frightened little girls the Chamberlains sacrificed in their temples. We've seen the bones. The Queen must have been far thirstier for blood in those days."

The Shepherd looked up at the face on the mural.

"Our Goddess is just as thirsty. Maybe more so."

Aleja stared hard at the Shepherd. He pushed the bag towards her. She noticed he was careful not to touch the mirror itself.

He's afraid of it.

Aleja smiled.

She held her wrists up to the Shepherd's face.

The Shepherd beckoned one of his men to come forward to untie her.

Aleja gently massaged the sore, reddened skin. The Shepherd impatiently shoved the pack to her chest.

Aleja looked over the crowd, some transfixed at the sight of the merchant, but the rest staring at her. She turned back to the Shepherd. He stared at her with wild, gleaming eyes. Aleja's own eyes betrayed none of the fear she felt looking into the madness boiling in his eyes.

"You've convinced them." Aleja said with feigned indifference as she took hold of the mirror and brought it out of the pack. The vibrations stopped once both her hands were on it. "Opal and Wren, people knowing my face or hearing my voice, and now me showing a shattered piece of a mirror. What is any of it going to really prove to them?"

"Oh," the Shepherd tittered, "that was just for fun. A bit of a show. I never thought that would convince all of them you are the Vessel. They're not that stupid."

"Really?" Aleja huffed. "So, what will convince them?"

The Shepherd smiled with his mouth opened wide, as if he were about to take a bite out of her. He held up his blade between them.

"What they see when you die."

CHAPTER 40

Aleja held the mirror up to shield herself from the Shepherd's downward swing. The blade pierced the mirror and stopped just short of her chest. Although it didn't touch her skin, she felt a cutting heat from the blade. Aleja twisted the mirror away from her chest when she couldn't push the weight of the Shepherd off her.

The hall filled with a crack of thunder as the Queen's Mirror broke in two. Aleja and the Shepherd were both sent flying across the stage in opposite directions. Aleja slammed unhurt into a group of onlookers that came on the stage to see the miracle of the merchant's undamaged eyes.

The Shepherd was not as lucky. When Aleja looked up he was sitting dazed, his blade now lying on the floor, after slamming into the pillar between Opal and Wren. It wasn't long before his bloodied head was topped off with Opal's spit.

Aleja looked for the pieces of the mirror as the Shepherd's men ran up to her. She saw one piece wedged into a large rock near one of the walls down from the stage. The Shepherd's men who were in the crowd blocked her from it.

The other piece had embedded itself into the mosaic, directly in the base of the woman's neck. As Aleja stood up, she watched as the mirror melted, and black, inky lines spread themselves over the woman's face.

The image of the Shepherd's Goddess let out an ear-piercing scream. The crowd fell to the ground and covered their ears at the sound. Only

Aleja seemed unhurt by it. Unlike the rest, Aleja was still standing, and watched the image transform.

The woman's wasp eyes returned, but her skin was now scaled and yellowed. The butterfly wings cracked and withered, and the mosaic began to crumble.

The inhuman scream reverberated through the stone walls. Once the last echo of it faded, the short silence that followed was interrupted by the sound of the mosaic exploding into thousands of glittering shards of glass.

The walls and floor of the cavernous hall quaked. Soon the hall filled with screams as large chunks of the ceiling fell upon the audience, and shards of tile from the mosaic flew like glass shrapnel into their bodies. Pieces of the black mirror flew into Aleja's body, and were absorbed painlessly by her skin.

Aleja stood trembling, unable to move. Everything in the hall changed. It was bright, beautiful and new. In place of the mosaic was an enormous, liquid mirror with the symbol of the lemniscate in the center. The bones in the walls and floors stood up and took on flesh. Soon she was surrounded by ghostly people unaware of her presence.

The large door in the back of the hall opened and Aleja saw the light and felt the heat of the sun on her face. A procession entered and walked between large crowds who stood on both sides of the hall.

Children, Aleja realized as she looked at the crowds and the procession, *there are no children here. Only the one leading this procession.*

The child with the veil on her face.

Aleja also noticed there were no people who could be described as infirm or elderly. All in the procession and the crowd were young, beautiful and vibrant creatures. Aleja remembered the pillar with the gutter at its base, and her heart filled with dread at the thought of what was about to happen to the child.

A woman, dressed like one of the Priestesses of the Queen's Memory, walked hand in hand with the child. Behind them walked a procession of people dressed in finery that Aleja had never seen before. Their soft yet metallic looking robes glimmered like the surface of a moonlit lake.

Aleja recognized one of the people as Ker, but with the female face Aleja saw just before Bao showed her the demon behind it.

Aleja saw another man with Taka's deep blue eyes. He walked beside a gorgeous, dark skinned man whose graceful movements made a mockery of the creature Aleja knew he would become.

Maran, Aleja thought with an anger building in her heart, *look at the beauty your evil has taken from you.*

Maran held a dagger in his hands. The veiled girl was chained to the post, and Maran took his place beside her.

The light pouring out of the liquid mirror lit the entire hall. But it grew dim as the priests picked up flutes and drums and began to play. The lemniscate began to spin, and created a black vortex that swirled in the middle of the liquid mirror. As the music reached a crescendo, the liquid darkness came out like a flood and consumed the light. Yet although the room was now dark, Aleja was still able to see.

The Priestess held up her hands and called out to the mirror in a language Aleja did not understand. Maran held up his knife. A liquid, both light and dark, poured out of the mirror and covered the knife. The crowd cheered at the sight of it. The liquid transformed the knife. Now Maran held two blades, one silver and one black, which sprung from both sides of the handle.

Maran held the blades up to the child's neck as the Priestess and the worshippers called out to the image of the lemniscate.

Forgetting she was invisible to the phantoms, Aleja ran screaming up to the stage for the Priestess to stop.

The Priestess was about to pull off the child's veil when the hall filled with shouting. Aleja saw others, dressed just like the worshippers, but armed with strange weapons that spiraled in light in dark just like that of the mirror.

Aleja saw two faces, untouched by time, which she recognized among the group armed with weapons. One was her father, the other was the Queen. Not the fiery Goddess who guarded the High Temple, or the motherly carving Bao found in its hidden passageways, but the strange woman who she saw in the rice fields. The one who spoke to her with such kindness and love.

Like a mother would.

They stood side by side, leading the armed crowd pushing through the worshippers.

The worshippers tried to slow them with words of reason, but failing that, drew weapons of their own.

A battle ensued. The two groups attacked each other with a strange light emanating from their weapons. Some fought up close with the light, others flung it from afar. Those hit by the light were knocked unconscious. None were killed in the battle. Gradually Aleja's father and the Queen gained ground on the worshippers, and threatened to take the stage from them.

Aleja looked back at the stage. Taka, Maran and Ker stood in front of the Priestess. The Priestess grabbed hold of the child as they unchained the girl and attempted to flee. Before they could, Aleja's father and the Queen, armed with fiery light spilling from their hands, sprang up onto the stage and blocked their way.

Maran lifted the veil and showed them the face of the child. It was a young girl, with sharp, intelligent eyes and a small bump of a nose. Maran smiled at the Queen, then laughed at her screams as he slit the girl's throat.

Aleja collapsed in pain unlike any she felt before. It was as if her life was being ripped from her body. Her vision went white, then returned just in time for her to see the liquid mirror explode the moment the child fell lifelessly to the ground. Pieces of flying glass shredded countless people in the hall. Taka screamed helplessly at the sight of the Priestess disintegrating into a stormy cloud of red. Maran and Ker crawled away from the hall, bloodied but alive. Most of the glass clattered against the walls of the temple, but the largest pieces tore through the stone walls and flew outwards into the sky.

Aleja screamed and covered her eyes. When she opened them Taka and the others were gone. A small group of people, some of those who attacked the temple, kneeled before the child and wailed. A loud, cracking sound sent the people running over the bodies of their comrades and enemies on the floor. Aleja followed them outside, and shared in their disbelief as they watched the city crumble around them and the temple sink into the earth.

The Yamanashi Mountains, which were almost twice as large as Aleja knew them, erupted in a deafening explosion. Smoke and flame flew into the sky, and then down upon the city. Even in the darkening sky Aleja saw small points of light flying off into the distance.

Pieces of the mirror! They must be everywhere in Corazon!

The chaos that once filled the temple was now in the streets. But Aleja's attention was drawn to the Queen sitting on the steps of a ruined building. She sat, eyes filled with tears and robe covered in blood, with the dead child on her lap. Aleja's father, Amedeo, was beside her. He begged the Queen to leave. She refused angrily. Aleja noticed she held a large shard of the mirror in her hands. Before Amedeo could stop the Queen she dug it into her chest. The Queen's blood became a black, viscous liquid as it poured over the mirror. Amedeo sobbed as he tried to stop its flow. The Queen rubbed the mixture over the child's throat. The girl's throat healed, and although her eyes did not open, her mouth took in air and chest moved rhythmically up and down.

The Queen leaned over and whispered into the girl's ear. Aleja watched in silence. Aleja was stunned to realize she knew what the Queen said. But not because she heard the Queen's faintly spoken words.

It was because she remembered them.

"I will always love you, Aleja." Aleja felt the Queen's gentle breath on her ear as she watched her speak. The mirror liquefied, ran up the Queen's chest and seeped into the child's eyes, nose, and mouth. The Queen cradled the child and died whispering into her ears.

"My child…my life…my miracle."

No. It's not possible. She can't be my mother.

She looked at the Queen's face. She saw it now, something in the eyes. It was like looking into a mirror.

How can it be?

Aleja ran up to her mother and father. But before she could reach them their images became distorted, like they were sinking in turbulent water. Then everything vanished as suddenly as it appeared.

Aleja was back in the Shepherd's crumbling temple. Everything seemed to be happening in slow motion. Aleja stared at her hands, then felt her neck. She could still feel the sting of Maran's blade, and the warmth of the Queen's healing touch.

My mother's touch.

Aleja shook her head violently, oblivious to the growing chaos of the panicked crowd around her. She felt as if something inside her was about to explode.

Whatever it was I saw, it was from a different age, a different world. I can't be that girl. I can't!

Who am I?

Aleja threw back her head and screamed. The stone walls and ceiling responded with a violent cracking sound, sending pieces of it crashing down onto the crowd. Amidst the shouts and screams Aleja heard Opal's voice ring out.

"Watch out, Aleja!"

Aleja turned to see the Shepherd charging towards her. She tried to dodge him, but his ample frame managed to knock her off the stage. The Shepherd rolled under an outcropping that burst from the wall. It almost crushed him, but also shielded him from an explosion of razor-like shards of rock.

Most of the Shepherd's men were not as lucky as their master. They shrieked and grabbed at their faces in pain after the shrapnel tore through their masks.

Bloodied but still conscious, the weakened Shepherd offered no chase as Aleja scurried away from him. Aleja moved towards Opal, but stopped herself. She turned back towards the panicked crowd now clamoring to get out of the hall. She went for the Queen's mirror embedded in the rock.

Blood curdling screams rang out at the sound of rocks crashing down from the ceiling, then were silenced with a thud that sent shockwaves through Aleja's body as she ran to the rock. She grabbed onto the mirror's jagged edges and felt it cut into her skin. Screaming in pain, Aleja thrust her hands upward and pulled the mirror free.

Aleja fell to the floor. She cradled the mirror, which was now in the shape of a crude dagger, to her chest. As the mirror vibrated in her embrace she saw shadows seep out of the cracks in the walls, human shapes but without features. Slowly and awkwardly, like fawns taking their first step, the shadows moved about the hall. The torchlight flickered in their presence, and then was extinguished as the shadows formed a cloud that blew through the hall and encased it in darkness.

Aleja saw the merchant, oblivious to the cracking stone above him, call out amidst the chaos.

"Light the torches! Light the–"

The stone broke free and the merchant was silenced with a sickening crunch.

The mirror began to glow. Aleja held it up, and was surrounded in a misty, grey light only she could see.

Aleja saw the Shepherd crawling on the floor towards what was left of the mural. After stumbling over the bodies of his men, the wounded and the dead, he found a door and fumbled out of the hall.

Aleja turned back towards Opal. She was still tied to the pillar. The Stick-man, his eyes wide with terror, clung desperately to the pillar with her.

There was another violent shake. The pillar broke in half, sending Wren and a large portion of the stone to the floor.

"NO!" Aleja screamed as Wren disappeared in a cloud of dust.

Aleja ran up to Opal, whose own rope hung loosely in the hole it was threaded through. She grabbed a knife from the Stick-man, who did nothing to stop her. In his fear he didn't even seem to know Aleja was there until she began to cut Opal free.

"I'm here, Opal."

"Aleja?" Opal said, her eyes blindly searching in the dark, "How could you find me?"

"Never mind that. Let's go."

Aleja cut through the rope and grabbed Opal by the hand.

"Wren!" Opal shouted through the din. "Where's Wren?"

"He's gone. I'm sorry, but we have to leave now!"

Aleja pulled Opal from the pillar.

"Don't leave me to die, Vessel! Please!" The Stick-man shouted out.

The fear in his voice filled Aleja with a pity he had not shown Opal. She thought of the young Guardian who fell to his death because of her. She thought of Bao.

I won't have another life taken if I can help it. Even if it's the Stick-man's.

Aleja, the jagged mirror stinging her free hand, thrust her arm to his chest.

The Stick-man clung to Aleja's arm as if it were a piece of driftwood in the middle of a stormy sea. Aleja, still able to see in the misty light that engulfed her, led them both to the door.

Just as she was about to follow them through, she heard Wren's voice.

"I'm going back for Wren." Aleja shouted. She grabbed the Stick-man by the face. "Get her out of here." The Stick-man nodded vigorously, his stubble scratching against the palms of her hands.

Aleja heard Opal shout for her as she turned to run. The sight in the hall was horrifying, beyond anything Aleja ever believed possible. Hundreds of people crushed under rock, and those still alive crawling over one another as they blindly searched for a way to escape.

Aleja blocked it all out as she descended from the stage to look for Wren. When she found him he was crawling on his knees and on one hand. His other arm was bloodied and broken.

Wren screamed in pain when Aleja pulled him to his feet. He followed her without question, even though he could barely stand, let alone run, on a badly twisted ankle.

The door was now caved in. Only a small hole remained to crawl through. Aleja saw Opal's face on the other side.

I told that man to get her out.

Her anger was quelled at the sight of the Stick-man's hands reaching through the hole to help Wren through.

"Now, Aleja," Opal shouted once Wren was on the other side. "Come with us!"

Aleja was about to take Opal's hand when she hesitated. She thought of Sara's warning in the dream, and how much danger she put Opal in. And now, if the vision was true, there was no telling what kind of danger anyone would be in if they stayed with her.

Aleja turned back and saw the door at the end of the hall was wide open. Some found their way through it, even in the darkness.

Aleja pushed Opal's hands back.

"Aleja! What are you do–"

In an instant, the rest of the stones caved in and Aleja was blocked off from Opal. Aleja pulled the mirror close to her chest, and ran for the door.

Unlike the others fumbling in the dark she could see the maze of rocks and debris that blocked their way. The mirror gave her light, but did not shield her from the shards of rock showering down from the ceiling and exploding onto the floor.

Aleja was far beyond the door, and deep into the passageways, when she stopped at the sight of two men approaching her.

It dawned on Aleja that, despite the destruction in the hall, the passageways leading away from it did not even tremble.

The men, one with a crystal lantern in his hand, stood only a few paces from Aleja.

"Get the Vessel." The man holding the lantern ordered.

Aleja held the mirror up, as if it were a torch. She felt a sting in her hand as the edge dug into her skin.

"I won't let you." Aleja said with a smile that halted the men in their tracks.

Through the mirror, she saw the bones in the walls and floor come alive. Shadowy creatures pulled themselves free from the rock and swept through the hallway like the wind. The man's lantern was snuffed out as the ghostly figures swarmed around them and dragged both screaming into the earth.

Aleja stared at the ground where the men once stood. They made her so angry, she could've killed them. She looked at the mirror, and saw the anger still burning in her eyes.

Maybe I did.

She did not dare get rid of the mirror, for she needed its light to see in the darkness. But Aleja wondered what it truly was she now held in her quivering hands.

Aleja moved through the remaining passageways almost in a trance. Eventually, almost by accident, she found a stairway leading up. With every step she took up the stairs she felt her shock subside and her senses return.

Aleja continued to walk in the light of the mirror. The light was not entirely clear, and dimmed the higher up the stairway she went. It was like everything was enveloped in a dreamlike fog. But it was enough. Aleja eventually found herself in an underground room with a ladder leading up in its center.

Torchlight from outside shone through the slits in the wood ceiling. Aleja placed the mirror back in her pack, and climbed up the ladder.

She opened the door above her only slightly. Just enough to see a group of the Shepherd's men milling about nearby. One of them had a fresh bandage wrapped around his head. It was clear they felt the tremors in the ground. They argued excitedly about who was to search the caverns for survivors.

Aleja waited. She tried to sense the moment when she could open the door and make a run for it. But every so often the men's attention was directed back towards her position, and she would quickly shut the door.

The men continued to argue. The fear was obvious in their voices. But Aleja knew it was only a matter of time before one was shamed enough to venture down into the caverns.

Aleja looked about the room for a place to hide, but there was none. The room was filled with piles of scythes and long poles fashioned into spears. It was clear the Shepherd was not just trying to build up support, but an arsenal as well.

She took one last look from the door, and saw a pair of the Shepherd's men rush up to the group. They were covered in dust, and told the men to come help.

"Others are trapped." One of them exclaimed in a loud, panicked voice. "You get down and help them or the Shepherd's gonna bury you with them."

The men refused. The argument between them grew heated.

They think the Shepherd is dead. Aleja realized. *Looks like he was right about one thing. The dead stand in the way of no one.*

Deciding this was her best chance for escape, Aleja quietly opened up the door and crawled out.

She was in the middle of a courtyard. Aleja was almost out of it when she heard a shout from above.

"Hey! Are you hurt? Are there any others down there?"

Aleja looked up to see a pair of men standing guard on the roof. They were not Guardians, but were armed like them. In the light of the full moon Aleja saw the glint of metal daggers hanging off their belts.

Then she heard another voice, one Aleja recognized instantly. She turned back and saw the Shepherd, his head bleeding, and one good arm wrapped around one of his companions.

"Stop her!"

Aleja did not stop to look up at the men leaping down from the roof. She ran out of the courtyard, through the halls, and into the streets.

When she came to a crossroad, and a foul wind blew her way, Aleja went against all her instincts and ran into the smell, and hoped the men who chased her wouldn't think to do the same. She had to get away. It wasn't just about escape or survival anymore. Aleja didn't just want to live.

She wanted answers.

CHAPTER 41

Aleja could hear the men closing in on her. The sound of their feet ricocheted through the maze of alleyways and skipped over the water in the canals like a smooth stone. Aleja was no less quiet. Without the light of the mirror, running through a walled passageway unlit by torches and untouched by moonlight, she knocked over crates of garbage in her wake.

Aleja turned a corner onto a street and came face to face with a donkey, its mouth covered with a feed bag. It stopped eating momentarily, looked at Aleja with complete indifference, and then resumed.

Aleja recognized the foul smell of the cart the donkey was leading. The cart was loaded with a mountain of decaying vegetables and fruits.

It couldn't be the same one, could it?

All at once it came to her. Not only a place to hide where no one would look for her, but a way to get out of Mir.

Aleja looked around for the cart driver but did not see him, nor anyone else on the street. She ran up to the back of the cart and climbed inside, wedging herself between the pile and the sideboards.

Once inside the cart she quickly scraped piles of rotten vegetables down over her, and dug her legs deep into the squirming filth. She pressed her face close down next to the sideboards and breathed through the thin slits between the planks.

Soon after she covered herself, Aleja heard a man talk affectionately to the donkey, remove the feedbag, then take his place on the cart.

Aleja's relief vanished when the cart stopped just as suddenly as it started.

The Shepherd's men shouted out to the cart driver.

"Have you seen a girl run by here?"

"Nah." The cart driver replied gruffly.

"You sure?"

The shadow of one of the men passed over the beam of light through the slit, momentarily returning Aleja to darkness. Aleja held her breath. She fought the urge to retch as the liquefied flesh of eggplants and tomatoes oozed through her hair.

"Yah." The cart driver said to the men with a crack of his whip. Aleja peered through the slit as the cart lurched forward. Briefly, she saw the silhouettes of the men.

"You go down that alley," one of them said, "I'll make sure she didn't double back."

Aleja took short, controlled breaths as she rode the cart through the streets. The ride on the cobbled road was bumpy. More than once she spat out the occasional piece of rotting cabbage that fell into her mouth.

The cart driver got off his perch and walked to her side of the cart. Aleja heard the sound of a latch being pulled.

Get ready. Not much longer now.

The cart lifted into the air. Aleja slid down with the rotten pile. In the two story drop there was no ground below her, only water, and a barge floating upon it.

Aleja fell off the cart in an avalanche of rotten fruits, vegetables, and decaying fish. She let out little more than a yelp as she fell down onto the barge and was promptly splashed with a waterfall of foul smelling juice and slush.

The pile from the cart covered Aleja completely. Her body sunk into a mass of decay. There were loud, sickening sucking sounds as she tried to push herself out of the heap.

Aleja retched as she clawed at the foulness covering her. Once free of it she breathed deep at the first taste of fresh air.

As the barge began to move she heard the bargeman call out to the cart-driver above.

"You hear something?"

The driver took his seat without looking down.

"Nah." he called back. And then, with a crack of his whip, went on his way.

CHAPTER 42

There were only two more stops before the barge reached the wall, and Aleja heard the bargeman call out for the canal gate to be opened. The Guardians walked onto the barge but only, it seemed to Aleja, out of a sense of routine. They did not examine the barge with anything close to thoroughness before sending it through the gate.

Aleja closed her eyes, as if shielding herself from the sight of the Guardians would also shield her from them, and waited with baited breath for the barge to pass under the wall.

At the sound of the gate creaking shut behind her, Aleja finally let herself peer out from under the layers of putrefaction on her head. She saw only darkness, the height of the wall blocked out all light. As the barge made some distance from the wall, the torchlights of the city looked like the sun rising over the horizon.

The barge, pulled by a team of donkeys on the side of the canal, moved steadily away from Mir. Gradually the Guardian's torchlights became an indistinct line of gold outlining the wall and the city it surrounded.

Aleja pulled herself from the garbage. Her clothes were soaked with foul-smelling water, her hair and skin covered with bits of indiscriminately colored mush. Aleja moved to the edge of the barge and looked down into the water. Her reflection flickered in the dim light emanating from the front of the barge.

Aleja almost didn't recognize herself.

There was a hardness to her eyes, or perhaps, just a weariness.

Aleja looked back at the High Temple. It stood out from the city like the tip of a red knife tearing through a golden sheer of cloth.

Lies. It is all a lie.

But knowing that now, Aleja was faced with the discomforting feeling she still needed to believe in something, even if there was nothing to believe in. But what? The visions of her father and mother? How could she believe in them? She never met them in her waking life, and only saw her mother in the strange shadow world that was either ages past or worlds away. And why did her mother pretend to be the Queen when she first saw her in the rice paddies? If she really was Aleja's mother, why did she lie too?

Why wouldn't any of them, her father, mother, or even her Grape Mother tell her the truth from the beginning? As she stared up at the few pinpoints of stars from her bed of filth, Aleja could almost hear Bao's voice calling out in the night with the answer to her questions.

"You not believe. You must see."

But even though she saw, she still didn't quite believe.

If you don't trust your own eyes, who or what can you trust?

Aleja closed her eyes and tried to force the thoughts from her head. She decided it was better to focus on the task at hand. When to get off this barge, and where to go next. Thinking about the practical problems of escape comforted her.

There were no lights on the shore of the canal, as if all life simply vanished outside the city walls.

Aleja rolled into the water. She tiptoed across the pebbled floor of the shallow canal and reached a stone wall that lined the edge. Just before pulling herself up onto the wall, Aleja dunked her head under the water. Her fingers scratched through her hair to free the fetid pieces of debris stubbornly clinging to it.

Even though the canal water was not as foul as the barge and Aleja managed to clean off the muck, the smell still clung to her. She would have to find another source of water, and change her peplos, if she was going to be presentable even to farm animals.

Aleja pulled herself over the wall and collapsed on a patch of soft grass nearby. Looking up at the moonlit sky, Aleja allowed herself a few deep breaths before she got up and walked away from the canal.

Not knowing exactly where to go, just that she wanted as much distance between herself and Mir as possible, Aleja followed a trail that ran parallel to the canal. She occasionally turned back to see if any barges came up behind her, and listened for anyone walking among the rocky outcrops or copses of trees as she walked.

But no more barges came up the canal, and she heard only chirping insects and hooting owls as she walked through the night. As dawn approached Aleja put more distance between herself and the canal.

Eventually Aleja came across a stream where she cleaned herself and her clothes properly. She found little food along the way, and tired from walking. She hid in a leafy thicket as she waited for her gown to dry.

When Aleja went through her pack for a dried piece of squid her finger grazed the edge of the mirror. She pulled the mirror out and then stuck a piece of tentacle in her mouth. In the light the mirror was unremarkable. Little more than a piece of broken, colored glass. There was no movement in the mirror, no strange humming sound as she held it in her hands.

And no visions.

Aleja looked at her reflection as she chewed on the now soggy flesh of the squid.

"Do you have nothing to show me now?" Aleja said aloud, and then laughed.

After finishing the rest of the squid she laid down and ran her fingers over the mirror. It wasn't long before she fell into a restful, dreamless sleep. The sun was high in the sky when she woke. She saw her gown was dried, if a little stained. She dressed herself and decided to walk on the road.

Aleja accepted a ride from a young woman wearing a simple, woolen tunic and a wide, straw hat. The young woman led a cart loaded with bags of onions and beets. The girl was curious about Aleja, and instantly noticed the distinction on her arm.

Aleja concocted a story that she was a Daughter from a small village in the north. She had gone to Mir to see the Vessel, stayed longer than her companions, and now had to find her own way home.

The girl accepted Aleja's story with wide, believing eyes. She asked for no payment for the ride, only for a blessing in return as she shared a loaf of bread with Aleja. The bread was old and tough, if felt like her teeth would be ripped out with every bite, but Aleja ate it gladly.

"I'm so honored to have a Daughter of the Queen ride with me." The girl said as she watched Aleja chew vigorously.

"I'm not really that important." Aleja replied. "Nothing like the Daughters in Mir. But thank you for saying so, and for the ride."

I forgot to say "this Daughter" Aleja thought with a chuckle.

The girl took no notice.

She may not even know about it. She's just a countryside farm girl. I might be the first Daughter she has ever met.

"I was heading to the port anyways." The young girl said with a gentle whip of the reins. "I could use the company."

"So could I." Aleja replied with a look around her shoulder to the road behind her. "The roads are empty today."

"They always are after a celebration." The girl gave the reins another snap. "But this one even more than usual. Everyone is still sleeping off the drink, my father included. That's why it's only me going to trade."

"What's your name?"

"You can call me Neera if it pleases you, Daughter."

"It does." Aleja smiled. "It's a lovely name."

Neera shrugged.

"It's the same name as all my sisters. My dad calls me number four."

Aleja laughed along with Neera.

"What's your name?"

"To you we are all just called Daughters." Aleja replied, thankful for the fact.

"Oh, yes." Neera said, clearly embarrassed. "Sorry to be so ignorant."

"Nothing to be sorry about Neera." Aleja paused, then chuckled. "I mean, Number Four."

Neera gave Aleja a queer look, and then broke out into a hearty laugh.

Aleja mostly listened to Neera as they passed through the rolling landscape. Neera spoke of the simple things villagers enjoyed. A rest from the harvest, the coming festivals, and the occasional visit from a traveler who told stories of faraway places in exchange for a meal.

Aleja relaxed and enjoyed Neera's company and the scenery. There was little land that wasn't cultivated, carved into endless rows of neat, symmetrical lines. But occasionally Aleja would admire a stream lined with moss covered stones, a rocky outcrop where farmers ate their afternoon meal in its shade, or thin woods sheltering families of deer.

As the cart ambled through the countryside Aleja did not give any attention to the flocks of birds that filled the sky overhead. She never saw Hermes hovering high above her, following the cart as if he were a kite on a string.

CHAPTER 43

Aleja drew in a relieved breath of salty, sea air at the sight of the port village of Edisto. Edisto lay at the bottom of a hill and was surrounded by a swath of green firs stretching down the coastline all the way to the Yamanashi Mountains.

Nearly hidden by the trees was a river that made a little island of the city. From the hill it looked as if Edisto were about to float out to sea.

There were no Guardians to stop them as they passed over one of the bridges into the town. Aleja accompanied Neera to the marketplace, where she found out from casual conversation that a ship would leave the next day for the larger port city of Andrid.

Aleja didn't need to ask where she could go on from Andrid. All Judges knew every phase of the moon two ships left from its ports. One to the Stone Islands for those who wished to leave the Queen's embrace, and another to the Wastes for those forced to do so.

Aleja had thought it would be a mistake to board a boat, even to a place as far away from Mir as Andrid. She originally intended to make her way to the Yamanashi Mountains, but now, after a day of hunger outside Mir, thought it was a foolish idea. It was best to get away fast.

But once I'm in Andrid, do I find Ivo, or hide from him?

After Neera traded the rest of her food for bags of rice and salted fish she took Aleja to the docks. There was only one ship in port. It was a wide, rather dilapidated one with sails that looked as if they were made from every piece of leftover fabric in Corazon.

The captain of the ship was a ruddy looking man sitting on one of the many barrels lining the deck. He was absent-mindedly chewing on a piece of squid, and spoke to Aleja with a stringy tentacle sticking out from the corner of his mouth.

"We sail in the morning." The captain squinted at Aleja as he spoke. "We'd be honored to help a Daughter to her home."

From the sound of his voice he didn't seem to believe it was an honor. More like a burden. If it was, Aleja couldn't blame the man for feeling that way.

I wonder how many Daughters or Guardians ate their share of his food, and slept in his bunk, without lifting a finger to help.

After her transport was arranged Aleja thanked Neera for her help and bid her farewell. It took some time for Aleja to convince Neera she helped enough. It was her first experience with the hospitality of the villagers of Corazon, which she found helpful but somewhat smothering.

It was not until Neera accompanied Aleja to a lodging house that she finally boarded her donkey cart and went on her way.

The lodging, a large thatched house, was already full of people sleeping on its open, common floors. Caretakers, while also tending the fire that warmed the room, walked delicately among the guests and handed out blankets and cups of soup and rice.

Aleja walked out of the house before any of the Caretakers approached her. There was still enough light in this dimly lit house for her to be recognized, and the Caretakers tended to sit with their guests and talk when they had the opportunity. Although it was likely none would recognize her as the Vessel, Aleja decided it would be better to return at night when she could ask for a blanket and space without any questions.

Wanting a warm meal, and feeling the need to disappear into a crowd, Aleja went out onto the street to look for a place to eat. She saw a blue tapestry hanging in the doorway of one of the buildings and walked towards it. Unlike the Queen's buildings, whose openings were shrouded in green, a blue curtain meant a tavern.

The tavern owner's wife stood in the doorway, her head peering out through the cloth. Upon seeing Aleja's interest in her establishment, she bid her inside with the promise of free food and drink.

"We'd be honored to have a Daughter of the Queen as our guest." The woman said excitedly. "Especially since one of your sisters just sacrificed so much for us."

Aleja forced a smile to her face, thanked the woman for her kindness, and followed her inside.

The tavern was crowded, packed with men and women sitting on the wooden floor by squat, rectangular tables. Some musicians played in the corner of the room. A few of the patrons danced, some sang, but most were engaged in conversation with those they travelled with.

The patrons stopped to bow towards Aleja. It took an uncomfortable amount of time before all eyes weren't on her.

The woman directed Aleja to a space on one of the thick mats laying on the floor. Aleja took her seat and thanked the woman. She rested her legs in a large, rectangular hole underneath the table. She felt the warmth of the heated stone on her feet. During the cold season the table would be covered with a cloth that would drape down around the waist to hold in the heat of the stones below.

Aleja took off her satchel and placed it by her feet underneath the table.

The meal was plain but hearty, and Aleja finished it off with a surprisingly good wine. She thought about having another but then changed her mind. Aleja was about to get up when she felt one hand on her shoulder, and another holding a pitcher in front of her.

"No need to leave now," said a voice that sent chills up Aleja's spine, "there is still much to drink."

Aleja struggled to get up but the hand held her firmly to the floor. She looked back at the woman holding her down.

In her shock Aleja momentarily forgot how she lost her friend. At the sight of Sara's kind, beautiful face Aleja called out her name, as if hoping somehow what happened back in the High Temple was just a horrible dream.

Sara's smile was bittersweet. She filled Aleja's cup and sat down beside her, then held out her cup in a toast.

"If we are to talk, let's talk truthfully." Sara said before tapping her glass to Aleja's. "You can call me Kalim."

CHAPTER 44

Aleja looked at the face that was once Sara's. It was just the same as the one in her memories.

Only the eyes now seemed different.

Although their color was unchanged, Aleja now saw Kalim staring out from them.

"So it's true." Aleja said.

Kalim nodded.

"How? Why?"

"Two different questions, both difficult to answer. Perhaps if you didn't run I might have entertained the idea of explaining it all to you. But not now. You've delayed us enough already."

Kalim spoke in whispers, yet her voice was clear to Aleja even in the noise of the tavern. She wore her palla around her shoulders and head. The musicians in the tavern played more raucously now, and several people joined together in dance.

Aleja tried to stand up, but Kalim held her down by the wrist. Her strength was incredible. It was as if Aleja's hand was trapped in-between the stones of the tavern walls.

"Enough of that. You may as well enjoy a drink with me. Perhaps it will loosen my tongue and you will get some of the answers you think you want. Or dull my wits so you can run out of here. Or whatever other feeble idea you have about escaping."

Kalim let go of Aleja's wrist. Aleja jumped at the sight of Hermes landing in front of her on her plate. Kalim fussily led the bird to the side of the table with a line of seeds.

"That's not how I thought to escape." Aleja replied with a grin. "Why dull your head with wine when hitting it with the bottle would do just as well?"

Kalim's hand went to the back of her head.

"You know," Kalim said with a smile after drinking her cup dry, "some of our Guardians have confided in me about the great anguish they feel chaining someone to the walls of a ship bound for the Wastes. They tell me that the person's screams and cries for forgiveness often call out to them in the night as they struggle for sleep. It's too bad what happened to Bao, because I for one was looking forward to hearing her screams in the night."

Kalim poured herself another drink, then held out the pitcher for Aleja.

"I wish I could rip that mask right off your face." Aleja blinked, surprised at the venom in her voice. She could not believe what she said. It was as if the hateful words did not come from her lips, but from another dark voice hidden inside her.

Kalim feigned shock.

"Such language coming from one of our people. I never would have imagined it. Hundreds of years ago perhaps, but not now. We've culled those who would even think such thoughts, much less say or act on them."

"Is that what we are to you? Pets learning your tricks? Just like your filthy bird?" Aleja nodded at Hermes, who was still perched on the edge of the table and picking at a pile of seeds, oblivious to Aleja's insult.

"I won't hear any such talk about Hermes. He has been a faithful companion, for a far longer time than you could imagine. Besides, you should be thankful it was Hermes who spotted you and reported back to me. If Taka knew where you were he would have tied you up by now, crowd or no crowd."

"You're here to take me back then."

"You think this is all about you?" Kalim tittered. "Such arrogance."

"I'm the Vessel."

Kalim sighed. Aleja saw through Kalim's showy act of indifference. She noticed the sideways glance Kalim gave to see if any heads turned at the mention of the word "Vessel."

Aleja and Kalim were alone at their table now. The people once seated with them now joined in the dance, but there were others still within earshot of their conversation.

"Yes, yes. You are one of many, my dear. But did you ever stop to think about why you were chosen?"

"Every day."

"Well then, did it ever occur to you that you were being made an example of?"

"What do you mean?"

"Like the one before you. Surely your gossipy friend Sara told you about Pallas. Like you she did not perform her duties in the way she was supposed to. Like you she displayed an unconscionable amount of ego and independence. We have many ways of punishing such transgressions, and when one such as you is chosen, enough of the more thoughtful Daughters realize to be a Vessel is not a reward, but a punishment."

"But I was celebrated."

"Yes, because you were the sacrifice they would not be bound to give. They will live out their lives with the knowledge they will never be claimed. But in the back of their minds they would know that the Queen's judgment for one who swayed from her path was to have her body taken and to be denied rebirth."

"But would that really have happened?"

"In a fashion."

"Is there really a Queen? One like you have preached to us?"

Kalim smiled.

"Why are you asking me? You know there isn't."

"So what about the rebirth? What happens to us when we die?"

"You rot. That's it. There is nothing for you, before or after."

Aleja didn't need to look into Kalim's eyes to see she was not lying. Whether it was true or not, Kalim believed it. Aleja thought of the visions, and the shadows that destroyed the Shepherd's sanctuary. She wondered if Kalim knew anything about them, or would admit it if she did. Did Kalim have the answers she sought? Even if she did, Aleja couldn't trust her words.

I need to see for myself.

Aleja pushed aside the wine Kalim gave her.

"But for you and Taka there is life after the body dies." Aleja said. "And for whoever it was that was going to take me."

"Yes." Kalim replied with frustrating succinctness.

"So if you're not here to take me, then why are you here?" Aleja said. "Why haven't Guardians stormed this place to get me?"

"There are no Guardians here because I did not bring any. And as I said, I'm not here for you. I'd be quite happy to see you board that ship tomorrow and make your way to the Stone Islands." Kalim drank Aleja's wine, then set the cup loudly back on the table. "Or, some other dismal place to live with people who lack good sense."

"Well what is it then?" Aleja spoke loudly, and it pleased her to see a level of discomfort on Kalim's face. "Have you just come to mock me with the face of my friend?"

"Quiet that talk. Once you give me what I want I will be on my way."

"What do you want?"

"The mirror."

"What mirror?" Aleja drew in the satchel with her foot.

Kalim's mocking tone became serious.

"The one under this table, in your satchel."

Aleja held up her hands.

"What satchel?"

"Don't even attempt to lie to me, girl. You know I can see through it."

"Yes, because you're such an accomplished liar yourself."

"What else does one have but lies for those who cannot face the truth?"

"What truths?" Aleja said with a sneer. "What are you hiding?"

Kalim broke out into a laugh. Aleja stared at her as if she had gone mad.

"Why, my poor, lost child, it is not the truth we are hiding. It's you. You and your people. You shouldn't be running from Taka and I, but kneeling before us in gratitude."

"For what?"

"For never being found."

"Who are you hiding us from?"

Kalim finished her drink. For the first time she seemed genuinely troubled.

"From yourselves."

"Such a clever response." Aleja said. "Yet still another lie."

"You mock me because you never saw the world as it was. Look at your people now." Kalim pointed to the crowd dancing and drinking by the musicians. "Look how happy they are. Nothing like they once were, back when they lorded over the Drowned Lands. Vain, arrogant. Vicious and cruel when they weren't simply indifferent to one another. They almost killed themselves off and took the world with them. But now here they are, simple, trusting, and good. Thanks to us, to our guidance."

"You speak as if you weren't one of us." Aleja said.

Kalim's smile was bittersweet.

"I was. Once. But that was a long time ago."

Aleja looked at Kalim skeptically.

"Bao said you are demons."

Kalim scoffed.

"Are you now so blind you can only see the world through the eyes of a simpleton?"

"I saw Ker's face. His true face. With my own eyes."

Kalim looked away from Aleja. She took another drink.

"I don't expect you to understand everything." Kalim said after drinking down all the wine in her cup.

"That's because you are not telling me everything. I can see the lies in your eyes just as you can see mine. If you did us this great kindness then why hide? Why create this lie about a Queen?"

"Because she binds us together. People need to believe in something greater than themselves, especially if they are sacrificing something for others. You people have received much from us. Safety, food, a roof over every head. But deep down all people know there is a price for everything, and someone must pay it. So they offer you."

"You chose me, not them."

"They allowed it, what's the difference? Those who offer a sacrifice are just as complicit in the killing as those who take it. For as long as we have lived on Corazon the people have allowed one of their own, a daughter of their blood, as a sacrifice so they may still receive the blessings of the Queen. They fear to disrupt it. For not only do they still want to be cared for, to receive the promise of rebirth, but to stop it would be to acknowledge what has been done in the past. It would condemn them all. It is why the Vessel is said to be denied rebirth. Her sacrifice must be total, so the people's commitment to this world will be as well."

"But it's a lie. Why hint anyone is taken at all?"

"For a lie to survive, it needs to feed on a bit of truth. Think of it as hiding in plain sight."

"You are just easing your guilt."

Kalim placed her hand to her breast.

"Why Aleja, I'm flattered you think I have any." Kalim took another drink. "But you're wrong. There is more in my life that I need to ease than any sense of guilt, my little dew petal."

"You have an answer for everything don't you?" Aleja reached down to the satchel. She would run if she had to, but would let Kalim delay her no more. The boat was no longer safe, she would have to leave on foot.

"If only I did." Kalim said with a sad smile.

"Well then, we have nothing more to say." Aleja started to stand up. Kalim placed her hand on Aleja's. The feel of Sara's skin sent needles of anguish into Aleja's heart.

"Leave the mirror with me child, and board your ship in the knowledge that none will follow you. Trust I will make sure of it. Make port in Andrid, find Ivo. Take him with you to the Stone Islands before Taka banishes him to the Wastes in retaliation for your desertion. Be happy with him. Begin to forget."

At the mention of Ivo, the needling pain in Aleja's heart became a stabbing dagger. Aleja stared hard at Kalim and bit her lip. She'd rather spill blood than tears in front of her.

Aleja felt she'd never known hate until now. The sudden softness in Kalim's voice enraged her more than any of her criticisms or mockery. Aleja's fingers itched at the sudden, violent thought she could somehow tear the mask off Kalim's face and expose her for what she was.

"I will never give it back to you." Aleja ripped her arm from Kalim and stood up.

"What do you hope to gain in keeping it? Giving it to me will grant you freedom. You can board that ship tomorrow and Taka will never know."

"I've seen its power, and I know it scares you."

"What do you know of its power? You have no idea what it is you have."

"It has spoken to me in dreams. Once I take hold of it, I will hear its music. It will show me the way."

"Really? And what has it shown you? You say dreams, but I'd wager they were more like nightmares. You don't know what you are asking for, girl."

"Maybe, but I know enough not to give it back to you."

"You've made a choice then? Running and hiding, always looking over your shoulder?"

Aleja held tight to the satchel. She looked Kalim in the eyes.

"Yes."

"Then you are a fool. I've had my fill of the chase, but Maran, Ker and Taka are still hungry for it. They have people loyal to them, those who know secrets you are only beginning to discover, and they will hunt you. You won't be safe, even on the Stone Islands. It may take time, but they will find you. And they won't offer you a choice like I have."

"I will always have a choice." Aleja turned her back on Kalim, and readied herself to break from her grip, but Kalim made no move to stop her. She walked out into the cool night and headed towards the bridge.

The streets were empty and poorly lit. The light of the moon was obscured by dark clouds. There was a rumble of thunder, and Aleja felt a few light, cold drops of rain on her skin.

Aleja's steps slowed as she approached the bridge. Fear crept into her mind. She looked behind her but saw no one on the street. The cloth covering the doorways billowed in the winds that blew noisily through the street.

Aleja imagined Taka behind every curtain, waiting for her with Guardians armed with staffs, knives, and ropes in their hands.

Aleja turned around and headed towards the ship.

I could stay by the docks. I could see if anyone is behind me. If any Guardian boards the ship before me, I'll see it and leave.

But to where?

In the distance Aleja saw two men on horseback. She heard the sound of horses behind her as well.

Aleja quickly ducked into a shadow. It was a good hiding place. Behind barrels that kept her out of view of the street, and next to an alley where she could quickly make an escape if she needed to do so.

But she didn't realize another thought it was a good hiding place too.

Aleja's scream was stifled by the thick, meaty hand that felt all too familiar to her. She smelled a strange, burning odor in the hand, and bit down on a piece of cloth.

Thunder echoed in Aleja's head over and over like the beating of a drum. She felt like she was falling.

Just before she fell unconscious, her head resting on the cold dirt, Aleja looked up and saw the smiling face of Ker looking down at her.

CHAPTER 45

At first there was only sound. It was muffled, like the sound of voices underwater.

Aleja could not see, but could feel she was seated on a chair. Her fingers rubbed against the armrests. The grain of the wood felt as rough as sharkskin.

Aleja tried to stand but did not have the strength. She felt heavy, as if pinned under a boulder. She couldn't even lift her head.

A hand ran through Aleja's hair. It was rough, calloused and pulled her head up with brute insensitivity.

The hand placed cold metal on her forehead.

The lemniscate. My silver headband.

The darkness left Aleja's eyes and blurred colors swirled before them. The colors gradually formed themselves into the shapes of people.

Behind them Aleja could make out a carriage draped in long green tapestries that looked like the shrouds used to cover the dead. Aleja could tell they were in some sort of grove, surrounded by tall fir trees whose branches seemed to be on fire.

Aleja felt no panic at the possibility of being encircled by a flaming forest, just a strange unease, as if her mind were slowly awakening to such emotions as fear.

Voices became distinct from the crackle of fire that encircled them.

"But why bring the girl's horse?" A voice like Maran's said. "I almost got kicked by the beast today. It's been wild as a wolf since we lost her."

"Exactly why it must be here now." A shape that looked like Taka replied. "They have formed a bond. It will be a test of transfer. If the horse rejects the girl we will know that Isla has taken her place."

"Isla is just as likely to drop dead from fright at the sight of that monster of a horse. Honestly Taka, with every new life she takes she seems more and more afraid of living."

"Well, we all react to immortality differently. Don't we Maran?"

Aleja's eyes focused just enough to see a look of distrust pass between the two men.

"Besides," Taka said, his face fading in and out of view, "when Isla feels the strength in this body, she will no longer be a prisoner of her fears."

"Or a prisoner of the High Temple, at least." Maran said with a laugh Taka did not share.

Another shape, squat and stocky, filled Aleja's bleary vision. The shape took hold of her and pulled her up into her chair.

"Go easy, Ker." Taka said. "The body is not to be damaged, nothing has changed about that, especially now."

Maran held up Aleja's satchel and pulled out the mirror.

"Too bad we can't say the same about this."

"It'll do." Ker responded gruffly. "And this body will heal quickly, especially once Isla takes it."

"Even so." Taka said. "Nothing more can go wrong. This body has caused us enough problems already."

Taka leaned in to look Aleja in the eyes. A mirror was attached to a chain dangling around his neck. Taka's fingers pulled down on the skin just below Aleja's eyes.

"She's waking." Taka said. "Are you sure you gave her enough to keep her still?"

"Enough to keep her still, yes." Maran replied. He stood slightly apart from Taka and Ker. He too wore a mirror around his neck, but that was not what caught Aleja's eyes. There was something else in his hand, long and sharp, that gleamed in the orange light of the fire. It was the hilt of the dagger Aleja had seen in her visions. "But if you want perfection," Maran continued, "you should've asked Kalim to drug her."

Taka took his hands from Aleja's face and looked back at Maran.

Maran stood with his arms across his chest, as if challenging Taka.

"Kalim has betrayed our trust."

"Not the first person to do so." Maran said with a grin. Aleja couldn't be sure, but thought he pointed in the direction of the Yamanashi Mountains as he spoke.

"That was long ago." Taka snapped back.

Maran shrugged.

"Still, no reason to exclude Kalim now. Especially for a transfer," Maran said with a smirk, "important as this one."

"Maran is right." Ker laid Aleja's head against the back of the chair. He did so gently, as if he took Taka's words to heart, and did not wish further reprimand. "We can't exclude Kalim, not when we've lost the power of so many others."

"We've lost none of our power." Taka's reply was quick and angry. Even as murky as her senses were, Aleja could tell Maran's words picked at some long, festering pain inside him.

"Only the unfaithful, who were never with us." Taka continued. "We have carried on without them. And without their parts of the mirror. Now enough of this bickering. It's time."

Aleja, her eyes now clear, saw others standing in a circle around her. They were draped in dark green, and wore gold, ceramic masks fashioned in a face like melting wax. The fires Aleja once thought were the burning branches of the trees surrounding the grove were actually torches held in their outstretched hands.

Maran drew in close to Aleja. The pungent smell of his breath burned her nose and eyes, and stirred her awake. Her eyes focused on his. Maran noticed how alert Aleja was, and he smiled.

"I'm glad to see you awake, little bird." Maran said with delight. "I was afraid I made you too sleepy for this."

Aleja followed Maran's eyes back to the carriage. Both Taka and Ker stood beside drawn curtains. Attendants walked to the carriage, pulled out a step, and opened the door.

There was no light inside the carriage, only darkness.

Taka called out to the open door.

"The Vessel is prepared. You are safe. Come forward and join us."

"Taka." A feeble voice called out from the darkness. "Help me out. The carriage is high from the ground."

Aleja strained to see inside the carriage. Taka and Ker moved forward and held out their hands into the darkness. Aleja heard Maran click his tongue.

"Sorry little bird, we can't have you watching. Seeing your Queen like this might diminish the sense of awe you should be feeling." Maran said with a snicker. Aleja heard him rap on a metal tray placed on her lap. "Look down here, please."

Aleja fought the urge to do as Maran said, but found it was of little use. Her head seemed to move independently from her mind, as if Maran's lilting voice were controlling her.

She saw a tray of beautiful, mirror-like silver. It was hooked to the chair and had a depression in the center. At the center of the tray was Aleja's mirror.

Aleja stared at her own reflection. There was a sleepiness in her eyes, and her head bobbed like a small boat floating on a rippling lake.

Then she saw Maran's leering face reflected in the silver tray.

"It's so good to look into those eyes. This is a moment I always look forward to."

Maran's black blade flashed as it struck Aleja in the neck. At first Aleja thought it was a trick of the light, but then her reflection was covered by streams of blood.

The sight brought pain, and the pain brought clarity to her mind. Just before the blood covered her face Aleja saw her eyes come alive.

"To watch the moment of death." Maran whispered in her ear. "Makes one feel so alive."

She wanted to scream but only gargled, choking sounds came out. Aleja tried to reach up to pull the knife from her neck, but found her arms paralyzed.

There was music in the air. The eerie, high pitched whistling sound of Aleja's dreams. The trees around her seemed to burst into flames. Although no flame touched her, Aleja felt the fire of the torches heat her flesh.

Maran still held the knife in his hands. He pulled it out gradually, letting Aleja's blood slowly drain into the tray.

Tears formed in Aleja's eyes. Death was coming, and she didn't know what she was dying for. She lived her whole life with a purpose, to serve her people in the Queen's name, and it was all a lie. It was not fair. She was not ready.

As the life drained out of Aleja, Maran whispered in her ear.

"Kalim tried to warn you, didn't she? She told you if you fought it would be this way. Painful. But that's the way death should be, shouldn't it?

For the pain tells you what your life is really worth. Be thankful this is the way you die, for now you truly understand your life's value."

Aleja felt Maran's hand caressing the back of her neck. His fingers tickled at the knots of her spine.

"I never thought I would miss that feeling." Maran said as he massaged Aleja's back. "But immortality is a blessing and a curse."

Maran drew the knife out slightly. The blood flow from Aleja's neck increased. The sound of the blood filling the tray rang out, like water from a pitcher filling a cup. She wanted death over this pain, and yet it came so slowly.

Aleja tried to scream, but could only manage a pathetic choke. As Maran's fingers ran down the base of her spine she scratched at the wood of the chair. Her hand lifted. Maran did not seem to notice.

Aleja heard the feeble, old voice again. It was closer, and she could see the bony shadow of the speaker approaching her.

"Hurry, Taka. I can feel this body dying. It hurts so."

Aleja's hand reached up and grabbed the knife. She heard shrieks of fear from the speaker approaching her.

Maran tried to draw out the knife, but Aleja's grip held. She looked at him in the eyes, and saw a growing fear.

"What's happening Taka? What's happening?" the feeble voice called out in panic.

Aleja looked towards the voice.

Both Taka and Ker were there. In-between them, supported by their arms, walked a pale, brittle creature who was little more than two wide and terrified eyes staring out from white wisps of stringy hair.

That body was once Pallas, yet it looks ages old.

The old woman struggled against Taka and Ker, as if she were trying to run away but lacked the strength to do so.

"It must be done now, Isla."

Taka urged Isla forward.

"She's fighting! She's fighting!" Isla screamed in panic. She looked around her. "Where's Kalim? She must help me. I'm not strong enough to take her on my own."

"We will be strong enough to help see you through." Taka said. "Be brave, Isla. Please. For all of us. For me."

Taka turned to Maran.

"Finish this."

Maran pulled at Aleja's hands but her grip held. Aleja turned to face him. She smiled. Even with Maran's knife in her neck, Aleja was now able to speak.

"You…will know….death….you will."

Maran's fingers pinched into Aleja's wrist. She felt his growing panic pulse down the blade. But she weakened, and he pulled Aleja's hand from the knife.

"Finish it now!" Taka yelled.

"As you wish." Maran replied, his breath heavy.

Aleja felt the searing pain of the knife cut across her throat, opening the puncture wide. Maran pulled out the knife and Aleja's head dropped to the tray along with the blood dripping from her neck.

Aleja's vision went dark. She no longer felt the heat of the torches. The voices around her became distant.

"You said it would be fast." Taka said.

Maran's laugh was an echo in Aleja's mind.

"Fast…slow. What is time to us, brother?" Maran's voice faded with his laugh.

The music grew louder, drowning out the voices, until it was deafening. Aleja's blood drained down into the mirror. She felt her body being pulled down with it, and was soon consumed by darkness.

But even in the darkness, there was a glimmer of light.

CHAPTER 46

A girl walked alone in the halls of a magnificent palace. All around her were objects of indescribable beauty. The shelves were lined with a kaleidoscope of finely wrought glass, ornate columns covered in gold held up towering ceilings, and smooth bronze statues of dancing angels.

She wanted to reach out and hold each piece but did not. Something held her back. A feeling, nothing she could describe. When she would get too close, the girl felt eyes on her and her fingers would stop just short of touching one of the objects. She would leave, and walk into another room deeper into the palace.

Each room the girl walked through was more extravagantly beautiful than the next, its objects more resplendent. And yet their origin, purpose, and meaning were a mystery to her.

In a room filled with objects made with impossibly smooth and curved lines she saw a box. Something resembling a large sea shell was on the top. There was a large, black plate inside the box and an arm with a tiny needle hanging next to it.

The girl's curiosity overcame her fear. She touched the needle, the only part of the object she recognized, and knocked it onto the black plate.

The girl jumped back at the eruption of sound coming out of the shell and covered her ears to block it out.

She was about to leave the room when, from somewhere within the odd, bleating sounds, emerged a hauntingly delicate and wondrous voice.

The girl stood entranced. She let go of her ears, her hands hung in the air as if she were trying to catch the sound. She moved closer to the box, her fear overcome by the joy the sound filled in her heart, and placed her hands on it.

Memories became flesh.

The girl was in another body, in another time, and locked in a passionate embrace. Her crown, covered in stones and long bird feathers, fell from her head as a man with beautiful blue eyes ran his hands through her short cropped hair.

The memory ended and the girl let go of the box. She touched another object, and found herself a part of another memory. Another life.

A life that was unending, one that led a great people to the sanctuary of a powerful island. The life's people kept alive by a magic harnessing the power of life and death and kept it contained in a large liquid mirror. The world outside their island was dying, but this life's people endured. Until the betrayal. The magic was corrupted by two of their own, two this life loved and trusted. A man and woman who selfishly chose to create a new life. A child was born, and death returned to the island.

The child had to die. It was the only way to restore the magic that kept them eternally young. It was the only way to save them all.

At the sight of the child's death the girl realized she was different from this life she was watching.

Isla. The name of this life was Isla.

The girl watched as Isla's body was ravaged by shards of glass, only to be kept alive, and in pain, by the one who loved her. One who hoped to find what Isla had lost. One who would heal the world, so he could heal the one he loved.

Taka. His name was Taka.

The images vanished from the girl's eyes. She was back in the room. It was dark now, and for the first time she saw windows. A figure stood by one of them, watching the girl, its features hidden in shadow from the light of the moon.

It spoke with a voice that crackled like dying embers.

"You are not supposed to be here."

The figure approached. The girl screamed as its featureless face, eyes and nose just lines of ash with only a slit for a mouth, came into view.

"These are my memories. You have none. You are dead."

The Ash-Woman reached out to the girl with claw-like hands. The girl grabbed a statue of a dancer, its ceramic skin smooth and cool, and swung it at the Ash-Woman.

The Ash-Woman flew backwards onto the floor, and screamed as the statue exploded into dust.

"Stop! Don't take my memories from me!"

The Ash-Woman got up and charged at the girl, and let out a shriek from her slit of a mouth. The girl dodged her attack, and then knocked over the musical box.

The box, like the statue, exploded into dust.

"Stop it! You're killing me!" The Ash-Woman clawed at her face in agony.

The girl felt no pity for the creature. She ran about the room, smashing every object she could get her hands on. The Ash-Woman rolled on the floor in frustration and pain.

"Don't do this to me! I'm afraid!" the Ash-Woman shrieked.

The girl picked up a small clay bowl that suddenly appeared in the place of one of the destroyed objects. It felt different from the other objects, strangely familiar. She stared at it, unable to let it drop from her hands.

The girl stood mesmerized by the bowl, and did not notice the Ash-Woman rushing towards her.

The Ash-Woman slammed into the girl and sent her flying out the window. All around the girl was a whirlwind of dust as she fell.

The girl hit the ground with a grunt. The walls of the palace surrounded her. There was no way out. She felt a stabbing pain in her side.

The girl screamed as she pulled a sharp piece of broken clay from her side. The piece was covered in her own blood. There were other pieces around her. She picked one up, and affixed it to the first piece. The two pieces fit. She ran her finger alongside the crack to wipe off the blood. To her surprise the pieces held, the blood disappeared, and the crack was gone.

The girl picked up other pieces. She dipped her fingers into the bleeding hole in her side and ran the blood along the edges. She placed all the broken pieces together and wiped it clean with her hands.

The bowl was finished, and looked as if it had just come out of the kiln.

The walls of the palace vanished into mist and the girl found herself inside a humble, windowless house.

I know this place.

She looked at the bowl in her hands. The hands holding the bowl were small. They were the hands of a child. The bowl changed into a black, jagged mirror. She was lying on top of a table, her eyes closed, locked in a deathless sleep she could not wake from.

A man sat at the table, staring at her. His face terrified the girl. It was pale, like that of the dead. His arm was held out over her, a large gash running up the length of it. The blood from the gash poured onto the mirror in her hands.

The man looked at the girl. His eyes were glazed. His mouth moved as if he searched for words he didn't have the strength to find. The mirror melted as his blood poured over it, and seeped into her skin.

The girl realized she knew this man.

Father.

As his life drained into her body his memories became hers. He was a loved member of a chosen people, until they lost their purpose. They were no longer guides and teachers, but vultures living off the carcass of a dying world. Her father found a new purpose in the love of another, and in the child they conceived. But the others, the vultures of the old world, took it all from him. The woman he loved, she gave her life to save the child. So he would give his life to give the child purpose.

Vengeance.

Over ages he watched the child sleep, her body alive, but frozen like ice, never to grow old. Countless seasons passed like the flutter of a sparrow's wing. Her father's anger grew. He watched from the shadows as Taka and the other vultures brought the refugees of the Drowned World to this sacred island. Brought them to Corazon to be slaves, to worship his consort Isla like a goddess, and to take their bodies as their own, never realizing their own souls were decaying inside them.

He knew he was weak. He should have killed himself, gave his life to his daughter long ago, but was not able until he found love again.

The love of a young, beautiful woman that he watched grow old and bitter. The girl saw the woman's face, and knew her name.

Grape Mother.

Grape Mother left him when she learned his secret, the child he kept hidden away like a forgotten doll. Over time, in his loneliness he finally found the strength he lacked for so long.

He held a knife to his sleeping daughter's finger.

"I'm sorry. I must."

The knife cut into the girl. The pain was intense. It was not from the sharpness of the blade, but from a heat in the knife that burned like fire.

The girl's blood flowed onto the mirror and mixed with her father's.

"Everything must have an end." Her father took her hand, and placed her finger on the mirror. "They will be drawn to you now. And you have the power to destroy them. Just remember who you are, and what I have given you. "

Over and over he traced a shape with her finger into the blood. Over and over he said the same thing until death finally claimed him.

"Aleja. Your name is Aleja. Remember."

When the last drop of blood left her father, the mirror melted under Aleja's fingertip. The inky blackness ran up her fingers and drained completely into the gash in her hand.

The cut sealed and left no mark on her skin. Her eyes opened. She looked at her dead father as if he was a stranger. Her memory of him vanished as his body crumbled into dust.

The girl took the knife and carved the name into the surface of the wood table. She read the name aloud, and remembered.

Aleja.

I am Aleja.

She heard Grape Mother's voice calling out to her from outside, yet when Aleja walked out the door she found herself alone in her own memory palace. She was no longer a child, but was surrounded by objects of her childhood in the Clay lands. The ones the Temple Maidens once made her destroy. One by one she touched each object until her memories returned.

Aleja walked across a plain of red clay. The memory palace of the Ash-Woman was alone on a hill. It looked small, diminished. Its power over Aleja's mind was gone.

Aleja walked to the door and opened it. She found the Ash-Woman cowering behind one of the columns in the main hall.

The walls were lined with immense, decorative tapestries that showed dramatic scenes of people crowded onto ships, fleeing burning cities plagued by the Shepherd's Goddess and her half-human children.

Aleja walked up to the tapestries, which burst into flames at her touch. The Ash-Woman screamed helplessly as the fire climbed up the walls. Soon the entire hall was ablaze.

Room by room she set each alight. She walked up to the Ash-Woman and embraced her.

"Do not fear, Isla." Aleja said as the Ash-Woman began to cry. "There will be no more pain."

Aleja watched the house burn around her, but felt no heat from the flames. Once the fire claimed the Ash-Woman the light from it became blinding.

Aleja closed her eyes, and then opened them again at the sound of Taka's scream.

CHAPTER 47

Taka knelt on the ground, cradling Isla in his arms. Her body was porcelain white, and her eyes stared into nothingness.

"Isla! Wake up! Wake up!" Taka cried as he placed his forehead on hers.

Only Maran noticed Aleja was conscious. The others were staring at the sight of Taka and Isla, her dead eyes reflecting the lightning flashing in the sky.

"You." Maran said, his eyes wide, the knife dangling in his trembling hands. "It can't be. You've been dead for ages."

Black liquid ran up into Aleja's throat. It filled her body with a paralyzing pain. Aleja was only dimly aware Maran stood watching her now, his eyes wide with unbelieving horror.

Just as quickly as it began, the pain stopped. Aleja stared down at her reflection in the now clean tray.

Aleja wiped her throat with her hand. Although the blood was still there, she felt no cut, no pain. She felt only a simmering hatred for Maran, stirred into fury by the incessant sound of her father's voice ringing in her head.

"Vengeance."

Aleja looked at Maran, and wrenched the knife out from his trembling hands. There was a crack of thunder as she plunged the knife through the mirror that hung from his neck and buried it into his chest.

The others turned at the sound of Maran's airy shriek.

Thick, black oil poured out of Maran's wound and covered Aleja's hand. The oil disappeared into her skin like seawater into sand.

Images of horror filled Aleja's mind as Maran's life left him and entered her. She saw his murderous crimes against the children of Jin. She saw a young man accuse him, only to be beaten by Guardians and led away in chains.

Ivo. You were right. I'm so sorry.

Overcome by the horrors of Maran's memories, Aleja pulled the knife from his chest with such force it flew from her hand. Maran fell backwards and flailed on the ground like a fish tossed onto dry land. Smoke rose from his chest where the blade cut through the mirror.

Aleja turned in time to see Ker swing at her. She caught his arm and pulled him forward. When she had Ker's elbow at her thigh she pulled down. There was a loud popping sound, followed by a scream, as Aleja bent Ker's elbow backwards.

Aleja wanted nothing more than to hurt Taka, Ker and all the others. Blinded by her rage, she was unaware of her smile at the sight of Ker lying helplessly on the ground.

Aleja knelt down and bent Ker's arm around her thigh, and finished him off with a head-butt to his nose. There was a satisfying crunch as a red spray exploded from Ker's face onto hers.

Aleja let Ker fall to the ground unconscious.

She stood over Taka. He was still holding Isla.

The Ash-Woman.

Taka looked up at Aleja with a hatred that was a mirror image of Aleja's own.

"Kill her!" Taka shouted at his Guardians.

There was a whistling sound. Aleja felt something slam into her shoulder. The force of it pinned her back into the chair.

Aleja groaned. She grabbed at the arrow sticking out from her shoulder. She saw Rhea, her face now unmasked, pull another arrow and notch it to her bow.

Aleja did not close her eyes. She stared hard at Rhea. The force of her stare gave the Guardian pause.

Rhea lowered her bow.

Taka kissed Isla on the forehead, then closed her eyes and laid her on the ground.

Aleja pulled at the arrow, but she could not remove it. The point had lodged itself into the wooden chair.

Taka walked towards her. His ocean blue eyes stared into Aleja's. Her fury grew with every step he took towards her. She let out a scream of pure, inarticulate rage.

The wind swirled around the grove. Trees swayed like kelp in a stormy sea. The roar of thunder and the whistle of the wind drowned out Maran's pitiful moaning as he writhed in agony in the dirt. The caravan's horses screamed in terror as the storm grew to a ferocity that matched Aleja's rage.

The Guardians removed their masks, and tried to hold their ground as the wind swirled around them.

Taka stood firm. He took one cautious step towards Aleja after another, and when he was almost upon her he pulled out a knife.

"You're nothing but a lie!" Aleja screamed at Taka. "You're not gods, not demons, just cowards!"

A powerful wind knocked Taka to Aleja's feet. He grabbed onto her chair and struggled to pull himself up to her. He clutched the knife close to his breast.

Aleja kicked at Taka's chest as he pulled himself up. Her hands left the arrow and went for his face. She could not hear his scream in the roar of the wind, but saw his face contort in pain as her nails clawed at his eyes.

An arrow whizzed by Aleja's head and planted itself into the chair with a thud. Aleja saw Rhea's trembling hand notch another arrow just before she too was blown off her feet.

Taka lifted the knife to Aleja's gut. She grabbed his arm and twisted the knife from his hands. Taka fell backwards onto the ground and was blown from the chair. Aleja picked up the knife and with a single stroke, cut the fletching off the arrow.

Aleja felt the wood burn through her shoulder as she pulled herself free from the arrow. The shattered splinters of the arrow picked at her muscles. The wound filled with a black, viscous blood, and quickly healed.

Aleja stood tall in the middle of the storm. Unlike the others she had no trouble keeping her ground. To Aleja it felt like walking through the airless halls of her memory palace.

There was a blinding flash of lightning, followed by rain that stung like icy needles.

A bolt of lightning slammed into Isla's carriage. The shock of the blast sent Guardians flying into trees. The carriage burst into flames. The heat was so intense that even in the pouring rain the fir trees caught fire. Horses screamed and broke free from their tethers. They charged through the glen and ran panicked into the forest, leaving saddle packs on the ground and knocking over wooden chests blown from the carriages.

Aleja's hair whipped her face in thin, stinging lashes. She looked at Taka lying helplessly on the ground. Anger burned in her hotter than the flame spiraling out from the carriage and now licking the tops of the trees. She found the knife with the double blades and left Taka's in its place, then walked over to him.

Aleja straddled Taka, who stared at her through eyes now caked with blood from his cheeks and forehead.

Aleja held up the knife over her head and readied her swing.

"You cannot do this!" Taka screamed. "You cannot kill! It is not who you are!"

Aleja took a deep breath.

"You do not know who I am." She screamed back at him.

Aleja tightened her grip on the knife.

"I do."

Aleja gripped the knife hard, but did not bring it down. She saw her face reflected in the mirror on Taka's chest. Her skin was a dark void, with only two blood red stones in the place of her eyes.

Do I?

She looked at Taka, who stared at her with a pitiful, horrified expression. At the sight of it Aleja struggled to find the hatred that would give her the strength to take his evil from this world.

Is this my path? To be the instrument of vengeance for my mother, my father, Sara, and Bao?

To claim vengeance for myself?

Taka relaxed. Aleja no longer felt him struggle against her hold. She looked into his eyes. She saw not strength or hatred in them. Instead she saw loneliness, a weariness of life.

"So you finally found us." Taka smiled sadly. "Go ahead, do what you will."

Aleja turned away from Taka's gaze and looked deep into the darkness of the forest.

A silver mist filled the forest. Aleja saw the shapes of people who seemed more shadow than flesh.

They called out to her.

"Kill him. Give his life to death."

The spirits in the mist threw the Guardians to the ground, and smashed through the carriages and trees that circled the glen. In them Aleja saw her own rage. The phantoms swirled around her in a vortex. They called out to Aleja.

"They made prisons of our lives, and have trapped us in death. Free us. Kill them."

Aleja felt as if she could reach out and hurl the spirits at Taka. She remembered the Shepherd's men who were dragged screaming down the catacombs by skeletal hands.

From somewhere in the storm Aleja heard her father's voice.

"Vengeance, Aleja! For what they did to your mother! For what they did to me!"

Aleja looked deep into the eyes of the souls spinning around her. She felt their pain and anger, and knew they felt hers. Whatever Taka and his followers were, they had taken from the dead, and through Aleja the dead would have their vengeance.

Is this all you gave me father? Is my only purpose to kill those who refuse to die?

There were two other figures in the distance. Unlike the other spirits they stood unmoved by the maelstrom surrounding Aleja.

Aleja cried out as their faces came into view.

One was her mother, the other was Bao. They were smiling at Aleja, and holding their hands to their hearts. Unlike the other spirits, who were separated from each other in their lonely bitterness and anger, her mother and Bao were joined. They drifted into each other's bodies, sometimes appearing as Bao, sometimes as Aleja's mother, and finally as a combination of the two.

"Follow your path." They said in unison. "The choice is yours."

Aleja looked at the dagger in her hands and cried out. Aleja looked away from them, then saw Maran's and Ker's wounded bodies. Her grip on the dagger loosened.

I'm not what Taka or my father tried to make me.

I'm not a victim. I'm not a killer.

I am Aleja.

Aleja looked at her reflection in Taka's mirror. The dark image of herself was gone. A fog rushed through the forest like a wave, extinguishing the fires, and freeing the Guardians trapped in the fallen trees. The deathly faces vanished from the mist, as did the faces of Bao and her mother.

Aleja placed the knife to Taka's throat. His blue eyes widened as it touched his skin. She cut the chain that hung on his neck, and pulled the mirror from Taka's grip.

Ker still lay unconscious, his barrel-like chest moving in heavy breaths ending in liquid gasps through his broken nose.

Aleja walked up to Maran. For a moment, as he drifted in and out of consciousness, she heard Maran's voice.

"It hurts, it hurts me so." He called out weakly.

As the guardians freed themselves from the broken tree limbs, Aleja walked calmly through the glen and placed Maran and Ker's mirrors in her satchel.

Taka and the Guardians surrounded Aleja.

Aleja stopped, and stared at Taka.

Taka, one hand in a fist, the other pointing to Aleja, called out to his Guardians.

"She cannot leave here."

The Guardians stepped forward with knives and bo sticks in their bruised and bloodied hands.

A low rumble grew in the forest. Aleja thought it was thunder from the storm that just passed. But the sound grew steadily louder, and shook the ground she stood on. The Guardians stopped and stared into the impenetrable blackness of the woods.

Horses charged screaming into the glen, the reins that held them to the trees now broken, and swinging from their heads like whips.

The Guardians scattered before the charge. Some tried to grab hold of the horses but were thrown to the ground.

Aleja saw Arrowchaser. He came straight for her, his nostrils and eyes open wide. Just as he was upon her his head went low.

Aleja grabbed his reins and her foot found the stirrup. She leapt onto his back and rode past the scrambling Guardians.

Taka screamed behind her.

"We will find you! There is nowhere you can hide from us!"

Aleja smiled as Arrowchaser stormed into the dark forest that surrounded the open, moonlit glen like a wall of night.

I won't hide. Never again.

CHAPTER 48

The glen now far behind her, Aleja rested her head against Arrowchaser's neck as she rode him through the forest. Clouds again covered the sky, and it became so dark that it made no difference to Aleja whether her eyes were opened or closed.

But, dark as it was, Arrowchaser never hesitated or stumbled as he charged through the thick woods. Aleja held on and trusted he would get her out of the woods safely.

Arrowchaser's pace slowed as dawn began to break. The woods thinned and they came to the banks of a river.

Aleja stopped, dismounted, and walked Arrowchaser down to the water to share in a drink and to clean herself off.

Aleja found some ginger root by the shore of the stream. She pulled it out, cleaned it, and bit into the pungent root with eyes tightly shut.

A strangely pleasant burn flared up through her nose. Aleja swallowed the root with some effort, and then tried to shake off the stinging sensation in her head.

There was a voice behind her. Aleja turned around calmly at the sound of it.

"Daughter?"

It was the village girl with the wide brimmed hat. The one who took her to Edisto on a donkey cart.

"Hello, Neera." Aleja said without getting up.

"Can I be of any help to you?"

"No, thank you. I'm fine."

"It's better ground up you know." Neera pointed to the ginger in Aleja's hands. "I can make a soup of it with some carrots I got. My cart is on the road just over there."

Aleja picked a few more roots and washed her hands. She walked up to Arrowchaser and adjusted his saddle.

"Beautiful horse." Neera said. Aleja could tell she wanted to touch the animal but was afraid. "Was it a gift?"

"Yes, he was."

"So…" Neera said, her curiosity finally getting the best of her, "…you didn't board the ship."

"No." Aleja placed the roots in her satchel.

"Because of the horse?"

Aleja nodded as she mounted Arrowchaser and started the horse in a trot towards the road.

Aleja stared down at Neera, who stood smiling pleasantly up at her as she followed along.

Aleja saw Neera's cart on the road. Like the day before it was full of food. Aleja stopped. Neera eagerly jumped onto her cart, pulled out a carrot, and held it out to Arrowchaser.

"They like this, yeah?"

Aleja nodded her head. Neera giggled as Arrowchaser took the carrot from her hand. She then pulled up handfuls of carrots and held them out to Aleja.

"I can give you more. Goes well with those roots like I told ya."

Aleja leaned down and took the carrots.

"This time I must give you something worthy in return."

"No, like I said," Neera shook her head, "you already gave us everything we need."

"I won't take no for an answer."

Aleja could see Neera's eyes twinkle at the thought of receiving a gift from a Daughter of the Queen. She refused it once, and now was free to accept.

Neera's mouth dropped open at the sight of Aleja removing her lemniscate headdress and stood speechless as Aleja placed it into her hands.

Aleja watched Neera admire the lemniscate in the warm, morning light. Neera seemed transfixed. She smiled as she turned the silver band over and over in her hand.

"I cannot accept this." Neera said finally, but Aleja was not there to hear her.

Aleja turned Arrowchaser and rode away until she came to a fork in the road. The moment Aleja thought to pull on the reins Arrowchaser slowed to a stop.

The road to her right would take her to the Yamanashi Mountains.

I could disappear there. Join the Yamanashi if they would have me. Live life my way.

She also thought about going on to Andrid and finding Ivo. Possibly even to take the advice Kalim gave her.

To go left meant getting closer to Mir and the world she left behind. But it also was in the direction of the Clay lands.

Maybe my Grape Mother is still alive. Maybe I can get answers.

Aleja leaned into Arrowchaser's mane and rubbed the hard flesh of his neck. She closed her eyes, and smiled.

Whatever it is, the choice is mine...

Aleja sat up straight and commanded Arrowchaser forward with a snap of the reins.

… and mine alone.

ACKNOWLEDGMENTS

Although writing is often a solitary pursuit this book was not completely written in isolation. I would like to thank my readers: Amy, Carla, Rebecca, Brianna, Keri, Jillian, Maureen, Brian, Becky, and Leilani whose invaluable support and input kept me strong. Special thanks go to my first readers Sara, Hallie, and Kathleen for their advice and support in the early years of my writing journey. If it wasn't for you, I wouldn't have made it this far!

I would also like to thank those whose own work has inspired me along the way. Thank you to Josh and A Sound of Thunder for writing the songs that inspired this book, and for giving me my first publishing opportunity with the *It Was Metal* comic anthology. I would also like to acknowledge the inspiration and support of the artists Rodrigo Pradel and Shino Hisano.

Thank you to Rachel and Dannet for your editorial expertise and advice along the way. Also, thank you to Shilah and the good people at Bublish for their support and assistance in getting this story into your hands.

Thank you Scott, Ash, Angel, Seleni, Aidan, Itzel, and Ryan for giving your time on the book trailer.

This book was written and revised to the music of School of Seven Bells and the Cocteau Twins when the coffee was working, and A Sound of Thunder and Ghost when it wasn't.

ABOUT THE AUTHOR

T.E. Dickason is a writer and teacher from the D.C. area. He has published the short story It Was Metal for the *It Was Metal* comic anthology and is currently working on a sequel to *The Illusion Queen*. In his spare time he indulges in his passion for silent films by drawing portraits of silent film stars and can be found lost in thought whenever the opportunity presents itself.

Follow T.E. Dickason on Facebook and twitter @tedickasonlit and visit his page at www.tedickason.com.